# Municipal Liaisons
## A Fortuna, Texas Novel

### Book 4

Rochelle Bradley

# DEDICATION

For Wrimos worldwide: If I can write, edit, and publish a
NaNoWriMo novel... you can too. Keep writing until you hit
"The End." Happy writing!

# ACKNOWLEDGMENTS

To the Honorable Brooks Compton Mayor of Centerville: Thank you for taking the time to explain the fundamentals of how a small town government works.

Dawn...Thank you for beta reading for me.
Your constant words of encouragement and love have helped me persevere through a tough time. You are an awesome friend.

Frau Sigrun Paust, Frau Britta Wunderlick-Herr, Frau Anja Marina Dean, and Sharon... Thank you for a fun evening of naughty German texting. I appreciate your willingness to help me.

Sharon and Frau Carla Gierke... thank you for double checking my German and for the suggestions. Danke schön.

# CHAPTER 1

## *Jasen*

JASEN DELAY HELD ONTO THE "oh shit" handle as B.J. Johnson bumped over the primitive road. "You aren't staying on the trail," Jasen yelled over the blaring country music as the truck hit a jaw-jarring rut.

Turning down the radio, B.J. said, "Relax." Both hands gripping the wheel, he smirked and jerked it, riding halfway on the dirt track.

"That's a little tough to do when every other second I'm catching air," Jasen growled.

The truck jolted to a stop and the pile of romance novels between them toppled to the floor. B.J. faced Jasen. "Look. You need to lighten up. This isn't a county-maintained road with lines or rules. It's a field. Cows shit in it."

Jasen huffed, crossing his arms. When had he last relaxed? Not since the flood. He sighed and peered out at the tall nodding grass.

B.J. raised an eyebrow. "Feeling more confident, are we?"

"No."

"Yeehaw!" B.J. whooped, flooring it. Jasen's forehead smacked the side window.

Jasen gasped and seized the handle again. They abandoned the trail and trekked west, flinging dirt clods and trailing a plume of dust.

"What are you, a hick?" Jasen teased.

B.J.'s brow crinkled. "I know you are, but what am I?"

"Prick," Jasen mumbled with a grin.

"I'm rubber and you're glue. Whatever you say bounces off me and sticks to you."

"You're a rubber?" Jasen asked, then laughed when B.J.'s mouth dropped open but nothing came out. "Wow. You're speechless."

"It was the visualization."

Jasen chuckled. "Whatever, asshat."

"Chicken," B.J. muttered.

"Sticks and stones, dude. Sticks and stones." Jasen said, shifting his bag. B.J.'s footfalls followed him toward the fire.

"Hey, Parker," Jasen said to the used car salesman as he unfolded a chair. He sat his backpack on the seat and picked up the tent box. On it, a family smiled as they posed before the perfect tent. He turned the box and swallowed. The blond woman reminded him of his deceased wife, Dee.

"Do you and B.J. want to put the tent up while I get dinner going?" Parker Ford asked.

"Sure, how hard can it be?" Jasen said.

B.J. pierced Parker with a brooding stare. "You don't like me, do you?"

Jasen slugged B.J. in the arm, making Parker chuckle. The large man continued setting out his supplies.

"Come on, Jase," B.J. said then ran his fingers through his thick, dark hair.

"Sure, let's get it done before Brad gets here." Jasen nodded and opened the box flap, pulling out the instructions.

B.J. carried the box away from the fire pit, stopping at a flat spot. Jasen bumped into him. "Watch it."

"Out of my way," Jasen said, waving.

Ignoring him, B.J. said, "What do you think of this place?"

Jasen circled around B.J. He'd never camped, let alone set up a tent. "Looks good to me."

B.J. dumped the contents then handed Jasen a small pouch with the metal stakes. The wad of polyester material sounded like a trash bag as B.J. unfolded it. Jasen glanced at the waning sun. B.J. handed Jasen a pole in pieces. "Put that together." Kneeling, B.J. huffed as he worked on one of his own.

"Should the door face the fire?" Jasen asked.

B.J. glanced at Jasen. "Do I look like I know outdoor feng shui?"

Jasen shrugged and turned the tent so the door opened toward the fire. B.J. took the poles and threaded them through sleeves. "Is it supposed to be crooked?"

B.J. tilted his head. "It's not if you look at it from this angle." He chuckled and extended his hand palm up. "Hit me."

Jasen slugged him in the arm.

"You hit like my grandma." B.J. said, but frowned and rubbed the spot. "I meant with a stake."

"Are you a vampire?" Jasen laughed and opened the cinched sack. He handed a stake to B.J.

"Yeah, love bites, and I'm a cold-hearted bastard."

A truck pulled in next to the other vehicles, and Brad Davidson emerged. He offered a wave before joining Parker and Forrest Greene at the fire.

"Jasen's hands might have grown soft being mayor," Parker yelled.

"Hey," Jasen tossed back. "We'll see if those potholes on your street get fixed now."

Arms in the air, Parker wiggled his fingers. "Ew. I'm so afraid."

"Shut up and keep working," B.J. said, struggling to push a pole into a slot.

"That looks wrong," Jasen said as B.J. dropped the ill-fitting pole.

"Son of a bitch, Jasen. Just hand me the damn thing," B.J. growled unseen from the other side of the lopsided tent.

Jasen shot back, "That's not where it goes."

Brad glanced at the long pole in Jasen's hand. "B.J.'s right."

"Thanks, Brad," B.J. grinned.

"Don't thank me. I'm here to make sure the tent gets pitched before it's time to leave." Brad stuck his hands in his front pockets.

As they finished, headlights panned the field. "Canon should set up the other one because he's late," Jasen suggested.

Brad, B.J., and Jasen walked toward Canon Berns' black truck. Canon hopped out with a large toothy grin. "Howdy, y'all. I've got coolers with beer." He lowered the gate of his truck and slid a blue cooler toward them.

"Grab a handle," B.J. told Jasen. They each heaved a side and carried it toward the fire pit. "What the hell did Canon pack in here? It's almost as heavy as a tote full of books."

"Wimp." Jasen pulled the handle, making B.J. stumble sideways a few steps.

B.J. countered, pulling then pushing the handle. "Wuss."

Jasen's knee buckled, but he caught himself. They sat the cooler down, and Jasen plopped into the chair, shaking his arms.

"Jerk," Jasen grumbled.

"Asshole," B.J. muttered.

With Canon's arrival, they could finally start the proceedings. At twenty-five Canon was the youngest member of the book club. He was perpetually late, although his job as a firefighter was sometimes the reason.

Forrest stretched his legs out as he lounged in a folding chair, staring at the flames. Parker stirred the pot, and Jasen's stomach rumbled. Brad accompanied Canon who carried a second cooler as if filled with helium.

Jasen cleared his throat. "Now that we're all here—"

"What's the status of the food?" Canon asked, opening the lid of the cooler. Jasen glared at Canon. The young firefighter hastily pulled out a bottle of beer, offering it to Brad.

B.J. crossed his arms and said, "Age before beauty."

"I've earned it, you whipper-snapper." Brad took the beer and twisted off the cap. He settled into a seat and raised his beer as Canon handed out bottles to the other guys. They likewise lifted their drinks.

"To my mother Undine Love-Davidson and her freakish book-hoarding tendencies. May the good Lord give her a big mansion with thousands of books." Brad clinked Forrest's water bottle then continued around the circle, tapping everyone amongst a chorus of cheers and here-heres.

Jasen sipped the cool beer.

Parker returned to the cast-iron kettle and as he stirred the delectable spicy smell wafted over the group.

"Now that we're all here—" Jasen said, narrowing his gaze at the latest arrival. Canon seemed to shrink under his scrutiny.

Parker sniffed the pot, closed his eyes, and grinned, "Soup's on."

Canon jumped to his feet. "Awesome! What can I do to help?"

"Get the fixin's out of the cooler," Parker said, pulling bowls out of a canvas bag. He handed one to Brad, then Forrest.

Jasen waited his turn. He had been looking forward to tasting the award-winning recipe since Parker had won the Nockerville chili cook-off. His stomach rumbled again, and he clenched it.

B.J. received his bowl and took a tentative bite. He picked up his beer and gulped.

"Too hot for you?" Jasen teased as Parker handed him a bowl. Jasen spooned in a mouthful. Flavor exploded, and he closed his eyes, moaning. "God, Parker this is fabulous. Holy cow."

"Mm-hmm," Canon agreed, holding out his bowl for more.

"Damn. How did you eat that so fast?" B.J. asked.

"He's not a pansy like you," Forrest said, shoveling in a spoonful.

B.J.'s jaw dropped, then he scowled. He took a large spoonful. Shifting the food around in his mouth, his face turned red. He finally swallowed. He lifted his bottle to his lips and chugged, then wiped his sweaty brow.

The men laughed. Parker ladled his chili and joined them. After the meal, Canon collected the trash while Parker unveiled a surprise.

"Lisa made these special for y'all. I hope you don't like them so there's more for me." Parker passed the homemade cookies.

Jasen moaned again, grateful Parker's wife could bake.

"Geez, Jasen you eat too much processed food," Forrest said. He nibbled a cookie, echoing Jasen's moan.

"I know, right?" Canon replied, swiping another cookie as the plate passed.

"Please give Lisa my compliments. These are excellent," Brad said, raising a cookie.

Parker smiled with obvious pride. "I'll be sure to tell her."

"How are you two doing?" Forrest asked.

Jasen stopped chewing and glanced toward Parker, then met B.J.'s gaze. Parker and Lisa had been on the brink of divorce until the romance reading fad had offered them a second chance at love. Now the Fords were the envy of the town. Parker acted out scenes from the novels, granting Lisa's fantasies.

Parker shifted backward. "Well, she's good. She recently discovered the books at city hall."

"Oh God," Jasen groaned, covering his hot face with his hands. Located near his office, the bookshelf housed the BDSM romances. When the Fortuna citizens mentioned the "mayor's books," Jasen couldn't help getting defensive.

Forrest inched forward. "Ivy has asked me about that stash of books too. Any luck?"

Parker chuckled and waved his hand. "A little. My suggestion is: let her pick something."

Jasen extended his hands. "I know you don't believe me, but just for the record, those novels are not in my office. I'll state once again I didn't ask to have a bookshelf or the BDSM books placed there."

"Says you." B.J. smirked and leaned back as he crossed his arms.

Jasen clenched his teeth. He shot his hand out and pushed B.J.'s chair next to his shoulder. Wide-eyed, B.J. gasped as he flailed his arms and legs, trying to right himself in utter futility. He landed with a satisfying thump and a small cloud of dust.

Jasen bit his tongue to hold back a laugh then popped another cookie into his mouth. B.J. jumped to his feet, red-faced and fists balled.

Brad motioned for B.J. to sit. "What are we going to read next?"

Forrest glanced toward the sky as if counting the stars.

"How about historical?" Jasen suggested. They hadn't read it in a while.

"Bodice rippers," B.J. guffawed.

"You like them," Jasen declared with a triumphant grin.

"Yes, you do, B.J. I've seen them in your office," Forrest said, pointing at him.

It was true. B.J.'s small office at Longfellow Property Management held stacks of romances.

B.J. shrugged. "I read everything. I don't discriminate."

"We could do western romance, but someplace like Montana or Colorado," Canon suggested.

"I'll make a list. We can read them all eventually," Jasen said, opening a notebook. He jotted down the suggestions.

"Cool. I liked *Sweet Vengeance*. It had vampires, sorcerers, and werewolves. Why don't we do werewolves?" Canon curled his fingers into claws and howled.

Forrest rolled his eyes. "Can we take a break from paranormal for a while? How about romantic comedy set in a small town?"

"You just want something easy to act out," Parker teased.

Forrest blazed red to the tips of his ears but grinned.

"Hot damn, Parker is right!" B.J. clapped his hands together then jumped to his feet and began pacing.

"Oh crap." Brad met Jasen's gaze. When B.J. schemed, it didn't bode well for the rest of the book club. Forrest stroked his beard then shared a look with Parker.

B.J. faced them, punching a finger into the air. "I have an idea."

"Here it comes," Jasen mumbled.

B.J. ignored him. "Let's draw."

"I don't have a pencil," Canon said with a furrowed brow.

"No, you goof. Like this..." He spun toward Jasen. "Can I use your notebook?"

Curious, Jasen handed the pad of paper over.

B.J. ripped out a few pages then tore them into thirds. He handed each man three. "On the top paper list a setting. Like a city, the mountains, or a diner. Whatever. Think where you'd like to read."

Forrest listed a setting then handed the pen to Brad. The pen circled the group.

"Brad, may I borrow your cowboy hat?" B.J. asked.

The oldest member of the book club, Brad, owned the Big Deal longhorn cattle ranch. Brad rarely removed his hat, but handed it over, and B.J. dropped his paper in then collected the others.

"Draw one and make sure it isn't yours. Keep what you receive to yourself. Tuck it in your cup holder." Jasen reached in but picked his own. He dropped it back and chose another.

"Now think of a subgenre you'd read or want to act out." B.J. wiggled his eyebrows, earning chuckles. "I guess it could be a common trope like the secret baby or friends to lovers."

B.J. held the cowboy hat in front of Brad and shook it. After they each drew a paper, B.J. announced, "Time to select a character. Not someone specific but like a clown or shop owner."

Jasen enjoyed the unconventional way to pick the club's next books to read, but he'd never voice his opinion to B.J.

They selected the final papers.

B.J. turned to him and said, "Jasen, write these down."

Jasen nodded, flipped the page then waited, pen poised. Silence stretched and B.J. stared into the fire. Jasen glanced around the group.

Forrest mouthed, "What the...?"

Jasen shrugged.

"Look at your papers," B.J. smirked and pointed at Forrest. "I dare you to act these out with your wife. And you." He jabbed a finger toward Parker. "The rest of us need to find someone."

Jasen met Brad's gaze. They were both widowers and presently single.

"I... uh," Canon stuttered, wide-eyed. "I don't have a girlfriend."

"Are you afraid of a little dare?" B.J. taunted.

"You don't have a girlfriend either," Jasen told B.J.

B.J.'s brows rose. "Don't worry. I'm looking forward to dressing up as..." he shuffled his papers and croaked, "a prince."

Forrest slapped his knee, laughing.

"Charming," Jasen teased.

Parker snorted. "Not."

"What's your trope?" Canon asked, leaning forward.

B.J. unfolded a paper. "MC. What the hell is MC?"

"Motorcycle club," Canon said.

"You get to be a royal bad boy," Brad grinned.

"More like a royal pain in the ass," Jasen laughed.

"Who likes leather," Parker said, then added, "you should visit Jasen's bookshelf for ideas." He winked.

"What's your setting, B.J.?" Canon asked.

"Haunted coffee shop." B.J. shook his head. "A coffee shop would be easy enough, but haunted? How the hell am I going to do that?"

Canon chuckled. "Are you afraid of your own dare?"

B.J. growled and plopped into his chair with a huff. He crossed his arms, appearing constipated.

"Listen, son—," Brad started, catching everyone's attention, "You could be a singer formally known as Prince imitator, who drives a Harley and sings haunting melodies at hipster coffee shops."

"Have you heard B.J. sing?" Forrest asked. "I have at church. It would be haunting, all right. It'd scare the shiznack out of them."

"Ha. Ha." B.J. rubbed his chin. "I like Brad's interpretation. I suppose we can manipulate our choices; as long as they're still deciphered from the original words. What did you get, Brad?"

Brad smoothed his papers and swallowed. "Alien, fairytale, and castle."

At the top of the paper, Jasen wrote "Fortuna Dare Society" and listed B.J.'s and Brad's dares.

Parker shifted and offered, "Mine are a dancer, a billionaire with a hidden past, and Scotland. I think Lisa will appreciate a kilt."

"Anyone want to switch?" Forrest asked, waving his paper like a flag.

"No switching," B.J. said with a smirk.

"This is such bull-crap." Forrest glowered at B.J. then sighed. "A vampire mystery at a club."

"That bites," Parker teased, chuckling. "What about you, Canon?"

"My character is a superhero, set in the past on a train." Canon blushed.

"That's easy," Brad said. "The Lone Ranger. You can skip the tights."

B.J. opened the cooler and offered another round. Brad accepted and lounged back, crossing his ankles.

"Jasen?" B.J. asked.

"I don't have a clue how to pull this off. A cowboy fantasy in the theater." Jasen sighed.

"Why?" Canon asked.

"The main reason is I don't have a wife, a girlfriend, or someone I'd remotely want to take to coffee, let alone cos-play." Jasen frowned and rubbed his chest. Even considering dating felt like a betrayal.

# CHAPTER 2

## *Jasen*

JASEN SAT ON THE CENTRAL park bench with his legs stretched out. The past months had been hard. He had hoped his wife would return from the grave, but after two years it was time to acknowledge the truth. *Dee wasn't coming home.* He rubbed his chin.

Sunshine warmed his body, and he inhaled the balmy Texas air.

He clenched his eyes as a wave of regret, followed by guilt, rolled over him, settling in the pit of his stomach. How the hell would he make good on the book club dare?

Jasen remembered the day when he had received the call from Colin Copper, the chief of police. Flash flood on Dry Run creek. The authorities had found his wife's car swept downstream, wedged by a tree trunk, and filled with clay. They'd returned only one of her shoes.

Jasen leaned forward, resting his elbows on his legs. Fortuna business and life continued regardless of how he dealt with Dee's death. Most people had stopped enquiring after him. Only his administrative assistant Jacklyn Hyde repeatedly asked after him. He appreciated the concern but felt mothered.

If he wouldn't have lost Dee, they might have started a family and attended fund-raising events and opening ceremonies of new Fortuna businesses. He shook his head and stared at his shoes.

Across the street, someone entered the Pink Taco, and the smell of Mexican food wafted over him. His stomach rumbled.

A vehicle door slammed. He glanced up. Two women carried bolts of fabric. Jasen raised an arm in greeting.

"Hi, Jasen," Jessie Barnes called.

Jasen rose off the bench and sauntered toward the ladies. Reaching them as they arrived at Jessie's business, he pulled the door and held it open. "How are you today?"

"Good, thanks," Piper Dart, Jessie's personal assistant, answered.

"I see you've got a lot of material. Working on a big project?" Jasen asked, curious.

Jessie beamed and nodded. "We've got to fill three large orders. But this new stuff is for a special prototype."

"The boutique Britches and Hose placed a gi-normous order," Piper said, squeezing past. She stomped up the stairs, her blonde bob swishing.

"That's awesome," he replied.

Jessie hesitated, glancing down before looking him in the eyes. "How are you doing?"

Jasen's heart hitched, but he plastered on the placating smile that had won the election. "I'm well, thank you." He gave a stiff nod.

Jessie's features pinched a moment, as if she didn't believe him. Then she nodded and headed into the building.

Jasen blew out a long breath as the door silently closed behind her. He walked away from the entry. Staring into the Gift Spot's window display, he tripped on the uneven concrete sidewalk. He shifted his focus to the ground as he crossed to the park once more.

The cracks in the pavement passed as he watched his shoes rise and hit. A chilly breeze blew, and he hugged his jacket tight. Spotting something blue on the ground, he reached to pick up the trash. He stopped halfway. A small bell-shaped flower, so tiny it almost escaped his notice, peeked out of the grass. Spring was a few weeks off, but apparently the plant hadn't gotten the memo.

Jasen straightened with a smile. Perhaps it was time to sloth off the winter of his life and come alive again. He sheathed his hands in his pockets. Returning to the park bench, he plopped down with a sigh and studied the large courthouse. A man hopped up the steps and disappeared through the wide entry. Moments later, he reappeared carrying a stack of paperback novels. The top book tumbled to the ground. He stooped to pick it up then dusted it off, turning it over to inspect the cover.

Jasen strained, trying to remember his name. Willie something. He worked at the feed store.

While Jasen had read a majority of the books on the municipal shelf, he opted for sweet romance novels. But only his book club knew that tidbit.

His book club. Jasen chuckled as he rubbed his face. They would tease him about his preferred romances. While the other men liked spicy, dramatic books, Jasen selected new adult stories. He enjoyed watching the characters find themselves and grow.

He leaned back on the bench. The dark green paint had faded to a dusty shade of mint.

Jasen considered his lunch options. Walking to the Kraut Wagon, the Pink Taco, or Hammered. He sighed. Birds chirped in the large oak behind him. The sunlight caressed his weary body. A gentle breeze fanned his face as he closed his eyes, drawing in a deep breath. He shook off any unease and relaxed. The humming of cars, murmurs of citizens, and the twitter of the birds lulled him.

Bang!

Jasen bolted upright. He swiveled his head, searching for trouble. As he blinked into the sunlight, he saw a large van. The occupants kept spilling out like clowns at a circus. They weren't children but gangly young men. Last out, a woman lunged from the vehicle and bent, placing her hands on her thighs as if she might get sick.

Jasen stood and stretched. He would have to report it if she vomited. He couldn't leave a mess on the sidewalk. Wandering in the van's direction, he took the path toward the side of the park where he could observe the newcomers.

While watching the clowns, he noticed a large black SUV parked behind the van. Two men dressed as if to stage a corporate takeover stepped out of the Escalade. "Which one is the ringleader?" Jasen mumbled.

When the gaggle of men parted, Jasen spotted two women. One was a dark-haired Barbie, and the other was shorter, but her long curls floated on the wind, entrancing him. Her laughter rang, and he focused on her face. The sound of her voice caused his heart to race.

Jasen shook his head. He shouldn't be interested, but curiosity had him stepping closer. *It's only because they aren't locals. Keep believing that, stupid.*

# CHAPTER 3

## *Michaela*

MICHAELA ARSCHFICK SUCKED IN A deep breath of Texas air and swore she smelled barbecue. She hated barbecue, but she would take it over the smell of the van. Stuck with six fresh-from-college men, the vehicle reeked of body odor, dirty feet, and farts.

"This trip can't be over soon enough," Michaela rasped.

"I know, right?" Kim Burr said with a Cheshire cat grin.

Michaela distanced herself from the van and the group of men. She stepped out onto the grass and arched her back.

"Frank is such a jerky driver," Kim uttered, throwing a glare at the oblivious man.

"Shut up. You're not in the back ricocheting around like a pinball," Michaela huffed with her hands on her hips.

Kim tossed her long ebony hair and laughed. "That's true, Mick. I'm not." She squinted devilishly.

Michaela slapped Kim's arm playfully, and they giggled.

Darren Arschfick cleared his throat. "All right, ladies, listen up."

Michaela and Kim stepped closer toward the vehicles. Inspecting her nails, Kim feigned disinterest. Michaela studied the goofy grin on her ex-husband's face. The IT gang quieted, listening to Saint Darren. He loved moments when the young guys leaned in, eager to learn at the feet of their mighty leader.

Darren's perfect sandy hair stayed in place even though the breeze tried hard to restyle it. His straight teeth glinted the winning smile that had sealed many deals. His dynamic personality had once enamored Michaela, but no longer.

Darren's dark eyes darted around, raking the square and the buildings surrounding it. Michaela knew his pattern. He would survey the buildings and businesses but not say a word. All the while his mind would churn ideas. He planned to set the IT gang loose and see if they'd come up with any ideas on their own.

"Let's form teams of two," Darren said, glancing at a clipboard his personal assistant Rodney Butkus handed him.

"Mick's with me," Kim announced, grabbing Michaela's hand and lifting it into the air.

Darren's eyes narrowed for a split second, and a few of the IT guys groaned.

"Sorry, boys," Michaela said, not sorry at all.

"We know the drill," Kim said, waving at Rodney and Darren as she turned, pulling Michaela away. They headed west and crossed the road. The old two and three-story buildings could be anywhere Main Street, USA. The closest building, housing Teed and Teed Law Offices, had a cornerstone that read 1864. They proceeded to the Pink Taco's brick facade.

Kim peered in the restaurant's large window. "Mm, it smells good. I wonder if Darren will let us eat here today. I'd kill for some authentic salsa."

Michaela nodded but continued toward the next retail shop. The grimy window bedazzled her. Not the grit and fingerprints but the handmade wooden toys on display. She took a step closer, tempted to press against the glass like someone else had. "Kim check it out. Look at the old-fashioned toys."

Kim snapped her gum and frowned. "Toys? What the heck?"

"Oh, come on." Michaela tugged her best friend to the door.

The red paint had faded to mauve, but the egg and dart patterned wood trim hinted at the store's former glory. A bell rang as they stepped inside. Michaela twirled on the hardwood floor, nostalgia washing over her. The store sold her father's childhood toys. On special occasions, Grandma had brought out the box of Michaela's dad's toys and let her play with them.

"Hello, can I help you find anything?" an elderly woman asked.

Michaela turned with a smile. "I love your store."

The woman's grin blossomed into a full-blown smile. "Thank you. It's been in the family three generations."

"Wow! That's amazing." Michaela glanced at a family photo hung on the wall. "I'll look around. I promised my niece and nephew a souvenir."

"Let me know if you have any questions or need any help." She walked behind the register and picked up a bottle of spray cleaner and started to wipe the countertop.

"I used to play with my dad's Lincoln Logs at my grandparent's house." Michaela reached for the container and inspected it.

"This is more my style," Kim said, pointing to a shelf of Barbie and other dolls.

"Is there a Texas Barbie?" Michaela asked. She decided on a pop gun for her nephew and a pretty cowgirl doll for her niece.

"You know, technically you're not their aunt anymore," Kim said, leaning against the counter and crossing her arms.

Michaela sighed and shook her head. "And you know Darren doesn't remember he has a family. The business is the only relationship in his life."

"That's true." Kim checked her watch then moved so she could see out the window. "But that doesn't mean you have to make up for his shortcomings."

"Where are you from?" the owner asked.

"Cincinnati," Michaela replied, reaching into her purse to find her wallet.

"You're a long way from home. What brings y'all to Texas?" the older woman asked.

Michaela shot a glance toward Kim, but she stared outside, watching Frank and his partner, Lance. Her eyes narrowed as they ventured into a gift shop.

"We visited Nockerville on a consulting job," Michaela replied.

"I hope it went well. How do you like Texas?" the woman asked, tucking a pencil into her silver hair above her ear.

Michaela rested her palms on the counter and closed her eyes a moment. Her heart had been trying to express something, but she'd ignored it. "It's nice."

The woman nodded as she punched the keys on an antique cash register.

"Is it hard to keep inventory using that machine?" Michaela asked, handing over two twenties.

"Tell her to chuck it," a disembodied male voice said from a backroom.

The woman laughed. "That's my grandson, Wyatt."

A tall dark-haired teen popped his head out of the doorway. "You need to update your system."

With a ding, the cash drawer opened. "The register is fine. We can't afford a new fancy machine, anyway."

Wyatt rolled his eyes before coming to his grandmother and giving her a side squeeze. She handed Michaela her change. "Oh, I forgot to ask, would you like me to mail this home for you?"

Michaela gasped at the thought. "That would be wonderful. Our van is cramped." She wrote the shipping address on a notepad.

Inspecting the young man who tapped on the screen of his cell phone, Michaela said, "I bet Wyatt could find you a system and set it up for you. He seems tech savvy."

"Yeah, Grandma, let me help you," Wyatt said. He put his hands together, begging.

The owner chuckled again and tussled his hair. "We'll see." She handed Michaela the receipt. "Enjoy your stay."

Kim continued to glare out the window. She'd cocked a hip and tapped her foot. "Frank's gone down that whole side."

Michaela met her at the window and watched the skinny man slip through another door. "So. He's not spending any time."

"Oh?" One of Kim's thin eyebrows shot up.

"Yeah. We've met the store owner and the possible future owner. We know how they both feel about the business." Michaela smiled triumphantly.

# CHAPTER 4

## *Jasen*

JASEN ADJUSTED HIS TIE. *WHO are these people and why have they descended on Fortuna?*

Jasen's gaze volleyed over several teams of two. One pair of men disappeared into the Tease Me Salon. He chuckled when they immediately stumbled back out. He imagined the receptionist Gloria Sass frowning and pointing toward the exit.

Another set entered the Gift Spot. With the romance phenomenon in Fortuna, the small shop had added adult costumes to their inventory. Jasen used to buy cards for the kind souls who'd made him a casserole after his wife died, but the card selection had dwindled to make room for more costumes.

He focused on the only two women as they toured the Tin Soldier toy store. When Jasen visited the old shop, the smell and squeaking floor triggered pleasant memories of his childhood.

One young man put a phone to his ear then elbowed his buddy as the women left the toy store and sauntered down the street toward the Tease Me Salon and more. The shorter wavy-haired woman yanked on the door handle, and the ladies disappeared inside.

The man on the phone nodded, and the men turned around, traipsing toward the converging group waiting at the corner. Jasen ambled down the sidewalk on an intercept course. Across the park, two others waved at the larger group.

Jasen pretended to read the ads taped to the windows of Sandy Beach's real estate business as the posse passed.

"I hope this restaurant is good," a voice said.

"I want a steak."

"Dude, that will cost a lot," the first voice responded.

"It's not like I'm paying for it," the second voice laughed.

"Yeah man, we're in Texas. They've got to have great…"

The conversation lagged out of earshot, and Jasen turned to inspect the newcomers. All sizes and body types. Wearing ripped jeans to joggers. Goofy novelty tees to polo shirts. The men hadn't stopped anywhere long enough to shop and appeared to be heading toward Hammered, Fortuna's favorite pub. Jasen squelched the temptation to follow them and find out why they visited.

The stylish men had stayed in the center of the park. They turned in varying directions talking. One pointed and rubbed his chin while the other furiously scribbled on a pad of paper. They appeared older than the crew but seemed close to Jasen's ripe age of thirty-two. The pointer stopped moving when the women exited the salon. The ladies laughed and headed toward Hammered.

Jasen watched a minute then followed them. Curiosity nagged, but also, returning to work wasn't an option. Jacklyn would chastise him if he came back before eating lunch. He stuck his hands into his pockets again and kicked a pebble into the street.

Across the way, the wavy-haired woman tugged on the restaurant's door. Jasen imagined the smell that hit her as she went in: comfort food and stale beer. He glanced both ways then crossed to the tavern. As he entered the building, he nodded at the owner behind the bar. Holden Dix wiped glass beer mugs and acknowledged him with a wave of a white towel.

Jasen slipped into a booth where he could observe.

The group of out-of-towners pushed together a long line of tables. The chattering young men left two empty seats on the end. Taking a chair on the far side, the tall dark-haired woman pointed across to an empty seat and the shorter woman nodded. Jasen forced himself to remain in the booth while the women sat themselves.

Holden's wife, Sharon, offered a menu, but Jasen shook his head. "No thanks, I'll start with a sweet tea."

"Sure thing." She smiled and turned to leave.

Jasen caught her wrist. "What's up with the crowd?"

Sharon threw the group a glance. "They're from Ohio on a big job for Nockerville."

"What kind of job?" He rubbed his chin, studying the young men again.

"They're some kind of consulting firm. I'm not sure. They were all talking at once." She gave a one shoulder shrug and left.

Piccadilly, the Dix's daughter, brought a tray of drinks for the large party. Jasen caught the wavy-haired woman's gaze and his heart skipped a beat. Blushing, she quickly glanced back at the other woman.

The men flirted with the women, and Jasen witnessed several eye rolls. Finally, the wavy-haired woman pushed her chair back and stood with her hands on her hips. "That's not funny, Chase."

"Ah, come on, Mick. You know I'm just playing," Chase said with a childish pout.

"Darren won't like it," the other woman stated.

"Darren isn't here. And Mick and Darren aren't a couple anymore, are they?" another man said, leaning back with his hands folded over his chest.

"That isn't the point," the other woman said in an irritated tone.

"It's okay, Kim, but you're right," Mick said. She pointed at Chase. "Darren won't like it. One of your cronies will rat on you." She turned away from the group and stalked toward Jasen. She smiled at him, and his heart fluttered again.

"May I join you?" she asked. Without waiting for a reply, she slid into the booth opposite him.

"Sure," he said, studying her heart-shaped face. She had pale green eyes and plump lips.

"What's good to eat?" She glanced over toward her group. Pixie started taking their order.

"They have great burgers and wings." Jasen swallowed when she swung her gaze back to him.

"Do you know this town well?" she asked, tilting her head.

Sharon set his tea on the table. "He's one of the most informed Fortuna citizens," she said with a wink, causing him to chuckle.

His guest's eyes widened then a genuine smile blossomed on her lips. "That's great. Do you mind if I pick your brain?"

"Will it hurt?" he asked before taking a sip of the tea.

"Maybe a little," she laughed then stuck out her hand. "Hello, I'm Michaela Arschfick."

He took her small hand and held it. Her warm skin was soft as silk. "I'm Jasen. I take it you're not from here."

The blush returned to her cheeks, and she pulled her hand back. "No, I'm from Cincinnati. We're from Ohio." She thumbed over her shoulder at the loud ensemble. "We're in Texas looking for consulting jobs. The Nockerville mayor invited us."

"Did you get the job?" Jasen asked, curious if she'd be in Texas for any length of time.

"We won't know until they receive and review the proposal. But they seemed to like what Darren had to say." She gave a small noncommittal shrug and inspected the stocked bar.

"Do you like the area?" Jasen asked.

Michaela studied him again. "Nockerville was okay. I'm more interested in this town. What can you tell me about it?"

Jasen rubbed the short growth on his chin and heated as her gaze followed the movement. "Why Fortuna?"

She glanced down at her hands. "I don't know." She sighed. "It feels homey."

Jasen liked the answer, and he nodded. "What do you want to know?"

"Anything and everything."

Jasen leaned back with a long whistle. Michaela laughed, her eyes crinkling into half-moons. The melodic sound sent waves of pleasure through him. He swallowed and looked away. A few young men from her group frowned at them. Jasen returned her smile. "That's a tall order."

She gazed expectantly, and he squirmed under the scrutiny. He cleared his throat. "It's an awesome place to live. There are several unique mom and pop places to eat. All the food is great." He ticked off a list: A Hole in One, The Pink Taco, Hammered, the Kraut Wagon, and Stitts. "The community is closely knit. We have ranchers and farmers, but many small shops too."

B.J. Johnson entered Hammered and headed straight to the bookshelf next to the bar. After reading the back blurbs, he settled on two books then left the building. B.J. had to be on his lunch break, because he hadn't glanced around and appeared on a mission.

"We, Kim and I, noticed that many businesses have bookshelves. Can you tell me about them?"

"Yes." Jasen smirked and crossed his arms. One of her dainty brows rose. She leaned over the table. He caught a whiff of a light floral scent. *Lilies?*

"Do tell," Michaela implored.

"It's a Fortuna thing. Jessie Barnes inherited a Longhorn cattle ranch from her grandparents, but she also acquired her grandma's hoard of romance novels. She dared that man, who you just saw, to read a few, and he liked them. He started daring other men to read them. Soon the whole town became obsessed with reading the things. Jessie donated the books, and as the phenomenon spread, bookshelves popped up here and there."

"That's interesting." She watched as another man came and perused the shelf.

"Can I buy you lunch?" Jasen asked.

Michaela's gaze lifted to his, and a pretty blush crept over her skin. She smiled and nodded. "That would be nice. Thank you."

# CHAPTER 5

## *Michaela*

THE RESTAURANT'S DOOR OPENED AND Michaela shrunk into the booth, holding her breath. Darren strode in, followed by Rodney. The men located their group and started toward the table, but when Darren saw her sitting with another man, he changed direction.

Darren's brow rose and his patented deal-closing smile appeared. He attempted to slide in next to her, but Michaela wouldn't budge. He balanced precariously on the edge of the seat.

Looking across the room, Michaela caught Kim's attention. Kim rolled her eyes then pretended to yawn as Rodney and Chase carried on a lively discussion next to her.

"I'm Darren Arschfick, Mick's husband," he said, offering his hand to Jasen, and they shook.

"*Ex*-husband." Michaela frowned and crossed her arms. She detested when Darren claimed her, especially after he neglected her during their marriage.

Jasen's gaze jumped from Darren to Michaela.

"So what's good to eat here?" Darren asked, glancing toward the bar.

"Nothing," Michaela said, giving Darren's shoulder a shove. "Jasen and I are going somewhere else."

She shoved again and, frowning, Darren rose. Michaela scooted out of the booth and pressed past Darren with her nose high. She hadn't intended to abandon Kim, and threw her friend an apologetic smile. Jasen stood and opened his wallet. He dropped a five on the table and followed Michaela out of Hammered. In the sunlight and fresh air, she inhaled deeply.

"I'm sorry. I hope you don't mind?" she asked, glancing at her shoes.

"It's okay." Jasen pointed up the road. "I know a place with great food. It's a food truck of sorts."

"Of sorts, huh?" She fell into step with his long strides as they headed away from Fortuna's central square.

"It's more a wagon." He glanced at her. "You'll see."

They walked in companionable silence. She inspected the different buildings as they passed the steps to the town hall.

"Darren wanted to meet with your mayor today but his assistant told us he isn't in this afternoon. I thought I might talk to him before Darren. Do you know him?" Michaela asked.

Jasen caught his toe on the sidewalk, stumbling. "Me? Yeah sure, I know him."

"Do you think he would be open to an outside consulting firm cold-calling?"

"I suppose." Jasen nodded, rubbing his chin.

If she could get inside information before her ex, she'd make Darren irate. Michaela smirked. "What's the mayor like?"

"He's a hot, young thing," a feminine voice said from behind her.

Michaela paused, turning toward a skinny, old woman with a cap of dark hair and an ornery grin. Jasen covered his face with his palm.

"He's young?" Michaela asked. Her father would be considered young compared to the woman.

"And hot," the lady reiterated while wiggling her eyebrows.

"What's he like?" asked Michaela, trying to stymie a giggle.

"He's single." The woman fanned herself.

"Desire Hardmann, let me introduce you to Michaela Arschfick," Jasen said.

"Nice to meet you, Michaela. So why are you interested in the mayor?"

Michaela sighed, glancing behind Desire to where Darren poked his head out of the restaurant. Thank God, they were far enough away that he wouldn't hear the conversation.

Jasen and Michaela shared a look before she answered, "I'd like to meet him."

Desire's gaze jumped to Jasen's then back. "Okay." The old woman shook her head. "Haven't you met him?"

"No, she hasn't," Jasen said then hastily continued, "We're walking down to Hamish's wagon for lunch. Would you care to join us?"

"Oh, that sounds heavenly. I haven't had Hamish's sausage in a long time." Desire clapped her hands.

They continued, passing an old fire station that appeared abandoned. "Is that building for sale?" Michaela asked.

"No. I don't know who owns the building, but it's rented by the city for storage," Desire said.

21

Jasen nodded. "Christmas lights. Props for the high school plays. Those types of things."

A pang of sadness hit Michaela. Kim had been on the lookout for a building where she could open a coffee shop. The old firehouse would be perfect; unfortunately, it was in Texas, not Cincy. "That's a shame it's not utilized. It's a cool building."

"It is," Jasen agreed. He led the women across the street and at the next corner a delectable scent had Michaela's stomach rumbling.

"Mm. That smells heavenly." Michaela smiled at Jasen.

A line wrapped around a chuck wagon shaped contraption enclosed with glass. Bags of chips hung like laundry. "Burger's Kraut Wagon" was hand-painted in an Olde English font on a sign over the window.

Jasen introduced Michaela to an older cowboy, Brad Davidson, and his daughter, Jessie, who stood in front of them in the line.

"Brad's in my book club," Jasen said.

"Wait. The books again," Michaela giggled.

"The men of this town are obsessed with my grandma's books," Jessie said with a wave.

"I'm waiting for someone to act out a hero for me," Desire said, staring at Brad. His gray mustache twitched.

Michaela spotted a man in camouflage pants sitting on a bench some distance from the wagon. He stared away from the people. Something about him made her suspect he was homeless. Before she knew what she was doing, she stood in front of him. He wore an old tattered t-shirt and had a grimy backpack next to him. His sunken eyes glanced up when she stopped and stuck out her hand.

"Hi, I'm Michaela," she smiled.

He hesitated then took her hand. A thin grin graced his lips.

"Thank you for your service," she said.

He responded with a stiff nod and pulled back.

"Can I buy you lunch?" she asked.

His features hardened, and he shook his head. "No, thank you."

She didn't want to push her luck or insult his pride, so she returned to Jasen's side.

Desire fluttered eyelashes at the man taking her order. "I'll take the Fortuna fire dog," she said. "Hamish, have you seen the mayor lately? This young lady wants to meet him." She pointed to Michaela, but Hamish stared open-mouthed at Jasen before Jasen shook his head.

"He's always around, miss. I'm sure you'll find him soon," Hamish replied.

Michaela nodded, reading the menu. "What do you recommend for a newbie?"

Hamish grinned. "I've got you covered. Just tell me the size."

"As big as I can get," Michaela said, standing on her tiptoes trying to see into the wagon.

"Wow, and I thought I had an appetite for wieners," Desire said, taking her to go sack.

Jasen insisted on paying for Desire and Michaela's food.

"Thank you, Jasen," Desire said. "It was nice to meet you. Good luck with the mayor." She waved as she strutted back the way they'd came.

Michaela placed a hand on his arm. "Thank you. Let's go sit by that man." She pointed to the homeless veteran.

He carried the food while Michaela held bottles of water. Jasen sat on one side of the bench opposite the man. She squeezed between them.

"I hope you don't mind if we join you, Tom," Jasen said.

"No, not at all." Tom glanced away as they unwrapped the sandwiches.

Michaela bit into the sausage-style meat with sauerkraut and other toppings. Flavor exploded in her mouth. She hummed as she chewed, making both men chuckle.

The conversation touched on Tom's service stint and then turned to Michaela's family.

"My grandpa was in the Army. My dad too. He's a long-distance trucker now. I don't see him much because he travels across the country all the time. He loves the west."

Jasen's thigh rested against hers, and as he moved to ball the sandwich wrapper, his arm brushed hers, sending tingles up it. She wished she didn't have to return to her traveling companions.

"Thanks for being willing to leave the restaurant. I'm sorry I acted the way I did." Michaela glanced down at her food, embarrassed she'd let Darren bring out the worst in her. She'd finished a quarter of her sandwich, but her appetite had fled.

"It's not a problem. I was craving the Kraut Wagon anyway."

She glanced hopefully toward Jasen. "Really?"

"Yes, but I don't blame you for wanting out of your ex-husband's space."

She nodded and peered down again, tears pricking her eyes. "He has a way of sucking the oxygen from the room."

Jasen's arm fell along her shoulder, and he squeezed her against him. Her wounded heart beat faster at his tender touch. She brushed a tear away. "You must think I'm crazy for working with him."

"You must love the work."

Michaela nodded again. "I do." She stole a breath and raised her head, examining the building across the narrow street. "We put together plans to revitalize small towns. We breathe life into them."

"You think Fortuna is dying?" Tom asked.

"No. But there are signs of decay." She twisted to face Tom. "This town has a steady heartbeat. It's crazy, but I feel it. I've never felt something in my gut like this. It's weird and scary."

Tom grinned and glanced over her head at Jasen. "It's home."

"Would either of you care for the rest of this? I can't eat any more." She raised it toward Jasen first.

"Sorry, I'm stuffed," he said, shaking his head.

Michaela lifted it to Tom. He smirked but took it. He made a similar humming sound while he chewed.

Jasen winked at Michaela, and she felt her face heat. She wanted to speak with the mayor, but she'd rather spend her afternoon with the handsome stranger, Jasen.

# CHAPTER 6

## *Jasen*

MICHAELA TOSSED HER HEAD AS she laughed, the sound music to Jasen's ears. She'd been clever, and Tom now had a warm meal in his stomach. She moved to the ground and wrapped her arms around her knees and talked with Tom. The veteran had opened up like Jasen had never seen.

Jasen relaxed back and studied Michaela. She had a smattering of freckles on a cute upturned nose. Her waves fell in layers around her shoulders, and the curls swayed as she moved. He longed to touch them to see if they were as soft as they appeared.

Michaela's phone rang. She glanced at the screen with a frown. A heaviness settled in Jasen's gut as she sucked in her bottom lip before hitting the button.

"Hey, what's up?" Michaela's brows knit together. "I'm getting a tour of Fortuna. Don't worry about me. Yes, I'm with Jasen. Why does that matter?" Michaela met his gaze and rolled her eyes. "If you want to leave, then leave." She sighed and put the phone away.

"Do you need to go back?" Jasen asked.

She stood and wiped her hands on her thighs. "No, but I should walk around the town more."

"What are you looking for?" Tom asked.

Michaela turned in a circle, taking in her surroundings. "Ideas."

"Ideas for what?" Jasen asked.

"Making this town better." She met his gaze.

"Name one thing you'd do on this street," he challenged.

She put her hands on her hips. "Easy. I'd move the Kraut Wagon over to

25

the square. There'd be more parking for the wagon's customers and it would bring business to the surrounding stores."

Jasen raised his finger to make a point, but as the image formed in his mind he lowered his arm. "That's a great idea."

She smiled with a blush. "Care to show me more of the town?"

Jasen jumped to his feet, earning a chuckle from Tom. "Sure. I need to call the office first." Her grin grew brighter. He stepped away and dialed the number. Jacklyn's familiar voice answered. "Hey Jack, I won't be returning this afternoon."

"There's a consulting firm in town, and the owner has requested 'an audience' with you," Jacklyn said in her lunch lady tone. Jasen envisioned her hackles raised. "Since the counsel meets tomorrow, I told him he could speak for a few minutes."

"An audience? Oh, brother." Jasen rubbed his chin. "I've met one of the consultants, and I'm going to give Michaela a tour of the town."

"You are?" Jacklyn said in a sing-song voice.

"She's only visiting for the day."

"If you say so. Michaela is part of the consulting company wanting to meet with you, right?" Jacklyn drawled.

"Yes." Jasen recognized the underhanded scheming in the older woman's tone. He'd bet on matchmaking. "Don't get any ideas."

"See if she will present their material instead of the other fellow. He was too pushy and got my goat."

"I'll work on her," Jasen said, slapping a palm to his forehead.

"I hope you will," Jacklyn replied then hung up without saying goodbye, her usual send off.

Jasen returned to the bench, noticing the faded color again. "Let's walk." He offered his elbow, and she slipped her small hand into the crook. He covered it with his, and they started off toward the library.

Jasen held open the library door. They slipped inside. "Ophelia is part of my book club," he said with a wave to Ophelia Cox behind the desk.

"Who's your friend?" Ophelia asked with raised eyebrows.

"I'm Michaela," she said, sticking out her hand. They shook, and Ophelia took over the tour of the library. Jasen followed like a loyal puppy.

# CHAPTER 7

## *Michaela*

As Michaela entered the hotel, a gust of stale air assaulted her. In a secluded seating area to her right, the IT guys huddled over a poster board. The door silently closed behind her. Kim stood in the background with her arms crossed and a smirk on her face. The only team member with any experience, Kim had let the IT gang create the proposal.

*They were so going to bomb and Kim will laugh the whole time.*

Michaela crept closer to the group, catching Kim's attention. Kim met her halfway.

"So did you have a good afternoon with Mr. Hottie McHot?"

Michaela glanced out the glass door as if Jasen might hear. "Yes, Jasen was fun. He gave me firsthand knowledge of Fortuna. I met half the town."

"Did you kiss him?" Kim asked.

"No," Michaela said, her face heating. She glanced outside again. Maybe she should have. It wasn't as if she would ever see him again.

"That sucks. You two had chemistry even Darren noticed it. It had his boxers in a bunch." Kim turned and swiped her hand in a grand gesture. "I've had to babysit these morons for the evening. You owe me, girl."

Michaela giggled and leaned against the door frame. The men began arguing over whose idea it was to add a clock tower to the courthouse. Buck rolled his eyes and then started drawing on the poster.

"That's not in perspective." Frank jabbed the sketch with a finger. "Darren wouldn't propose something like that, anyway. It's a waste of resources."

"It's beautification with function." Buck's tongue stuck to the corner of his mouth as he hunched closer and added detail.

"Is that the University of Cincinnati's clock tower again?" Frank asked with a huff.

Red-faced, Buck glanced up at the light before answering, "No." He shrugged. "Maybe. Darren can sell anything."

Michaela pushed off the doorjamb and pulled Kim into the lobby. She leaned and whispered, "Darren *can* sell anything, but Jasen suggested I make the presentation."

Kim's eyes narrowed as she studied Michaela's face. "What are you thinking?"

Michaela sighed. She threw her hands into the air and turned around to pace. "I don't know. This is crazy."

"Spill it, Mick." Kim tapped her designer-clad toe.

Michaela stopped pacing and grinned. "The municipal building already has a clock." She shrugged. "I think I want to see if Fortuna will hire me as a consultant."

"You? Not New Wave Designs?"

"Yes. I'll come back another time." Michaela's heart raced.

"But you have a no-compete clause if you leave the company." Kim shot a glance to the room full of guys.

"Only three months." With a shrug, Michaela crossed her arms. "This place feels like home. I can imagine a life here."

"With Mr. Hottie McHot?" Kim's bright red lips twisted into a smirk.

Heat flared on Michaela's face, and she glanced at the floor. "He's a nice bonus but not the reason."

Jasen had asked her if she felt obligated to remain loyal to New Wave Designs. She loved the work, but if she could do the same thing somewhere else, she'd make the switch. Moving hadn't occurred to her before, but suddenly the change sounded thrilling. Darren wouldn't want it, but she didn't care.

"Uh, huh? Go find Mr. Hottie McHot," Kim said with a wave of dismissal. "I don't want to listen to you sighing all night."

With her backside, Michaela pushed against the door but hesitated. "If you wouldn't mind, pick slides for the Power Point that show work that I've contributed too."

Kim stalked toward the gang with another wave.

"Oh, and I found the perfect building for your future coffee shop," Michaela offered. Kim's head whirled around so fast she stumbled in her high heels. "I'll tell you about it when I get back."

Kim narrowed her eyes. "You'd better."

Michaela slipped out into the dark, cool evening. She hugged herself. Glancing both directions, she didn't spot Jasen. She took a guess and headed toward the square. On the corner, she inspected the small park but couldn't see anyone. Doleful, she crossed to the green space. The black street lamps lit the paths. She stopped before the bronze statue of Fortuna's founder. After reading the plaque, she ventured to the fountain in the center. The soft light caressed the bubbling water, luring her close.

She relaxed. Her mind wandered toward Jasen. She'd been attracted to him and found his scruffy, strong chin sexy. His dazzling smile and expressive hazel eyes were nice, but his willingness to ditch Darren and the IT gang without question warmed her heart. He hadn't pried into her personal history and had been genuinely interested in her work, even when she had rambled on. When she had apologized, he waved off the apology and asked intelligent questions that proved he had listened.

Joy bubbled in her soul. His attentiveness validated her. Michaela glanced at the silhouette of the large oak, its branches yawning overhead, and took a deep breath.

Texas. Who'd have thought she would like Texas? Especially some small town with the mighty fire ant as its mascot. Michaela chuckled and leaned back. Her eyes sought the sky littered with more stars than she'd ever seen. Lord have mercy, there was a lot about Fortuna she liked.

Michaela hated to admit it, but Kim had been right. Jasen would be one hell of a perk if Michaela moved to Fortuna. She sighed. Why hadn't she kissed him?

Goosebumps formed on her arms, and she hugged herself and studied the area. The fountain had several tiers. The highest with a Greek deity, maybe Justice, stared down at her in silent judgment.

What was she doing wandering around a strange town looking for the boy next door, Mr. Hottie McHot, when she should join the IT crew working?

Jasen had most likely arrived home by now. Unzipping her purse, she searched for a coin and tossed it into the water, making a futile wish. She rubbed her face then shuffled the circumference of the fountain, returning to where she had started. Gazing up from the water, Michaela met Jasen's eyes.

Her wish had come true. Michaela's lungs declined to work, and she froze. She refused to blink in case he vanished. His wide eyes and smirk made her heart jump.

Jasen stepped forward. She leaped into his arms.

"What are you—?" she began, but he brushed his lips against hers.

Heat consumed Michaela, and she tiptoed, claiming his lips with territorial aggression. For the night, he was hers. His hands plunged into her hair, holding her head.

When they took a breath, he lifted her and they sat on the bench. Cradled on his lap, one hand playing with the hair at the nape of his neck, she opened for him and his tongue swept in. She clutched his shirt.

He moaned. Their ragged breath split the silence and drown out rational thought.

After a while, she snuggled against him. She dragged in large gulps of air. It had been a long time since she'd kissed anyone with the ferocity as she kissed Jasen.

"Don't leave," he rasped. His heart thumped rapidly through his shirt.

Michaela twisted so her nose was in the crook of his neck. She stole a deep breath as tears stung her eyes. "I have to go home."

Jasen sighed. "Come back."

"I will if we're offered a contract."

"I want you to take the job, not the firm."

Michaela rested a moment as he stroked her hair. Could she find enough work in Fortuna to survive? "We'll see how it goes tomorrow when I meet the mayor."

# CHAPTER 8

## *Michaela*

SHADOWING DARREN, MICHAELA STRUGGLED UP the steep steps, clutching a stack of paperwork and a messenger laptop bag that bumped her rump with every stride.

Darren's pants clung to his hindquarters and while appealing, she recognized the extra swagger for her benefit. He effortlessly opened the thick wood door and disappeared into the vestibule. She hurried up the last step to catch the door before it closed. Her fingers stretched for the handle when the door thrust open. Darren had remembered her and, out of breath, she staggered through.

Filled with paperback novels, two eight-foot by four-foot bookshelves hugged the right wall. Trade sized and smaller, all romance like Jasen had mentioned. She glanced at the spines. *The Forbidden Room*, *Daddy's Naughty Assistant*, and *Bound by Love and Ligatures*. She chuckled nervously and scrambled after Darren.

The long paneled hallway reminded her of elementary school. Their footsteps echoed as they approached a large desk. The seal of Fortuna hung on the wall behind it. A spotlight highlighted the metal disk with a landscape, longhorns, and stars. A woman cleared her throat.

"Can I help you?" she asked in a voice that reminded Michaela of her third grade teacher. The woman's dark eyes scanned them and Michaela shifted. A brass nameplate on the desk read: The Boss.

Darren smiled and nonchalantly leaned against the desk. "Hello. I'm Darren Arschfick with New Waves Design. We have an appointment with the council and the mayor."

The boss glanced at her computer screen. "Ah, yes." She pushed the chair back and stood, smoothing her navy pencil skirt. "Welcome, I'm Jacklyn Hyde. Please follow me." Jacklyn crossed the hall ten steps and opened a white six paneled door. She clicked on the light to a small conference room. "You can set up your equipment here."

Darren took the bag from Michaela and opened the laptop. He plugged in the machine and tapped the device awake. In the work zone, he dropped into a chair and powered up the presentation.

Jacklyn cleared her throat. "Do you have everything you need?"

"Yes, fine." Darren waved her off like he would shoo a fly.

"Michaela?" Jacklyn asked, her gaze bored into Michaela's, yet her lips held a faint smirk.

"Yes?" Michaela stepped closer to the woman.

"Come with me. The mayor wants to see you." Jacklyn crooked her finger and left the room.

Michaela shot a glance at Darren, but he remained absorbed in his work. Rolling her eyes, she left the room.

Jacklyn pointed to another door. She smiled and nodded as she twisted the knob and pushed it open.

Michaela hesitated when Jacklyn leaned close and confided, "I don't know what you've said or done, but I wanted to say thank you. He hasn't been this happy since his wife died." She left Michaela gaping.

The office seemed dark compared to the corridor, but as her eyes adjusted she noticed a desk, filing cabinets, and two chairs. She advanced into the room, recalling what she'd learned about the mayor. Young, widowed, good-looking. How could he know of her?

A man rose from behind the desk.

She blinked. "Jasen?" She smiled and clasped his hands in greeting. Her heart did somersaults. "Did you tell the mayor about me?" she asked as she hugged him.

"Michaela, I have a confession. I am the mayor." His gaze raked her face, his brow knit with concern.

"You?" She pushed back. "You want me to..." She turned away and glanced at her shoes. Her head started to pound.

"Stay. I want you to stay." Jasen took her elbow and moved her to one of the chairs. "Please, have a seat."

Michaela sunk into the navy armchair and leaned forward with her head in her hands. "God, Jasen. Darren will think I've been scheming this whole time. Why didn't you tell me?"

"I didn't want you to think of me differently. The only thing New Waves wanted with this town was to talk with the mayor." He sat at the desk across from her and fiddled with a pen. "I'm surprised you didn't figure it out. Every time you asked someone about the mayor they looked at me."

"That old lady called you a hot young thing," Michaela laughed.

Jasen turned red but smiled. "Yeah, she likes most of the male population. So how are we going to proceed?" he asked with raised brows.

Michaela locked her fingers together. Was he referring to them or the meeting? She sighed and glanced up. "I'm not going to say a thing."

His shoulders relaxed, and he leaned back in the chair. "Okay."

"I'm not doing this for you," Michaela snipped. "I couldn't ethically continue even if Darren didn't want the limelight but—"

"He always takes the spotlight, doesn't he?" Jasen reached his hands across the desk as if he wanted to console her.

Michaela drew back, examining the pile of the beige carpet. "It's his company. I just work for him."

"Do you do everything he says?" Jasen's gravelly voice held a hint of accusation.

Michaela's gaze snapped to Jasen's. "What do you mean?"

Jasen's eyes narrowed. "Last night, did he require you to work late?"

She gasped, and her face flared. "After our..." she paused, waving her hand. They had done a little more than make out, but "groping session" didn't sound eloquent. "...time together, I went back to the hotel. Kim pestered me about details, especially after she saw this." Michaela pulled her collar away, revealing a hickey. "She can be very persistent, so I spilled the beans then I probed her about what the IT gang had envisioned. We had a good laugh. They suck." A dry laugh escaped.

Jasen's gaze softened.

Her face pinched. "I don't serve my ex-husband. Since we've divorced, I have a strict new rule." She stood and pointed at him. "I won't sleep with my boss. Now or ever again." She twisted and stalked out of the room.

Michaela's breath came in short huffs as she returned to Darren's side and tried to appear relaxed. He was too busy to notice other than to nod.

Distracting herself from remembering Jasen's fingers in her hair and his lips on hers, she surveyed the room. One long oval table with twelve plush chairs on casters. Wood straight-back chairs lined the outside wall. The United States, Texas, and Fortuna flags hung on poles at the end of the room. The tan walls displayed several aerial photographs of the town.

Michaela sat in the seat and pulled out her phone. She texted Kim, and within ten minutes Kim sat next to her, patting her hand. "I've got this today," Kim told Darren.

Darren's gaze shifted to Michaela, but he nodded then shrugged. "If Mick wants to hand you the reins, then that's what we'll do."

The council started filing in, shaking Jasen and Jacklyn's hands then Darren, Michaela, and Kim's. Michaela noticed Jasen was the youngster of the group. He could easily be the son or grandson of the others. He called the meeting to order, and they went about their business.

Jasen stood. "We have guests all the way from Cincinnati. They were working in Nockerville, and Mayor Krystal Baals referred them to us. They are restorative consultants and want to pitch their ideas. Their team came and spent the day yesterday touring the town. They've made some observations and would like to share where they might be of assistance. Mr. Arschfick."

"Thank you, Mayor DeLay." Darren strutted to the podium and clicked the remote. "As the mayor told you, we consult but we aren't just city building or city planning consultants. We are life consultants. We want to improve your way of life." Darren clicked the small remote he had hidden in his hand. The screen lit up with a picture of a children's museum with overgrown bushes and a drab facade. "This town hired us to update and make one of their area's top moneymakers into a shining star." He flashed to the next slide and used a pointer to show off each thing the company updated.

"We had the yews removed and replaced with boxwood bushes. We focused on ornamental grasses that the children could touch, but nothing poisonousness or with thorns." A new slide showed another angle. New paint and more pathways leading to the front entry.

"Who designed these changes?" Jacklyn asked.

Kim replied, "We had several team members contribute, but the lead was Michaela Arschfick. Her number one priority was the children. She insisted that they add elements that encouraged kids to explore the world."

"What sort of elements?" Jasen asked.

Michaela squirmed in her seat as council members glanced at her. Her temperature rose, and she took a drink of water.

"A stepping-stone path. Box wood maze. A bridge. Funny cut outs."

Darren changed to the next example and once again Kim and Darren both were singing her praise to the council, even though she hadn't been the only member on the team.

A few council members nodded and made notes. Michaela sunk back into the chair, trying not to call attention to herself. Her knee bobbed up and down. It sounded more and more like a job interview, and Jacklyn kept smiling at her. The slides proceeded through jobs, highlighting what the company had done. Kim's melodic voice honed in on about Michaela's contributions. At the conclusion, Michaela remained as still as a statue, wishing for an invisibility cloak.

The presentation concluded, and the council peppered Darren, Kim, and Michaela with questions. Michaela excused herself to find the bathroom. She took her time. Kim finally went to retrieve her. "You all right?"

"Did you see who the mayor is? Jasen is the mayor. No, I'm not all right. God, Darren probably thinks I tried to shut him out of the job." Michaela wrung her hands.

Kim examined her eyebrows in the mirror. "Actually, Darren thinks you charmed the mayor into a job."

Michaela gasped. "He what?" She pressed her lips together to keep the profanity from flowing.

"Chill girl," Kim said, turning toward her. "You're as red as a fire ant." Kim burst out laughing. She leaned over until she had to wipe tears from her eyes.

Her laughter calmed Michaela until she was chuckling too. "I'm going to give Darren a piece of my mind," Michaela said.

"Just don't give him another piece of your heart." Kim held open the door for Michaela. Her high heels clicked on the tiled floor. They mingled in the hall, waiting for Darren to pack the laptop. When he emerged, Darren handed Michaela the messenger bag. Kim took it from her as she subtly pointed to Jasen.

Jasen was classy, yet casual in his white button-down shirt, navy and red striped tie, gray suit jacket, and dark jeans. His scruff was more of a beard. He glanced over and caught Michaela's gaze and blushed. If Darren noticed, he didn't react. With a final handshake, the New Waves Design team was ready to leave.

Michaela threw a glance over her shoulder as she left the building. It stung that Jasen hadn't told her. And it frustrated her that he stood there with his hands in his pockets watching her leave.

The van waited at the curb. Chase pushed up his glasses but held the door open for Kim as she climbed into the front passenger seat.

"Michaela," Jasen called from the door of the courthouse.

She turned and glanced at him. He seemed to be breathing heavy. "Yes?"

"May I have a minute of your time?" Jasen asked.

Darren glanced at his watch. "Hurry. We don't have time for lovesick heroics today." He and Rodney got into the SUV.

Michaela frowned and glanced at the van occupants. Kim had rolled down the window. "I'll be back in a few," Michaela said.

With a bright smile, Kim leaned out. "Screw Darren. Take your time."

Michaela grinned; Kim always had her back.

Michaela strode toward Jasen. His tentative expression softened, and a timid smile hinted at his lips. He opened the door, and she stepped back into the building. When she whirled around, she ran into his broad chest. He held her close, his hands gripping her arms gently.

"I've been wanting to do this since last night," he rasped. She tipped her head and glanced into his hazel eyes. Warmth from his fingers spread up her arms, and she pressed her hands against his chest. The tender expression on his face took the wind from her lungs. "Oh, Michaela." His lips brushed hers like a blessing. Soft and whispering, the touch set her on fire.

Over her shoulder, the SUV and van could see through the glass. She stepped out of their line of sight.

"Jasen, I—," words stalled as his lips found hers again. His scruff tickled and one hand plunged into her hair, holding her close. His tongue plundered her mouth, and she moaned. She clutched his dress shirt and pulled him closer. She hooked her leg around his as he pressed her against the bookcase. He shifted, and she slipped, causing a few books to clatter to the floor. They didn't break apart but tried to consume one another.

Someone started to clap. Jasen and Michaela broke apart, resting their foreheads together.

# CHAPTER 9

## *Jasen*

MICHAELA KEPT INVADING JASEN'S THOUGHTS. Her melodic laugh, soft lips, and silky waves were some of her features that had him staring into space with a silly grin. It didn't help that Jacklyn harped on him to call or text Michaela. He redirected Jacklyn by assigning her a task. Too bad his thoughts weren't as easily dissuaded.

Jasen opened his mailbox to answer citizens' emails.

Someone on Elm Street reported the same pothole that Jasen had already forwarded. He made a note to check and see if a work order had been placed. The pothole could cause a flat tire if a driver hit it too fast.

He clicked on the next email. Jasen blinked and read it again. He started laughing. A high school club requested the city pay for and maintain a colony of fire ants since it was the school's mascot. What a preposterous idea.

His phone pinged. *Michaela.* She'd handed in her resignation. "Thank you for helping me to see past the present. I've been spinning my wheels. I'll call you later," she texted.

Jasen kept watching the time, unsure when later was. The day dragged on. Around five, he turned off his light and left city hall. The sun had warmed his black sedan. He started the engine and rolled down the windows.

As he rounded the corner with the Kraut Wagon, Jasen's phone rang. He touched the car's screen to accept the call.

"Jasen, how are you?" Michaela said.

"I'm good." He paused, envisioning her brilliant smile. "How are you? Kim couldn't have been happy."

"No, but she gets it. She's been bugging me since the dog issue."

"Dog?" Jasen slowed at a stop sign and glanced both ways. Bunny Hopkins waved at him as she turned left. The equivalent of a Fortuna rush hour. "What breed of dog?"

"I don't know," she huffed. "A small, white yappy one. It's a crap story. Would you like to hear how romantic Darren is?"

"Not really."

Michaela laughed until she snorted.

"Now I'm curious," Jasen said. He turned onto the road that ran parallel to Dry Run creek.

"After Darren and I had been married a few years, I complained about his lack of attention to me, to us. You know, he wouldn't come home but stayed at the office all night. If I wanted any kind of physical touch, it happened at the office. It wasn't romantic, and I didn't like it. He loved that damned business more than me. So after I'd complained again he bought me a dog so I could cuddle with something at home."

Jasen chuckled. "What a dip-shit."

"I didn't have time to train it because I worked almost as much as Darren did."

"What happened to the dog?"

"Oh," Michaela squeaked. "Darren's cleaning lady was fond of it. Hopefully, she found it a home. That's just one story. Once I decided to separate from Darren, I found a small apartment and moved my stuff out. I didn't tell him that I'd left. I wanted to see if he'd notice."

"How could he not know you had gone?" Jasen asked, shaking his head.

"He doesn't go home, that's how. Darren found out two weeks later, when his personal assistance, Rodney, let it slip I'd gone. Darren suggested working on our marriage, but his idea of fixing the marriage meant having sex in his office." Michaela laughed dryly. "It was easy to not fall for Darren's charm after he hadn't realized I'd moved out. Geez, I can't believe it's been a year now."

Jasen could envision the small V on Michaela's forehead when she frowned and the way she rolled her eyes when she said Darren's name.

A squirrel darted across the road. Jasen slammed on the brakes and pulled over. His thumping heart drowned out her words. He blew out a breath, angling the air-conditioning vent at his face. "What did you just say?"

"I have to wait three months for the no-compete clause to expire before I can work in this field again. That sucks, but I will survive."

"Come to Texas," Jasen breathed.

"Jasen," she whispered. "What would I do?"

"I'll set up an interview with the city."

"You're a little biased," Michaela teased with a laugh. She quieted. "You know, I have an idea."

"I'm all ears." Another squirrel ran across the road, and a car swerved and honked.

"Is there something, some problem facing the city, that it needs to overcome? Maybe I can prove myself helping with that?"

"I'll have to consider it." Jasen rubbed his chin. "I'll let you know when I think of something."

They ended the call, and he closed his eyes, smiling. Her voice warmed his soul.

When he opened his eyes, his body went numb. He had pulled off at the entrance to Stanton Cove Park. The park where his wife had lost her life. The location still unnerved him.

With a shaky hand, he shifted into drive and eased away, clamping the wheel.

He parked then went straight to the fridge and downed a beer. On the sofa, he sat with his head in hands.

Why did the guilt still get to him?

Jasen hadn't forced Dee to go to the park to take a walk in the rain. But they'd had an argument, and she'd stormed out. The squabble had been Jasen's fault. Dee tried to explain, but he had kept harping. Reaching her boiling point, Dee had yelled "it's over" and thrown a photo of them at his head. He'd dodged it but the glass had shattered and the frame splintered when it hit the wall.

Jasen ran his fingers through his hair. That broken picture had reflected their marriage.

The phone rang, bringing him out of his morose thoughts. He plodded to the kitchen and picked up the handset. "Hello?"

"Hey Jasen, how are you doing?" Brad Davidson asked.

"I'm fine." Grateful for the distraction, he plopped onto a ladder-back chair. "I'll get *The Rancher's Daughter* back to you soon. I only have a couple of chapters left."

"Listen, son, I'm not calling regarding book club business," Brad said. "Coming home from the grocer I saw you stopped at Stanton Cove Park."

It felt as if someone slapped him, and Jasen rubbed his face. "I had a call, so I pulled over. I didn't realize where I was until the call ended."

"Everything okay?" Brad asked.

Jasen sighed and slumped forward. "I was shocked I'd ended up there, but now I'm fine. It was probably a good thing; it's been a long time."

"Probably." Brad coughed. "You've been holding on for a while. You've held it too close. I don't think Dee would want you to flounder."

"You didn't know her well." Heaviness settled in Jasen's gut.

"Well, son, if Dee would have preferred you to wallow in misery, then she wouldn't have been a woman worth holding on too."

Long after Brad had ended the call, Jasen laid awake on his bed, alone and empty. On his nightstand, his phone vibrated. He glanced at the screen. Michaela.

Instantly, the weight lifted, and Jasen could breathe again. He replied, and they texted well past her bedtime.

When Michaela stopped texting, Jasen set his phone aside and fell asleep dreaming about a different house and a new wife.

# CHAPTER 10

## *Michaela*

SOMEWHERE A MUFFLED BUBBLEGUM VERSION of the Flight of the Valkyries played. Michaela opened her bedroom door and peered down the hall. The song abruptly ended.

The heavenly scent of bacon tantalized her nose, and her stomach rumbled. She followed the smell.

A cabinet shut with a bang and pans rattled. Reaching the kitchen, Michaela spied Mierda Vaso, the pretty Hispanic woman who had checked her into the Dungogh Inn Bed and Breakfast, putting dirty dishes into the sink.

With a phone pinched between her ear and shoulder, Mierda said, "I'll be there soon. Thank you." She turned, frowning. "I'm sorry, Ms. Michaela. I have to leave and pick up my daughter from school. She's sick." Mierda swiped hair away from her face.

"Of course." Michaela took the empty plate Mierda handed her. "You need to take care of her."

"There's juice in the pitcher. Coffee and sugar is there." Mierda pointed to the counter with the condiments.

"It's fine. Just go." She waved as Mierda nodded, running out the door with her purse swinging.

Michaela glanced around the room and found a plate of bacon and a box of fresh donuts. She'd prefer a bowl of oatmeal, but at the moment her stomach demanded attention. She plucked a pastry from the box. The powdered sugar melted when it touched her tongue. The soft dough oozed jelly. She ran to the sink as it dribbled down her chin. A dollop dropped into the basin. She wiped her face and washed the confection down the drain.

Michaela poured a glass of orange juice then returned the pitcher to the fridge. The large Victorian home's kitchen was cozy yet modernized. Michaela cleaned the counter and put away the perishable items.

"What do you think you're doing?" A masculine voice startled her.

Michaela whipped around, nearly dropping the sponge she held. "I... uh." Her gaze raked the man's body. He was approximately six-feet tall with a muscular build. His short cropped hair and cop uniform had her smirking. "Are you really a police officer or is this some kind of RPG?"

"RPG?" he asked with a crinkled brow.

"Role playing game." Michaela put her hands on her hips. "I've heard about the men in this town. They like to act out their favorite heroes."

The man turned bright red but smiled. "You are right about the town, but I'm really an officer of Fortuna." He opened a cabinet and pulled out a mug and poured coffee. "I'm Ben Moore. My fiancée Kelly and I own this place."

"I'm Michaela Arschfick. I met Kelly yesterday." Michaela leaned against the counter and sipped her juice. She was the lone guest since Ben and Kelly had only remodeled one bedroom so far. "Mierda will be back in a few minutes. She had to pick up her sick daughter from school."

"Oh? I hope Cali is okay," Ben said. He swigged his coffee. "You don't need to clean up. I can get it."

"It's not a problem. I'm almost done. You could start the dishwasher. It's full."

"Thanks, Michaela. Are you enjoying your stay" Ben put his empty cup in the dishwasher and started it.

She moved to the large window, glancing out on the backyard with a gazebo. "There's something about this town. It feels like home." She turned and smiled at Ben. "Your house is lovely. Thanks for letting me be the guinea pig."

"We appreciate your understanding. I'm glad we could help you." The doorbell rang. "That's the electrician."

Michaela drove her rental car the long way, meandering down back roads weaving in and out of the Fortuna community. She found the elementary school where Kelly worked, and later she passed the high school.

She stopped at Stanton Cove Park. It had an interesting shaped lake, with a trail wrapping around the bank. She examined the sign with a map, noting it connected to a path that followed a creek away from the lake and main park. The trail led to a ridge. Michaela decided she'd jog the trail someday. On the flip side of the sign, pictures of fauna, regional animals, and a canyon dotted the surface.

At the courthouse, she hopped up the stairs but hesitated inside where Jasen had kissed her. Being pressed against the bookshelf had turned her on. She heated, remembering the slide of his hands through her hair.

Someone cleared their throat. A peripheral glance revealed Jacklyn typing at the keyboard. A small smirk graced the older woman's lips. Michaela swallowed and concentrated on keeping a neutral expression. Jacklyn had been the one who'd clapped for Jasen and Michaela's very public make-out session.

"He's waiting for you." Jacklyn giggled as Michaela walked past.

Michaela readjusted the bag on her shoulder. She wasn't exactly sure what task the committee would assign her, but Jasen had warned her it had involved property development. She had favors she could call in. The husband of her childhood best friend was one such person. She'd forwarded many opportunities to his company over the years. When her old friend found out about Jasen, she'd told her husband to be on call.

The door was open, and she entered. Three people glanced up, one elderly man and two women around her dad's age. "Hi, I'm Michaela." She recognized one woman from her earlier visit.

"Welcome," the older woman said. "This is Walter Mellan and Bunny Hopkins. I'm Sandy Beach. Nice to have you back in Fortuna. Please take a chair." Sandy indicated the only empty seat at the round table. Bunny passed her a thick folder.

"I hear you have a mission for me?" Michaela said, glancing at the folder.

Sandy and Walter shared a look. "What has the mayor told you?" Sandy asked.

Michaela leaned back. "He told me I'd have a task and it would have to do with property. Usually it does." She smiled.

"Take a look and see." They all opened their folders. Michaela glanced at the line drawing of a map of someone's land. It wasn't a large plot but sat adjacent to Stanton Cove Park.

"Has someone willed it to Fortuna?" Michaela asked. Some people considered it a legacy to pass their property on to the community.

Rubbing his chin, Walter laughed. "Yeah, I wish."

"That would make it a helluva lot easier," Sandy agreed.

"Michaela wouldn't have a task then," Bunny reminded, then giggled.

Once they sobered, Sandy took the lead again. "It's a dilapidated old farm and an eyesore. A sneezing longhorn could knock over the barn. The couple have refused to sell or even consider the option."

"Mr. Saks is a grouch, but truthfully, the property is too big for the couple to manage. It's going to kill them." Bunny's lips pinched.

"What do you want me to do?" Michaela asked.

Bunny glanced at Sandy, who glanced at Walter.

"I can't force them to sell." Michaela crossed her arms.

"Not force them. Get them to consider it." Sandy smiled. "They need to think about the future."

Walter flipped through the folder and picked out a paper. "If the city could find a developer, then maybe we could get a nice townhome community. With the park across the street, it would be a good sell for families."

"You'd like more tax dollars?" Michaela asked with a frown.

Sandy shook her head. "We need more affordable housing near town. The residents from the Saks' community could walk into town, to the park, or to school. It would help the downtown businesses."

Michaela nodded and pointed to the wall map of the city limits in the county. "Show me."

They stood and, while holding the property parcel map, she learned the layout of the land, town, park, and couple's home. She closed her eyes, visualized a subdivision entrance near the park. "So just townhomes? Or condos, apartments, and houses too?"

# CHAPTER 11

## *Jasen*

JASEN GLANCED OVER HIS LUNCH at Michaela as she smiled at Clint Torres. She chatted with the owner of the Pink Taco as if they were old friends. Clint winked and returned to the kitchen.

"What an interesting man," Michaela said.

Jasen had a mouthful of food and couldn't answer. A sour feeling twisted in his gut as she rambled on about the restaurant's decor, the food, and the owner engaging in his business. "Did the pink statue story really happen?" she asked between bites of her taco salad.

"Yes, the town prankster created a spectacle," Jasen laughed.

"I bet. It was absolutely ingenious. Brilliant marketing strategy. I would have never thought of that." Her eyes sparkled as she grinned.

He relaxed, letting the strange jealousy fade. "The town prankster has been hitting varying businesses for a few years."

"What a great promotion to get people into the town." She sipped her sweet tea as she glanced at the patrons. She raised a hand at Ben Moore when the officer walked in. He nodded and joined another officer, Indigo Black, at the counter.

Jasen studied her profile. The corners of her eyes crinkled. A slight blush fanned her cheeks, and rose-colored lips flashed a smile. She tucked a wayward curl behind her ear. He sighed.

Her gaze turned to him and her smile grew. "What are you thinking?"

Jasen pointed to himself and leaned away from the table. "Me?"

Her eyes narrowed, and she fingered her glass. "Yes, you."

Jasen shifted on the booth. "I noticed how easily you make friends here. It's like you belong. The community has accepted you."

Michaela's face went blank for a minute then her lips quirked into a smile. "Yeah." She pulled her glass forward and took a sip of tea while keeping her eyes locked on his.

"Hiya, I don't believe we've met." Nellie Neus plopped onto the seat next to Michaela, causing her to scoot in. "I'm Nellie. I work for Fortuna's one and only newspaper, the Fortuna Forum."

Jasen kept from snorting his tea. Every time the city had a function, Nellie would show up and berate him to answer questions. He knew it was her job but her "in your face" personality irritated him like petting a cactus.

Michaela hid her wide-eyed shock with a faulty smile. She quickly recovered and introduced herself.

"What are you doing here?" Nellie asked.

"I'm visiting a friend and looking for a job." Michaela didn't breathe before asking, "What do you do at the Forum?"

Nellie's face lit up, striking Jasen as pretty. If Michaela could illicit such a change in Nellie nettles then maybe she could reach Mr. and Mrs. Saks.

"I do whatever they need me to do. I mostly write articles regarding important events in town. Jasen and I see a lot of each other." Nellie winked at him, wiggling her thin brows as her cheeks flamed crimson.

Jasen tilted his head, pulling on his collar. He kept his lips clamped. When Dee had disappeared, Nellie had implied he had been a suspect. During the flood, Jasen had been at town hall and Nellie knew it. Still the grief and guilt topped with the article had made him wary of anyone giving him sidelong glances.

After the hubbub of the funeral, Nellie had offered to buy him a beer. *What the hell?* Not that he wouldn't have minded a friend, but Nellie would have twisted anything he said into whatever story the Forum thought would make the most money.

Michaela planted her chin in her palm. "Sounds exciting. Do you get to meet a lot of people?"

Nellie blushed and giggled. "Sometimes."

"What about all those men who act out heroes?"

Nellie gasped and stretched her arms out. "I could go on." She giggled again.

"I'm sorry, Nellie, you'll have to catch Michaela another time. She has an appointment." Jasen stood, taking the bill to the register. He watched the women as he paid.

Nellie's demeanor changed from welcoming to abrasive. She clasped Michaela's wrist. "Be kind to Jasen," Nellie's loud, nasally voice warned. The occupants of the nearest booths turned. Jasen grit his teeth and covered his face with a palm. Nellie continued, "His wife died, and he hasn't gotten over her. I don't want him hurt."

"It's nice that you care," Michaela said. Her face remained neutral as she pulled her arm away. "I don't intend on breaking his heart. I'm leaving in a few days."

Walking to the car, Jasen pulled Michaela aside. "Don't mind what Nellie said."

"You heard?" Michaela asked with wide eyes.

"She's loud." He stepped toward the car, but she stopped him, holding his arm with her hand.

"I think she has a crush on you," Michaela said with a smirk.

Jasen tipped Michaela's chin. He hovered his face over hers. Her eyes widened, and her gaze dropped to his lips. A fire ignited in his blood. He stepped back before he pulled her into his arms. "You better watch out, then; she might not like you."

One side of her lips twitched before her brow dipped, and she frowned. She crossed her arms. "You're very sure of yourself."

With a smirk, Jasen shrugged and opened the door for her.

As they drove, he wondered how his life would change if two women were interested in him. *Yikes.* He didn't want any cat fights. Especially between Nellie and Michaela. Poor Nellie. It wouldn't be a contest. He'd take Michaela hands down. Suddenly air was in short supply despite the vent blowing in his face.

The Stanton Cove sign came into view as they rounded a corner. "Oh, there's the park. You know the trail that runs along the creek?" She'd twisted toward him expecting an answer, but his tongue stuck to the roof of his mouth. He kept clutching the wheel as he turned into the driveway of the Saks' property. She continued when he didn't answer. "I'm going to hike it."

Jasen slammed on the brakes, coming to a jarring stop. He whipped around. "You will not walk, run, jog, or skip along the river. Do you hear me?"

Michaela searched his face with wild eyes. Her mouth had fallen open, but she made no comment. He tempered his tone and ran fingers through his hair. "Please, Michaela, promise you won't do it. For me," he pleaded.

She'd closed her mouth, tilting her head, and continued to study him. He felt the questions coming and squeezed his eyes shut. He shook his head, not wanting to have the conversation here or now.

Michaela touched his arm, startling him out of his thoughts. "They're waiting for us," she said, gesturing toward the house.

The couple stood on the stoop. Jasen blew out a breath, never so happy to see Mr. Saks.

They walked toward the small clapboard farmhouse.

"Hello, asshole," Mr. Saks said to Jasen.

"Milo, that's no way to greet the mayor," Mrs. Saks said, crossing her arms and tapping her foot.

"I didn't vote for him," Milo grumbled.

"Apparently," Michaela said with a giggle, and Milo blushed.

"I apologize for my crude words and rude behavior, little lady," Milo said. He led them into a tiny but cozy living room. The house smelled old, and fried chicken supper lingered in the air. Jasen tried not to wrinkle his nose.

"Mr. and Mrs. Saks this is Michaela Arschfick," Jasen introduced. She nodded with a gracious smile and offered her petite hand.

"I'm Artis," she took Michaela's hands in both of hers and squeezed, then continued, "and this grouchy old fart is Milo."

Milo reclined in a lounge chair, and his wife sat in a Wedgwood blue rocker. Jasen and Michaela lowered to a plaid sofa with worn arms. While Artis had been civil, Milo had been argumentative to any talk about his property. They didn't have any kids, so it was an impending problem.

"So," Michaela said, slapping her knees, "I appreciate your willingness to meet with me today. You—"

"We ain't selling," Milo said with a frown. "Nothing that fancy-boy says will convince me otherwise." He huffed and crossed his arms.

Michaela glanced at Jasen. He frowned and put his hand on her leg. A warmth started in his chest and crept to his face.

"Why don't we get rid of the fancy-boy asshole so we can talk straight?" Michaela said with a grin.

Jasen whipped his head around. "What?"

"Your presence is no longer required. I'll call you when I'm finished, and you can come pick me up." Michaela stood. "Or I can walk back to the Dungogh Inn, if you'd like?"

"Uh," he stood, fumbling for his keys. "I'll go. When you need me, call and I'll return." He touched her arm, then he walked out of the house. Glancing over his shoulder, he admired Michaela's gall. If anyone could win the Saks she could.

# CHAPTER 12

## *Michaela*

MICHAELA GLANCED AT MILO AND smiled. "It's just me. I don't have an agenda or work for the city. They just asked me to speak with you." She scooted to the edge of the sofa. "I want you to talk to me. I want to know your hopes and dreams. Tell me what you want and how you'll achieve it. Everything we discuss is speculative. Just talking and dreaming."

"Okay," Artis said. She smoothed out her pink sweatshirt.

"The city would like to develop the land," Michaela said, pulling out the property map. She handed it to Milo. "Are your property lines correct?"

He grabbed the paper but didn't look at it. "We are not selling."

"I know," Michaela said, studying his grizzled chin. "I'm not here to make you sell. Let's play a game for an hour and make the mayor sweat the whole time."

Milo narrowed his eyes, then a loud guffaw escaped. "I like you."

Artis chuckled and stood. "Let's go into the kitchen and get some tea." While Artis set the kettle on and Milo stood with arms crossed, Michaela spread the folder of papers over the round table.

"That realtor Sandy Bitch—"

"Milo!" Artis scolded, hands on hips.

He rolled his eyes. "Well, she is. Sandy Beach is a pushy, pompous, plump—"

Artis spun, waving a wooden spoon. "Hells bells, Milo. Behave."

"Fine." Milo sighed. "Sandy has come around here needling us to up and sell. She's found me in the barn and cornered Artis at the grocery."

Artis poured them each a cup and joined them at the table. "We don't have anywhere to go," she said, frowning into her teacup. Milo patted her hand. "The land is getting too much for us."

"Artis," Milo growled.

"Milo, it's the truth. I worry about your health. Remember last winter when you fell and hurt your ankle? I didn't find you for three hours." Artis clamped her hand on her husband's arm.

Milo's gruff tone softened. "I know you worry. We aren't spring chickens anymore." He patted her hand again.

The Saks talked about their health and aging concerns, and Michaela listened while they expressed their worry. Compassion bubbled under her skin. She wanted to find a compromise to benefit all parties, but more importantly she wanted a feasible solution for the Saks. "I'd like to propose an idea. An experiment. This does not mean you will sell your property."

"Ah, is this the game you referred to?" Artis asked.

"Yes." Michaela lowered her cup and leaned closer toward the couple. "When is the last time you played pretend?"

The old man raised his eyebrows as he gazed at his wife. Artis blushed.

Michaela cleared her throat. "Pretend not related to romance books," she specified.

Artis wrung her hands, staring at the table. "A long time."

"For a newcomer, you sure know this town." Milo rubbed his chin, his lips curled in a smirk.

"It's an interesting place. Romance reading and acting men are an unusual thing in this world." Michaela tapped the paper, refocusing the discussion. "I have a property developer friend in California, Peter Moss. If you don't object, I'd like him to assess your property and give us some scenarios. I'd like you to take a look at his work."

Michaela opened her laptop and started a slide show of Pete's buildings. The Saks watched as a movie theater, warehouse complex, large houses, and condo communities scrolled.

"What are you thinking with a California yahoo?" Milo asked. He folded his arms over his plaid shirt.

"He's good at what he does. Pete uses local materials and outsources to regional companies. So it would help Fortuna and the surrounding area. He's fair and keeps costs low." Michaela smiled. "He likes Fortuna. It appeals to him as a place to retire."

"Retirement?" Milo said. "That would be nice."

"With the park across the street, he could build condominiums or a townhome community on the property. They'd have a clubhouse with a pool," Michaela said, handing Artis a brochure of Pete's latest patio home development.

"I still have my Speedo," Milo said sarcastically.

"Pete has made swaps before." Michaela folded her hands on her lap.

"Swap?" Artis said. "I don't understand how that would work."

"Basically, you trade the land for housing." Michaela leaned back and smiled. "Well, we could call him. He could shed light on the specifics." She shrugged.

Milo crossed his arms again. "I'm not selling to a bean-sprout-eating-weirdo."

"He's from Cincinnati, Ohio, like me."

Milo harrumphed. "They've got weird chili."

"Everything is better with cinnamon and chocolate. Even chili." Michaela laughed at the grimaces on their faces. "Seriously, it's awesome. There are only minute amounts of cinnamon and chocolate."

"We're pretending, dear; let's call the man. Maybe if we talk to him, he'll talk to the committee and tell them it won't work." Artis' eyes held a mischievous glint.

Michaela sent a text then connected the video call. "Hello, Michaela," Pete smiled at her. He had thick glasses and wispy, thinning hair. "It's nice to see you again."

Michaela made the introductions and explained what she'd shown the Saks.

"Basically, we'd deduct the value of the property. There are several contributors to that figure. Surrounding property values and sales. I hope you don't mind—I've worked up a few floor plans and layouts based on the property elevations and schematics that Michaela emailed me. The park across the street will be a main selling point."

The doorbell rang.

"That should be your delivery," Pete said. "I had them mailed to you so you could see how it works."

"Wow," Artis said as Milo stood to leave the room. "You work fast."

"Anything to help Michaela. She introduced my wife and I," Pete grinned.

A moment later, Milo returned, struggling to carry an awkward shaped box. "Lord almighty, what's in here, the kitchen sink?"

"Everything but," Pete said, earning a chuckle.

Milo retrieved a Swiss Army knife out of his pocket and cut the tape. He dug through the packing peanuts and pulled out a packet of information and a cardboard tube. He popped the lid off and slid a large set of blueprints out. Artis flipped through the housing brochure. Milo moved the box to the floor, out of the way.

Michaela smoothed the pile of blueprints. The first was a two bedroom patio home.

"This is like our house," Milo said, pointing to the paper.

"There are examples of each of the floor plans in the booklet. These are floor plans I've used before in a community."

"This kitchen is beautiful," Artis said, shoving the book into Milo's face.

"Fancy-schmancy," he said, then whistled.

Milo pulled out the next floor plan and leaned in, studying the room configuration. The design had a walkout lower level, perfect for a sloped lot. Michaela let them sort through the papers. They spoke with Pete regarding the land, his company, and the designs.

"So how would this work?" Milo finally asked.

"I'd need to come visit the property and have it surveyed. If we decide it's mutually beneficial, then we'd see about zoning."

Artis and Milo exchanged a look.

"Your land is zoned one type. It would have to be changed to another. It's a process." Michaela walked around to view Pete on the screen.

He nodded then pushed his glasses up his nose. "It can take several weeks or even months to get it through the first committee meeting, then the city manager needs to review it. On my end, once the zoning has been changed and permits gained, then the building begins."

"What about us?" Artis said. "If we barter the land where would we live?"

"You can theoretically stay in your home until the first phase is completed. It will depend on the sewers and underground utilities," Pete said.

"We have a septic tank," Milo said.

Artis motioned to Michaela, and the women left the room. "I think Milo might want to ask a few questions privately."

"A test." Michaela giggled. "Don't worry. Remember, I don't mind if you keep your land or sell it. It's your choice. You are helping me by just talking to me."

After a few minutes, Pete promised to be in touch and ended the call. The Saks and Michaela relaxed at the kitchenette, sipping tea and studying the floor plans. Michaela sent a text to Jasen.

Out the large sliding glass door, Michaela studied the slope of the yard. The long gravel driveway snaked toward the road. In the distance, a large grove of trees marked the entry to the park. Jasen pulled onto the drive, and Michaela's heart raced. She gathered her items. Artis and Milo walked her out.

Remembering Jasen's emphatic request about the canyon, she turned to Artis. "What do you know about the mayor's wife?"

Artis tsked and shook her head. "I didn't know her, but I know he hasn't been the same since the flood."

"It was a tragedy. So many deaths, most of them livestock, mind you, but a darn shame nonetheless," Milo said.

Jasen parked, and Michaela lifted a hand in greeting. His worried expression shifted into a smirk. "So how'd it go?" he asked.

"I like your girlfriend better than you," Milo grumbled.

Artis elbowed him in the ribs. "Hush, Milo."

Jasen rolled back on his heels with raised eyebrows. His boots crunched on the gravel drive. He glanced at Michaela.

A wave of heat rushed through Michaela and pooled in her gut. She sized him up. With his jeans, boots, and belt buckle, he could be a cowboy. The button-down dress shirt and tie balanced the wild wind-blown hair. Civilized versus wild.

He blushed under her scrutiny. "So…?" Jasen started again.

"Don't worry about it. Milo and Artis have a lot to consider. They'll call me if they want to talk more." She winked at Milo, then hugged Artis. "Thank you for hosting me and for a great game of pretend."

She waved as they drove down the driveway.

Jasen's phone rang as they came to a stop. He glanced at the screen. "Oh, crap."

# CHAPTER 13

## *Jasen*

JASEN'S PHONE RANG. HE RECOGNIZED the in-laws' number flashing on his car's display screen. He tightened his grip on the wheel and glanced at Michaela. "Sorry, I need to take this."

"Do what you got to do," Michaela said. Her sweet smile had him wishing he could disregard the caller and focus on Michaela.

"Hello," Jasen greeted, accepting the call. Only the third call from them this week. First, it was storage containers for food, then lotto tickets and now...?

The booming voice of Jerry Mander over the car speakers made him wince. Jerry was hard of hearing and forgot others didn't have the same issue. "Jasen, your mother needs some things. You can pick them up from the store."

"What does Sally need?" Jasen asked, turning onto Main Street.

"Butter, sugar, foil, green beans—oh, and something else." Jerry paused and the unmistakable deep nasally voice of his mother-in-law yelled "toilet paper" from another room. "Toilet paper. Yes, that's it."

Jasen repeated the list. "I'll stop by after work."

"What did he say?" Sally shouted.

"He'll bring them after work," Jerry yelled. Michaela swiveled her head with her hands over her ears. Jasen twisted the volume control down.

"That won't do. I can't wait until later. I have to go now," Sally whined.

"What do you want me to do? The man is at work," Jerry thundered back.

Jasen glanced at Michaela, who nodded. He sighed. "Jerry, I can come now," Jasen said.

"Bless you," Jerry said then yelled, "He's coming now."

"Oh, he's a good boy. She shoulda kept that one."

"Goodbye." Jerry hung up without waiting for a response.

Michaela covered her mouth, her glittering eyes squinted with mirth.

"Sorry about that. The in-laws." Jasen couldn't offer more explanation.

"Do they always shout like that?" she asked. "It reminds me of my grandparents."

Jasen took the opportunity. "Tell me about your grandparents."

A small smile flitted over Michaela's lips. She sighed and pressed against the seat. "After my mom left, my grandparents took me in and raised me. My dad worked full time as a long-distance trucker. He was gone for long stretches of time. My grandparents gave me a home and my dad a home base."

"And your dad?" Jasen turned into a mini mart.

"Dad is still a trucker. Actually, he loves the west and drives to Texas and New Mexico often. We might see him later if his load is on time." A smile brightened her face.

"I'll be quick," he promised. Michaela waited in the car while he purchased the items from Sally's list.

Jasen drove the winding road past Chatwell fields, but it was too early for the butterflies. Near the Manders' trailer, the pavement turned into a one lane road that eventually became dirt. They bumped over the ruts.

"They live out in the sticks," Michaela said, grasping the handle.

"Not really. We're approaching Nockerville from the backside."

"The backside of Nockerville is crappy," Michaela mumbled after a jaw-jarring, man-eating pothole.

They crested a hill, and a community of shanties appeared. She stared open-mouthed. The hovels were wood frame or trailers. Weeds dominated and rusty cars littered the area like lawn ornaments.

"How are these not condemned?" she uttered.

Dust swirled around the vehicle when they stopped. He cleared his throat. "You can stay here in the air conditioning."

"I'm going with you." With a nervous chuckle, she pushed the door open.

Jasen carried the bags in one hand while hugging the toilet paper to his chest. He shifted the bag to knock, making the rickety wood stoop creak. As long as he'd known Dee, the doorbell hadn't worked.

Jerry opened the door, and the smell of stale cigarettes and fried food assaulted him. Jerry's ribbed, sleeveless white tank had an orange stain on the crest of his pot belly. The wispy white fuzz surrounding his bald spot and his brows looked as if he'd stuck his finger in the socket. A cigarette hung off his lips. "Jasen, my boy," Jerry said, exposing yellowed teeth with a few gaps. His brows morphed into one when he noticed Michaela.

"Here's your toilet paper," Jasen said, pushing the nine rolls toward him.

"This ain't the kind she likes," he said, shaking his head. "Who's that?"

"Who's who?" Sally hollered from inside.

"Jasen has a pretty girl with him," Jerry yelled.

A large thump and scurrying met their ears. Sally's bulging brown eyes with blue shadow blinked at Michaela. Her judgmental gaze raked Michaela head to foot. She tilted her head and her white curls bounced. "That's not a social worker, is it?"

Michaela shifted side to side holding her purse. Jasen smirked and leaned on the door frame. "This is Michaela. Meet my in-laws Jerry and Sally Mander."

"Is she your girlfriend?" Sally's eyes narrowed.

Michaela blushed and glanced at him.

Something came over Jasen. Possession mixed with orneriness. With a one shoulder shrug, he held out the grocery bag. "Could be."

Jerry took the bag and opened it. "Canned green beans. She's not going to like it."

Sally grabbed the bag, and the thin plastic ripped. One can fell and landed on Jerry's toes. His face turned bright red and he sucked in his lip. Hobbling inside, he landed on the sofa and put his foot up.

"I need fresh green beans." Sally pursed her lips like a child. "Get me some."

Jasen clenched his jaw.

Michaela's eyes narrowed, and she'd stepped closer to Jasen. Her shoulder brushed his.

"How about you say thank you for what you have? Jasen stopped his plans to get you these things, and if you can't appreciate them, then I don't think you should ask him for anything." Michaela glared with her hands on her hips.

Jasen's heart raced. Michaela had his back.

Sally's face turned beet red, but her bottom lip trembled. Her eyes filled with tears. "We ain't got no one else but Jasen. Our daughter is dead. He took her away from us." A tear slipped out and slid down her cheek. She dipped her head to wipe the tears away.

Sally's words twisted like a knife in his heart. He had taken Dee to Fortuna.

Michaela's anger diminished when she glanced at him. She opened her arms to him and he crumbled against her. She stroked his back in soothing circles, cooing in his ear.

Jasen sucked in a deep breath. Despite the Texas heat, Michaela's body pressing against him had his heart working overtime. He breathed in the scent of lilies. She smelled like summer and felt like sin. He wrapped his hands around her back, squeezing her tight. She squeaked and tipped her head upward. He kissed her temple.

"Let's go," Jasen said, taking her hand and pulling her toward the car.
"Don't forget my check," Sally called, cupping her hands around her lips.

# CHAPTER 14

## *Michaela*

MICHAELA'S FIRST VISIT TO STITTS' travel center proved ripe for people watching. Every time the bell over the door sounded she'd glance up from her Architectural Digest magazine. There was a steady flow of men visiting the bookshelf by the entrance.

Jasen had to make a work related call, and stepped outside with the promise to return shortly.

Michaela checked the time. Midway through her second cup of coffee, a deep voice that rumbled like an idling truck called, "Mick!"

Michaela flew into her father's arms. "Dad, finally." He squeezed her in a bear hug.

They sat and ordered. "So, have they hired you?" her father asked.

Michaela glanced into her coffee. "Not yet, Dad. I only met with the committee today. They asked me to talk to an older couple about future land development. Things went well."

"That's good. They'd be fools not to hire you." He sipped his iced tea.

"Thanks, but you're a little biased." Michaela folded her arms and smirked.

"Michaela, who is this handsome hunk of a man?" Desire asked as she slid into the booth next to her.

"This is my father, Tim Wheeler." Michaela waved her hand. "Dad, let me introduce Desire Hardmann."

Her father took Desire's small hand and shook. "Pleasure, little lady."

Desire blushed and glanced away. "How long are you in town?"

"I'm only staying for a few hours, but I'll be back in a couple days. I want to see Mick before she goes home." Tim took a bite of his sandwich.

"Home, huh?" Desire examined Michaela's profile. "I thought you belonged to Fortuna now."

"Not yet." Michaela bit her lip then smiled. She turned to Desire. "If I get hired, I'll need a place to stay. At least temporarily, until I can learn the area. Do you have any suggestions?"

Desire's ruby-red lips parted in a brilliant smile. "It so happens I might. I have a friend, Elberta Deeds, who's planning to winter in Florida. I don't know what the draw is with the humidity, alligators, and all those old people."

Tim almost inhaled his tea and coughed. Michaela covered her mouth to hide her grin.

"Although, she might find a man and get lucky," Desire said with a shrug. "Elberta has a small Cape Cod on Second Street. She might rent it while she's in Florida. I think she plans to move to Florida permanently after what happened to Piper."

"Who's Piper?" Tim asked.

"She's a lovely girl." Desire glanced around the diner. "I met her right here. She was new to town, like you, dear." She patted Michaela's arm. "One of Brad Davidson's ranch hands took a hankering for her and soon she was swooning. He was gorgeous and single just like our mayor, Jasen." Desire elbowed Michaela. She continued, "Just when things began to progress, a stalker from Piper's past showed up in Fortuna. I saw through that snake's charms, but he wormed his way into Elberta's heart, doing odd jobs for her and flattering her with attention. He borrowed Elberta's van and kidnapped Piper. Ever since Piper's kidnapping, Elberta has been looking to escape Fortuna."

"That's terrible," Michaela said. "Poor Piper."

Michaela caught movement at the back of the room, and a broad smile broke out. Jasen's laughter floated through the restaurant, and her gaze honed in on his stooped shoulders as he listened to an older man. They shook hands and Jasen nodded. He patted the man's shoulder before moving on to the next patron.

"Natural born politician, that one," Desire said, watching Jasen high-five a kid.

"So, that's your Jasen?" Tim asked.

Michaela gasped, but Desire grinned and replied, "Yes, sir. He's one hot tamale. Makes me wish I was a few years younger." She hummed as Jasen waved and smiled at their table.

Jasen approached them, and Tim stood. Her father was six-foot. Built like a lineman, he could be intimidating. He wore his typical driving uniform: a plaid short-sleeve shirt with breast pockets, jeans, and a Cincinnati Bengals ball cap.

"I'm Tim Wheeler, Michaela's father." He offered a meaty hand which

Jasen took.

"Nice to meet you, Tim. I'm Jasen DeLay. I'm glad you could coordinate your schedule to meet Michaela here. She's been looking forward to seeing you." He turned to the women. "Ms. Hardmann, as always, it's a pleasure."

Desire elbowed Michaela again. "See—born to be a politician." She giggled and stood. "Mayor DeLay, I voted for you, and if you'd like to come over for dinner sometime, I'll let you convince me to vote for you again."

Jasen laughed as he turned crimson and rubbed the back of his head.

After Desire left them to join another men-filled table, Jasen slipped into the booth next to Michaela. "Is Ms. Hardmann always so...?" Michaela asked.

"Forward? Perverted? Yeah, she is." Jasen chuckled and gave Michaela a side hug under her father's watchful eyes.

"So are you using protection?" Tim's eyes narrowed on the couple.

Michaela shared a look with Jasen, and her face heated. She sucked in a deep breath before replying, "I left my hard hat, goggles, and gloves in Cincinnati, Dad."

Her father smiled but shook his head. "You know what I mean, kids."

Michaela had been married for years and hadn't conceived. At the ripe age of thirty-one, Michaela was a far cry from inexperienced.

Jasen threaded his fingers with hers under the table. The erotic sensation caused her heart to flutter. She swallowed and curled her fingers. Michaela wanted to pinch her nose and tell her father to mind his own business.

"Jasen will be my boss, Dad. You know how I feel about workplace relations." She frowned and leaned forward, pulling her hand free.

"I know, but the heart is a funny thing. Especially when it overrules the mind." Tim shrugged. "I'm only trying to help."

The door chimed, and a man stalked to the bookcase. He chose something and put another book back. Michaela shook her head. "Have you heard about the romance phenomena happening in Fortuna, Dad?"

Tim raised an eyebrow. "Between you and Jasen?"

Glancing at Jasen, she hoped he'd explain. He caught the hint. "The romance *book* phenomena. Fortuna residents read romance novels." He glanced at Michaela, and she motioned him to continue. "They also act out favorite stories and heroes."

"The men, Dad." Michaela giggled. "The men are the romantics. Amazing, huh?"

"Oh, I don't know," Tim said. His hand disappeared under the table to the side. He pulled up three books. "I thought I'd try it."

Michaela squealed then buried her face in Jasen's shoulder until she could contain her laughter. She breathed deeply, trying to memorize Jasen's spicy scent.

"Mick," her father said, pushing away an empty plate. "I need to get going. The traffic in Austin set me back."

They left the dining room and walked Tim to his semi. Jasen waited while Michaela hugged her father goodbye. She watched her father's truck until it disappeared from sight. With a sigh, she turned toward Jasen. He pulled her into his arms and held her. Warm and comforted, Michaela could have stayed there the rest of the day.

Her father's line of questioning scrolled through her thoughts: protection. Her blood rushed. She swallowed, and knew if she tipped her head she could claim his lips and more if she wanted. It had been a long time. She wouldn't mind having the pleasure of a man in her bed, but not her soon-to-be boss.

"Come on," Jasen said. "Let's go back to town."

With a nod, Michaela sighed again.

# CHAPTER 15

## *Jasen*

JASEN SHIFTED FROM FOOT TO foot in the baggage claim. His beard itched. He hadn't shaved since he'd seen Michaela three months ago.

Her flight had been delayed from St. Louis by an hour. He paced the crowded room while he watched the travel-worn folks mumble and fight for a space to grab their luggage.

The monitor showed her flight had landed, but no passengers emerged from the hallway. He wrung his hands and stared at the space, desiring to see her brilliant smile again.

There had been progress in the zoning acquisition of Milo and Artis' property. It had passed the initial committee and when it had reached the city manager, Cam Payne approved it. At the public hearing, someone threw a stink regarding job outsourcing and the noise of the construction. The developer Peter Moss had provided brochures for the citizenry and a model. He answered the questions posed and allayed many fears.

Jasen grinned recalling how Milo and Artis sat in the front row. Peter's supporters. The old coot Milo sure sung the developer's tune now.

Fortuna would benefit all the way around. And it was Michaela's doing.

A business man with a laptop bag and a phone pressed to an ear exited, followed by a family pushing a fellow in a wheelchair. Then the crowd flowed from the hallway. He rose on his toes to find Michaela.

Halfway through the mass, he spotted her wavy lengths. She inclined her head toward an elderly woman. She smiled and nodded as she shielded the frail woman from the throng. Someone broke his line of sight and he lost her.

The baggage turnstile lurched. The crowd amassed at the hole where the conveyor regurgitated luggage. Jasen swept his eyes over the travelers. After the throng thinned and three quarters of the flight had retrieved their bags, his gut churned. Michaela had disappeared.

Jasen panned the bathroom entrance, the missing luggage window, and baggage claim room, but with every minute that passed his anxiety rose.

His cell vibrated, startling him. Pulling it out of his pocket, Jasen saw a text from Michaela. Relief washed over him. He hurried through the long room, weaving in and out of the people.

Michaela waited near the pickup door, scanning the vehicles through the glass. Her fingers drummed the handle of her small rolling bag.

Jasen stopped beside her and shoved his hands in his back pockets. After a peripheral glance, she ignored him. She hadn't recognized him with a beard.

She retrieved her phone from her purse and hastily typed something. His phone vibrated and chimed. He chuckled, and she peered over but quickly turned away.

"To your left," he replied.

When she glanced up, her mouth dropped open. "This is new," she said touching her chin.

"Yeah, like it?" Jasen swallowed.

Michaela cocked her head, inspecting him. Her brow furrowed. "I don't know. Give me a few minutes for the shock to wear off."

"You travel light for moving here." Jasen took the handle of her suitcase and motioned for her to follow him.

"I shipped a few boxes of necessary things, but my dad is bringing the rest. We'll put it in storage," she said.

Jasen slowed his gait so she could keep pace. Heat radiated off the hood of his car. He opened the trunk and deposited her bag.

"How was your flight?" Jasen asked, turning onto the highway entrance ramp.

"It was fine. Thank God for noise canceling headphones," Michaela chuckled. "They drowned out chainsaw snoring and screaming babies alike."

She kept her nose to the window, examining the foreign landscape. A comfortable silence fell as the prairie rushed past.

An old-fashioned telephone ring startled them. "Sorry," she said as she fished inside her purse. The sound threw him back to his childhood. His grandparents had an olive green rotary dial phone.

"Hi, Dad," she smiled and glanced at Jasen. "Jasen picked me up and we're heading to Fortuna."

While she chatted with her father, Jasen caught glimpses of her profile. The slope of her cute, slightly upturned nose with a smattering of freckles. Her bright eyes, crinkled with a smile. She tucked a curl behind her ear, making Jasen long to plunge his finger into the silky length. He tightened his grip on the wheel.

Tim informed her of his itinerary, something Jasen knew because they had scheduled everything together. Tim would arrive in Fortuna the next day.

In Nockerville, they stopped at a coffee shop. While they sipped cold brews, Michaela's phone played, "I'm sexy and I know it." She giggled with a slight blush and answered. "Hello, Kim." Michaela rolled her eyes. "Fine. I'll put you on speaker."

Michaela covered the mic and whispered "sorry," to Jasen before tapping the screen. "You're on speaker. Happy now?"

"Hi, Jasen. How's it going?" Kim asked.

"Fine," he replied, leaning and inspecting the picture of Kim sticking her tongue out.

"Kim, you'll never believe where we are." Michaela smiled and pulled the phone closer.

"A hotel?" Kim guessed, giggling. Jasen started coughing.

"Whatever. No, a coffee shop like you want. The guy behind the counter is just your style, too." Michaela winked at Jasen.

"Oh really? Tall, dark, and handsome," she hummed. "Hang up and FaceTime me." The line went dead.

Michaela sighed. "She's going to demand to talk to the barista. I should warn him."

Jasen glanced at the bar and met the man's gaze and motioned him over. The tall Native-American smoothed his dark green apron and approached their table.

Michaela twisted her napkin. "I'm so sorry. I mentioned this shop to my friend. It's her dream to open a coffee house, and she wants to FaceTime me so she can see it."

"That's cool," he responded.

"She's single." Michaela glanced at the ringing phone. Lifting an apologetic gaze to the employee, she picked up the phone and tapped the screen. The barista stood behind Michaela and waved as she greeted Kim.

"He is cute." Kim gushed. "I'm Kim."

"Thanks," he mumbled, blushing. "I'm Glen."

No one waited in line. Michaela handed her phone over and said, "Here you go. You can give Kim the tour."

"Uh, okay." Glen took it with a grin. He walked and talked the rest of Jasen and Michaela's visit. He set the phone aside when he served a customer.

Jasen threw his empty cup away. Michaela did the same then turned to leave. "Forgetting something?" he asked.

"Oh!" Michaela squeaked, retrieving her phone. "Kim will visit Texas soon. We better start the zoning application for the firehouse on the square."

Jasen stopped walking. "Are you serious?"

"You don't know, Kim. She'll have a coffee shop, and she'll hire Glen. Mark my words." Michaela eyes sparkled when she smiled at him.

Jasen longed to please Michaela. He planned to call the Longfellow Property management team to inquire about the building's zoning.

# CHAPTER 16

## *Michaela*

"WHAT WAS I THINKING IT'S hot here. I won't wear those sweaters again." Michaela declared as she studied the Pink Taco's menu.

"You'll acclimate," Desire said. "It might take a season or two."

Michaela doubted she'd ever be cold in Texas unless she stood below an air-conditioning vent. The Cape Cod house had been perfect for her. Miss Deeds had moved her knick-knacks and clothes up to the attic. The house didn't feel like a home, but it didn't have to. It was temporary.

"Thanks for helping me unpack today," Michaela said. The least she could do was buy the older woman lunch.

"You're most welcome," Desire replied, watching Clint Torres. "When is your father coming into town again?"

"A few weeks." Michaela focused on the a la carte items.

"Michaela."

She glanced up. The bustle of the restaurant dimmed the sound. Ben Moore raised his hand, his fiancée Kelly with him. A petite lithe woman with auburn hair, she appeared to ooze good vibes when she smiled.

"Welcome to Fortuna," Kelly said. "You'll have to stop by the Double D Intimates office down the street from here and try something."

"I'm sure Jasen would approve," Desire said, wiggling her eyebrows.

Heat crept to Michaela's face and she took a drink of her iced tea. As if saying his name summoned him, Jasen opened the door. His gaze roamed the building, and when he found her, he grinned. He shook Ben's hand. "Looks like there's a party."

"Join us," Desire said, tapping the table. Kelly slid in with Michaela and Jasen sat with Desire. Ben placed a chair at the end of the booth.

"Are you all moved in?" Kelly asked.

"Mostly. My furniture is in storage for now."

Michaela let Desire lead the conversation, trying to get wedding details from Kelly and Ben.

Ben turned to Jasen and asked, "What's with the whiskers, mountain man?"

Jasen smirked and stroked his mustache. "Something new."

"Leave him alone, Ben," Kelly said. "I think it makes him look sexy."

The tease left Ben's face, and he raised his brows.

"He doesn't need a beard to be sexy," Desire said, "Isn't that right, Michaela?"

Michaela's jaw dropped. She nodded, agreeing with Ms. Hardmann.

"Don't worry. You'll get used to Ms. Hardmann," Kelly giggled.

After lunch, Michaela walked toward town hall with Jasen, then headed to her new office. She breathed in the warm air.

Hamish Burger's Kraut Wagon had moved to the far corner near the park. The aroma of his wieners teased her senses. It was nice to know the Fortuna council had taken her suggestions.

Inside the small office, taller than it was wide, a big metal 50s desk hogged the floor space. The mint green monster proved hard to push three inches. When Michaela sat in the desk chair, she could see the corner of Jacklyn Hyde's desk. Jacklyn leaned and waved.

"Are you sure you'll be all right in this space? It's claustrophobic." Jasen glanced around the room.

Michaela rose and peered out the large window. "It's overlooking the green space of the square." She turned to Jasen. "It's perfect."

His gaze roamed her body, lingering on her ballerina shoes. She wiggled her toes and crossed her arms.

"Don't you have work to do?" Michaela asked. "You don't need to babysit me." She waved him away and shifted, resuming her inspection. His shoes tapped the tile floor as he disappeared from the office. She whirled around and hurried to the door calling, "Jasen."

As she reached the door, he stepped into the room and they collided. She bounced off his chest, the wind knocked out of her, but he caught her. He held her arms gently as she took deep breaths. Her hands splayed on his chest, feeling his heart racing. Warmth spread, covering her like a blanket and the room became stifling.

Michaela tipped her head back. Big mistake. Her gaze met his sparkling hazel eyes. Again, air refused to fill her lungs.

"Yes, Michaela?" Jasen asked.

She focused on his lips, and they curled into a smirk. She blinked not remembering how she had become enclosed in his embrace. Pushing against the muscled wall of his chest, she put distance between them.

"Oh yeah." She swallowed, finding oxygen at last. "Can I hang things on this wall?" She flopped her arm in the general direction of the solid off-white wall.

"What sort of things?"

"Lists, pictures, or whatever."

"Do what you need to do," he said, releasing her.

Michaela nodded dumbly as Jasen left again. Her hand clasped the warm spots where he had touched her, and she stared after him. Jacklyn's fingers flew over the keyboard as she watched with a grin.

"Ah hell," Michaela said.

# CHAPTER 17

## *Jasen*

FROM JUST INSIDE HIS OFFICE, Jasen inspected Nellie Neus while she waited outside near Jacklyn's desk. Nellie glanced at the wall clock. He took a deep breath and stepped into the hall.

Nellie rose and smiled. She'd swept her golden curls into a French twist. With a button nose, round gray eyes, and rosebud lips she wasn't unattractive but… the way she puckered her lips and tapped the pen on her pad of paper annoyed him.

"Welcome, Nellie," Jasen said, taking her petite hand.

"Thank you for agreeing to see me today, Jasen," Nellie said, squeezing his fingers. Her lilac sundress ballooned out as she stumbled in her heels trying to strut into his office. "I had hoped we could get lunch—"

"I've been busy. There are many things in the works for the upcoming holiday season," Jasen said, offering her a chair then returning to his across the desk from her.

"How is this any different from last year's or any other past Christmas season?" Nellie asked with pen poised. The underlining tone of her voice had a whiny lilt to it that grated on his nerves. She tilted her head and smiled.

"As you know, Fortuna has hired a consultant," Jasen started.

Nellie's eyes narrowed as she scribbled. "Yes, was she expensive?"

"Offhand, I don't know the specifics of her contract. However, the city manager, Cam Payne, would be the one to ask about those details." Jasen steepled his fingers and pasted on a placating smile.

"There's a list of community events and how people can get involved on Fortuna's website and our Facebook page." He glanced out the window, watching leaves on the oak wave. They mocked him.

"Is *she* responsible for increased expenditure?" Nellie looked through her bangs.

"Ms. Arschfick is responsible for recruiting the community for the committee's approved plans. She also helps with coordinating and implementing their ideas." Jasen leaned back and grinned, reminded about the Halloween event Michaela had planned. Michaela oozed enthusiasm, exciting everyone around her.

"About the city Halloween festival. Anything special you'd like me to mention?" Nellie's pen remained poised over her pad of paper.

"It will be fun for the whole family. The kids will have a safe place to trick or treat around the square. The business and restaurants will have goodies and stay open later. Everyone in Fortuna is encouraged to dress up. Let's face it, you know they have costumes."

Nellie stared at him. "Do you?" She cocked her head and sucked in her bottom lip.

Jasen ignored the question. "Let's add *family friendly* to that costume part." He chuckled then shuddered, trying not to think of the individuals, mainly his book club buddy Parker, who had been caught cos-playing with their significant others.

By the end of the interview, Jasen's throat was dry. As he opened the door to let Nellie out, he froze spotting B.J. Johnson. Jasen was glad to get rid of the reporter, but the relief diminished because of B.J.'s unscheduled visit coupled with his patented scowl. The Longfellow property manager had his hands on his hips. He'd stepped away from work early.

"What do you want?" Jasen asked then turned around and escaped into his office before B.J. could answer. Jacklyn had ears like a jackal.

"Nice try, but you can't get away from me." B.J. followed him into the small space. His strong cologne scented the area. "Did you have a friendly chat with nosy Nellie?" He plopped down, leaning forward with his elbows on his knees.

Jasen inspected B.J., but his neutral expression remained impossible to read. "She interviewed me about the upcoming events and the things in place to fix up the town."

"She was getting the scoop on the new girl, huh?" B.J. scratched his chest.

"I guess." Jasen shrugged.

"Everyone thinks you're sweet on Michaela," B.J. said, watching Jasen with narrowed eyes.

Jasen hoped he didn't give Johnson what he wanted to see, whatever that was. "Michaela doesn't want a relationship. Not while we're working together." He sighed. "I'll admit it's nice being around someone who doesn't know my grandparents' history or the names of all my classmates."

"You around her a lot?"

Jasen shrugged again. "Here and there. I don't see her all day, if that's what you're asking."

"Jasen," Michaela bound into the office but stopped short. The large grin on her face dimmed when she saw B.J. "Oh," she squeaked. "I'm sorry. I didn't know you were in a meeting."

"It's okay," Jasen stood to make introductions. "Michaela Arschfick, meet B.J. Johnson."

"It's a pleasure," Johnson said, taking her dainty hand in his. He held it while a blush bloomed on her cheeks. Her gaze shifted to Jasen, and she pulled her hand away.

"Nice to meet you. I'll come back later, Jasen." She blinked twice and bolted.

Jasen frowned; the room seemed hotter than before. B.J. wore a devilish smirk. "Hmm," he said. "Maybe I should ask her out. I'm not working with her. I could show her around and things."

Jasen narrowed his gaze. "Why are you here?" Jasen asked.

"Getting the inside scoop, just like nosy Nellie." Johnson crossed his arms and chuckled.

Jasen sat back at his desk and woke his computer, trying to appear calm and casual. "I'm not sure what you're about but I've got things to do."

"Icy." B.J. chuckled. "Does that mean you don't want me to ask Michaela out? Or that you don't mind?"

Jasen's stomach gurgled, and he clamped his jaw. He began typing, hoping B.J. would get the hint.

"It must be nice to have two girls you could ask out for your dare," B.J. said with an inkling of a wistful tone.

"Two?" Jasen glanced up from the computer screen.

"Michaela and Nellie. Didn't you notice Nellie's skimpy dress?" B.J. hummed. "She's got nice legs."

"No. I didn't notice."

"Right." Johnson drawled. "Did Michaela burst in here while Nellie interviewed you?"

"Once."

B.J. covered his face with his hands. "Christ. That's spells trouble."

Jasen sat rigid. "What do you mean?"

"Nellie's had the hots for you since…" B.J.'s voice trailed off. He cleared his throat. "Since forever. She won't like your interest in Michaela, no matter how friendly you say you are. If I can see it, she can."

"See what?" Jasen said.

"Oh, brother," B.J. chuckled. "You're hopeless."

Jasen rubbed the spot over his heart.

"Here, I finished the book earlier than I thought. I knew you are keen to read it." B.J. tossed the paperback onto Jasen's desk.

The cover had the headless bodies of a couple in business wear. In heels and a black skirt, the heroine tugged the tie of the hero. Inches apart, they leaned against a desk. Jasen wouldn't mind being stuck in that position with Michaela.

It had been a good thing he'd had guests each time she'd visited him today. He hadn't noticed Nellie's, but he had noticed Michaela's legs and the dark gray slacks that appeared painted on. A small pocket on the rear drew his eye when she walked in front of him. Maybe it was his imagination, but she'd tossed a look over her shoulder as if she'd wanted him to like them.

Jasen set the book aside. B.J. had gone, leaving him alone.

"Jasen," Michaela said, poking her head in the door. Relieved, she sauntered in and dropped into one of the empty guest chairs. "You've been busy."

She tilted her head and studied him. "Are you all right?" Her gaze slid to the book on his desk. "*Work Hanky-Spanky*?" She covered her mouth to hide a giggle.

"Is something going on?" Jasen inclined his head, watching the way her chestnut hair fell into waves as she moved.

"Oh, earlier." She blushed and glanced at her folded hands. "That reporter stopped in to see me on her way out. She asked a bunch of things that made me think she didn't approve of me."

Jasen leaned over his desk, his stomach once again churning. "Such as?"

Michaela lifted her face. "She wanted to know about us."

Jasen rocked back in his seat. Michaela sucked in her bottom lip and appeared to pale, but as he studied her face, it turned crimson.

"What about us?" he finally asked.

"That's what I said, but she wouldn't accept that I didn't want a relationship right now. Especially with you." Michaela arched a delicate brow. "I think she likes you." She drummed her fingers on her arm, staring at the book cover. "I'm worried."

"Don't be. Nellie asked me about the scheduled improvements and the Halloween event." Jasen shrugged when she didn't look convinced. "Listen, Michaela, don't worry. If she likes me, as you suggest, then she won't do anything to upset me. You and I are friends, and writing something defamatory would definitely piss me off."

Michaela's eyes flashed. She pursed her lips for a moment before her brilliant smile shined again. Jasen blinked at the transformation. Joy radiated from her expression.

"Are you ready for the Halloween festival?" he asked.

"I have a costume." She stood. "Guess I should get back to work." She started for the door but paused, staring at the doorknob.

"Your friend B.J. asked me out." Michaela met his gaze.

His stomach rumbled, and he clenched it. It felt as if he'd been punched. Oxygen was insufficient.

Jasen sucked in a rasping breath to reply, but Michaela had gone. For the second time, someone had mysteriously disappeared from sight.

# CHAPTER 18

## *Michaela*

MICHAELA ROASTED IN HER LONG medieval green crushed velvet dress. She couldn't wait for the sun to set. The pleasant sound of families having fun was the backdrop for the information table where she volunteered near the courthouse door.

On the narrow lawn beside the building, children lined up for pony rides. The little munchkins smiled, at least the ones without masks.

The square pulsated with life. Moms and dads held hands while taking their children from store to store begging for treats. The stores varied in decorations. Some played spooky music and had strobe lights flashing while others had orange and purple light strands. The Tin Soldier remained open. Families ventured inside, but the store also had a table on the sidewalk manned by Wyatt. He passed out coupons and small toys instead of candy.

The north-south streets had been closed for the fall festival. Where the streets intersected, food trucks sold dinner and sweet treats. A black Sleepy Hollow carriage and a silvery-blue Cinderella pumpkin carriage offered rides.

A couple approached the information table. "Happy Halloween," Michaela greeted.

"Happy Halloween," the tall man echoed. He smiled and stuck out his hand. "I'm Cole Dart."

Michaela glanced at his costume, taking his hand. "You must be a cowboy."

Cole chuckled. "This is my everyday uniform, and my wife Piper has just arrived from Oz."

"And this is lady Arwen of the elvish realm of Rivendale." Piper bowed,

74

sweeping her arms out wide.

"I'm glad I'm not the only Lord of the Rings fan. Greetings, I pray your evening fares well," Michaela said in an accent.

"It does, m' lady," Piper said, curtsying her Dorothy Gale skirt, then giggling. "I wanted to welcome you to Fortuna. I moved here from Chicago. Thanks for taking over the position of newbie."

"Oh, I've heard a little of your story from Ms. Hardmann."

Piper glanced around, her blond bob swaying. "I hope she behaved."

"If that was behaved, I want to experience misbehaving." Michaela shared a giggle.

Jasen, dressed in a Wolverine costume, stepped up to Michaela's side of the table. He nodded to the Darts. "Where's your costume Cole?"

"In the bedroom, I'd wager," Michaela smirked.

Piper blushed and slapped her husband on the back. "Michaela certainly has Fortuna's number." Cole's face reddened, but he didn't say a word.

Jasen shook his head and tidied the stack of papers in front of him. "Here's a list of concerts happening this fall." He pointed to another. "These are the other events over the holidays."

Michaela had straightened her hair for playing the part of an elf. She'd also added pointy ear tips. The thin, woven metal crown she wore on her head itched and caught her hair.

"Uncle Cole, Aunt Piper," a high-pitched voice screeched. A little boy dressed in brown and carrying a bright yellow pillowcase ran up to them.

"That's Beau," Jasen whispered. Michaela acknowledged with a nod.

Cole picked the boy up as if he weighed nothing and tossed him into the air. The boy squealed in sheer delight. Giggling, he regained his footing.

The boy's face sobered and pointed. "That's an elf."

Michaela rounded the table. Furry patches covered his gym shoes. Her first hobbit. She stretched out her hands to him and said, "To you, master hobbit, I give you the light of our star. May it shine on your path in dark times. Or freshen your breath if it's stinky."

Beau tilted his head and gazed up with awe. He nodded and gasped when she removed her hand. His face scrunched. "Hey, this is gum." Cole tapped Beau's head, sending his dark curls bouncing. "Thank you, ma'am," Beau said.

The Darts moved on, leaving Jasen and Michaela alone. They stood in awkward silence.

After a while, Jasen uttered, "I'm sorry, Michaela."

"I told you," Michaela's voice cracked as she turned away from him.

Jasen's fingers brushed her shoulder then fell away. The back of her throat ached as she kept the sob at bay. She couldn't cry, wouldn't cry out, where Nellie could find her.

"Nellie was unfair." Jasen's soft tone only twisted the knife in her heart.

"Unfair?" Michaela snorted, crossing her arms.

"There are children about or else I'd tell you what I really think," he growled.

The low rumble of his anger touched her primitively. She swiveled and flung her arms around Jasen. She buried her face in his costume's puffy fake muscles. He stroked her head and back. The irony wasn't lost as she took comfort in the arms of the object of conjecture.

"I can't believe she called Darren," she mumbled, turning her nose away from the funny-smelling synthetic material.

"She contacted the previous company you worked for and spoke with your former boss. It's a normal procedure to get someone's credentials. What I don't understand is why Darren dumped your personal information. It was underhanded and not professional. Your childhood or your parents' relationship shouldn't have been an issue."

"*Not professional?*" Neither was hugging her boss while working. Michaela laughed, pushing away from him. Her laughter rang bitter and she hugged herself. "The town will think the worst of me. I didn't take this job to get revenge on Darren, and I'm not afraid of magicians!"

"Her article says a lot more about her than about you. Fortuna folks are used to Nellie's rants. They'll understand."

Michaela couldn't help her skepticism. An outsider whose purpose was to shake up the town, even if it was for the better, was still a pushy outsider.

"And who's going to believe you're afraid of magicians? Seriously, what adult is afraid of magicians? Clowns maybe, but not magicians. Magicians are cool." Jasen nudged her elbow.

While she appreciated his effort to lighten her mood, she couldn't shake the gnawing dread. It was as if Nellie had picked the scab off an infected wound, leaving it exposed and seeping.

Michaela wanted the wound to remain hidden from the world. But since her past would always be her past, she couldn't run from it. Moving away from Ohio hadn't distanced her from the past.

"I'm not afraid of magicians. I don't like them." Michaela scratched at an invisible itch on her arm. Her gaze snapped to Jasen's. "I loathe them," she spit. She might as well admit the truth.

Jasen rocked back on his heels with wide eyes. "It's understandable, considering what happened, but they're not all monsters."

"My mother performed the ultimate disappearing act with a magician. She abandoned me and my father for some guy with something up his sleeves, so please excuse me if I don't care for magicians." With her hands on her hips, she cocked her head and glared, daring him to rebuke her. Michaela shook her head. She didn't want to dwell in the bitterness of her childhood.

Michaela needed to get a grip. She clenched her eyes shut and took deep breaths, dropping her arms she rolled her shoulders. When she opened her eyes, Jasen's gaze had dropped to the low scoop neckline of her dress. She sighed. Raising her hand to breast height, she snapped her fingers, earning his attention.

Jasen-blushed and gave her a lopsided grin. "Sexy dress," he offered, eyes raking her gown.

"Nice try." She shot back. "It's not too low, is it?" Michaela glanced around.

"It's fine. I just have a nice angle, that's all." Jasen wiggled his eyebrows.

"I'm trying one of the Double D's pieces. I think Jessie called it the Hallelujah bra, but it's basically a demi-bra."

Jasen's jaw dropped and he examined her cleavage anew.

"Do you know what a demi-bra is?" Michaela asked.

"I—," Jasen smirked. "No. Care to explain?"

"A demi-bra lifts the girls and hugs them, enhancing cleavage. It works perfectly for a dress like this."

Someone cleared their throat. Bare-chested with strapped on white-feathered wings, B.J. Johnson stared at her cleavage as well.

Words clogged the back of her throat. B.J. 's black hair curled around his ears. She appreciated B.J. 's sculpted chest and abs, sprinkled with a light covering of dark hair. His jeans hung low on his hips. She hadn't noticed what a hunk B.J. had been before; then again, he had been wearing more clothes.

Michaela had learned about *The Visitation,* a favorite novel of Fortuna's residents. The hero falls for his neighbor and visits her at night; posing as an angel, he whispers to her while she sleeps. Angel-men visiting their ladies to make their dreams take flight had become the trending Fortuna fad. According to Jacklyn, there had been several arrests. Men caught with wings became a badge of pride for the ladies. Other women turned envious gazes toward the lucky individuals who'd received a visitation.

"Where's your halo?" Jasen asked with a frown.

"You don't want to know," B.J. drawled.

A few more people joined them, picking up the event list and asking questions. The townsfolk didn't stare at her with contempt, but complimented her on her costume.

"Come here a minute," B.J. said to Jasen. They moseyed toward the town hall steps out of earshot. Jasen frowned. B.J. wore a cocky grin.

"Where's the ice cream truck?" a man asked.

"There's a dessert truck right over there. Look for the pink truck with the unicorn." Michaela pointed to the southwest corner.

The sky darkened. The DJ ramped up the volume on the amphitheater's stage. She tapped her foot in time with the bass. The older crowd roamed the streets. Couples danced and churned on one side of the square. Scents from the food trucks made her mouth water.

B.J. met Michaela's gaze and curled a finger, beckoning her over. "Ready to go dancing? Jasen said you can go," B.J. said.

"You said I can go with him?" Michaela found it hard to breathe.

"No," Jasen said, crossing his fake muscled arms, his foam claws sticking out. "I said we're done here."

Michaela glanced down at her dress and pulled the skirt up on both sides. "I don't think I could dance in this dress anyway. It's a little too long."

"Take it off," B.J. said with a wolfish grin.

"Don't be ridiculous." Jasen's frown morphed into a scowl.

"I wish I could, but I didn't bring anything else to wear," Michaela said swirling around. Her skirt flared. "If I spin, I won't trip on it."

"Come on," B.J. held out his hand.

She reached for it then pulled back, studying his body. "Where would I put my hands?"

"Darling, you can put your hands anywhere you'd like, and I mean anywhere." B.J. opened his arms to her, and she giggled.

Jasen shot his arm out and caught Michaela's wrist. "Wait a minute." He glared at his friend.

"B.J. and I had a talk while Nellie interviewed you," Michaela said.

That stunned Jasen. "Why?"

"I dared him."

"You what?" Jasen's gaze shifted to B.J. and back.

"I dared B.J. to make you jealous. Of course he agreed, being the origin of the Fortuna Dare Society."

"It worked," Jasen muttered.

"I told Jasen about my plan, and he didn't like it one bit. Giving me the older brother, jealous boyfriend routine," B.J. said.

"Boyfriend?" Michaela couldn't help the smile on her face. She stepped toward Jasen, but stopped when a car came screeching to the barrier.

"Help!"

# CHAPTER 19

## Jasen

JASEN'S HEART LEAPED TO HIS throat, and he surged toward the vehicle. B.J. followed, close on his heels. The doors to the hatchback opened in unison. Three teens with wide eyes and pale faces spilled out.

Winded, Jasen slowed beside the driver's door. The passengers converged on him and began talking at once. They gasped short phrases.

"A ghost."

"Moans."

"Haunted."

"Reaching arms."

"White lady."

"Shrieks."

Jasen glanced at Johnson. They shared a skeptical look. Were they getting punked?

Hand gripping the hem of her dress as not to trip, Michaela met them at the car. She opened her arms for the girl, and the youth fell in and started sobbing. Not punked.

"Slow down," Jasen told the driver.

The kid took a deep breath and glanced at his friends. He ran his hand through red-tinted hair. He wore a tattered clown costume. Although his lips were purple, it wasn't makeup.

Something had spooked the living tar out of the kids. Jasen frowned and opened his mouth, but Michaela said, "I'll go get Ben. I know where he is."

The girl wiped at her face, and the clown boy took her hand.

Michaela disappeared into the throng of dancers and Jasen waited anxiously for her return. After what seemed like hours, she emerged with a determined look followed by an inflated T-Rex. Ben peered out of a hole in the neck. He waddled over and unzipped the costume, stepping out. He straightened his Hammered T-shirt and squared his shorts.

"What's going on?" Ben asked the teenagers.

They all began speaking again. "The park. There was a woman. A ghost."

Ben held up his hands and pointed to the girl. "You first."

With a glance at her friends, she nodded and leaned against the clown. "We were at Stanton Cove Park and we saw her."

Noise faded into silence. Lights dimmed into darkness. Oxygen. Where was the oxygen?

A small tug on his elbow had Jasen glancing into Michaela's worried eyes. The subtle touch made him remember to breathe. He sucked in a ragged breath and gave her what he hoped was an appreciative smile.

Jasen refocused on the girl. "She was white. The lady called to me then disappeared like smoke."

The boys dumbly nodded.

"There was a horrifying moan," the clown boy said.

"I heard it too," said the second boy.

"Oh God." Jasen groaned. His heart raced, and he couldn't move.

Ben's voice was even. The officer wasn't panicking, but they needed to hurry and get a search party organized. Collin Copper, Ben's boss and the chief of police, appeared next to Jasen.

"A ghost," Collin chuckled. He rubbed his face and shook his head.

The girl's parents showed up and joined the group. Once the story had been told, the parents led her away.

Anxiety threatened to erupt. The police weren't moving fast enough. "Aren't you going to search for her?" Jasen blurted.

"Who?" Ben asked.

"The woman. What if she needs help?" Jasen wrung his hands.

Ben motioned for Jasen to follow him away from the crowd. "Listen, Jasen, they saw a ghost on Halloween. Someone was just having fun trying to scare the dickens out of them. It worked. They went there to see a ghost and that's what they saw."

"Halloween? You think it was a prank?" Jasen stepped back and bumped into Michaela. She'd been his shadow since she'd retrieved Ben. She rubbed small soothing circles on his back.

"We'll send a car over to double check, but it looks that way. With the newspaper running that stupid article about the canyon ghost, I'm surprised we haven't had this happen more often. It wouldn't be the first time someone has been tricked instead of treated on Halloween."

Jasen folded his arms and gave a stiff nod.

"It's not a real emergency," Michaela cooed, "and if it is, it's not the same as before, and the police will deal with it accordingly." She continued to rub his back and the tightness started to subside.

Jasen nodded again, hugging her to him. He breathed deep, smelling lilies. Warmth filled him and he gazed down into her green eyes.

"Are you okay?" she asked, studying him.

Jasen swallowed and nodded. "I just," he cringed. "Just saying the name of the place puts me on edge."

She lifted one eyebrow, her eyes taking on an impish glint. "Well, you have to practice saying it, because I've got plans for that park." Her voice had taken a husky tone that shot straight to his groin. She had his attention.

"Plans?"

She elbowed him in the gut. "Not those sort of plans."

He hummed, and she giggled. "Tell me about them tomorrow," Jasen said, grateful for the distraction.

Michaela tilted her head, and with a small grin she whispered "I will."

Jasen found it hard to nod off. He kept fantasizing about Michaela, his desk, and the green elvish dress. "Get a grip," he groaned as he rolled onto his side. The drone of the furnace finally lulled him into a restless sleep.

*He stood on the top of a cliff, gazing down into the raging torrent of the Dry Run creek. Anything but dry, the water crested the banks, rushing over boulders and shrubs. The gray sky boasted neither daybreak nor twilight. Michaela called to him, and he whirled. Scanning the tree line, he saw no one. The long centennial shadows stretched for him.*

*"Jasen," his dead wife's voice echoed from the turbulent depths. Frantic, he spun.*

*Levitating in the fog, Dee opened her arms. "Come," she beckoned. Her wispy blond hair swirled and bellowed as smoke from an extinguished flame. The beguiling smile on her pale lips promised reward, yet her opalescent eyes were hard and cold.*

*Again, Michaela's voice floated on the wind. Dee glowered, and her fists became lost in balls of luminescent vapor.*

*Jasen twirled once more and Michaela stumbled free from the forest, her face a mask of abject horror. Jasen's heart raced. He longed to protect her, but his feet wouldn't move. "Don't go," she shouted. Struggling toward him, she fought against an unseen force. Her forehead glistened with beads of sweat. Closer. Her arm stretched, fingertips touching his. A timid smile flitted over her lips.*

*Warmth spread up his arm, pooling in his heart. Jasen returned her grin.*

*Dee laughed, a mocking hollow sound. A cold mist descended, encapsulating them.*

*Jasen reached for Michaela, unable to jerk his gaze away from her ruby lips as they parted, exhaling little clouds.*

*Michaela's gaze jumped behind him, her eyes widened. "No!" she screamed, lunging for him, but it was too late.*

*Fiery pain erupted from his spine as Jasen was yanked backward. He gasped. His shoes scraped the rocky edge. Dee's laughter met his ears. His clothes fluttered as he clawed at air. Useless. His stomach lurched as he fell.*

*Michaela peered down, her face wet with tears.*

*The floodwater roared.*

*Dee's face hovered before him and she reached into his chest grabbing his heart, her evil laughter echoing.*

Jasen pushed away sweat-soaked sheets and sat up. He scrubbed his face. Christ. He hadn't dreamed about Dee in months. His feet touched the cool floor, and he switched on the bedside light. With his heart and mind racing, he wouldn't find sleep anytime soon.

He plucked *Work Hanky-Spanky* off the nightstand and opened to the dogeared page. He'd rather fantasize about an office affair with Michaela than be haunted by his dead wife.

# CHAPTER 20

## *Jasen*

MICHAELA STRETCHED, THE VIEW OF her lithe legs ending at her running shorts. Her white sport bra and tank barely covered her back. Jasen longed to touch her smooth skin, but he'd striven to keep his hands to himself since dating her wasn't an option. He understood based on her previous relationship to her boss and Darren's devotion to the business and not the marriage.

Michaela didn't want a repeat. He could sympathize, but he was not Darren. He wasn't as flashy or as rich but he loved his job. Jasen endeavored to do his best. The residents of Fortuna counted on him. Michaela was a citizen now, even if it was temporary. He wanted her to stay after the consultant position ended. He'd use any means to persuade her.

Like now, visiting Stanton Cove Park. He wiped his damp palms on his shorts.

Time to let Dee go. Jasen hadn't been responsible for her actions or the weather. Still guilt hung over him, shadowing his thoughts.

Jasen could have been nicer to Dee and less angry. Nowadays he strove not to get angry, holding his temper in check. Letting others vent before offering an opinion. Sometimes he ended up zoning out, other times he just bit his tongue to hold the tirade back. Whatever the method, it had to work. He wouldn't be responsible for another person's death.

Michaela lunged, stretching. He mimicked her movements, letting her lead the exercise. "I like those shorts," he said.

"Thanks," she grinned, catching him staring at her butt again.

"I like the color periwinkle." Jasen shrugged.

She straightened. "Sure you do. So you like purply blue."

"Personally, I think it's more bluish-purple. But yes, I do." Jasen sipped from a water bottle. "I have that tie."

Her face scrunched. "Oh, the Easter one."

"It's not eggs. They're dots." Jasen shook his head. She'd teased him about the eggs the day he'd worn it.

"Are you ready for this?" she asked, pointing to the trail. Her brow etched with concern as she picked up her backpack. They had planned to picnic at the shelter.

Jasen sucked in a deep breath. He nodded and smiled. "I am." He slid the straps of his backpack over his shoulders.

Michaela's face lit up when he locked his car. He stuffed the keys in his pocket. "Let's roll."

She started at a slow pace he could easily match. They passed couples, singles, and families out enjoying the sunshine. The Dry Run creek was low, and he tried to keep his gaze averted.

Michaela stopped and relaxed on a large boulder. Rapids bubbled. She stared into the water as if it had trapped her thoughts. Without glancing at him, she said, "I love this place. It's so tranquil."

He breathed deeply, taking in the fresh air. "It's a little noisy to be peaceful."

One side of her lips quirked up, and she patted the rock beside her. "Come and sit. Close your eyes and listen."

Jasen obliged, sitting on the cool stone. He closed his eyes. The rushing water threatened to consume his senses. The sound from his nightmare.

"Feel the sunshine on your skin." She touched his thigh. A whisper of a touch, but it was enough to set his body on high alert. Her breath caressed his ear. "What else to you hear?"

"Your breathing," he replied.

"Very good," she said, placing a kiss on his cheek near his ear.

"What else?"

"A bird. It's a hawk."

Michaela kissed further down his jaw line, closer to his mouth. He liked this game. "Branches rustling in the wind." She kissed the corner of his mouth. Besides his heartbeat, he couldn't hear another thing.

He imagined her expression, brows raised and lips tilted in a smirk, waiting for him to say something, anything.

Her breath fanned his cheek. Jasen swallowed. He touched her face. Then he heard them.

"People."

A quick peck to his lips, and she was gone. He opened his eyes and saw a couple holding hands strolling toward them. They were older but appeared fit enough to hike the steep trail ahead. The couple greeted them then passed.

"Are you ready to climb to the overlook?" Michaela asked, beaming. "The view will be beautiful today."

Jasen nodded.

Would she have kissed him like they had kissed at the courthouse? He stood and turned from her, pretending to shake stiff limbs, but trying to hide something else stiff. "I'm ready. Lead on."

She took off at a steady clip, and Jasen enjoyed the view. Her shapely calves, the curve of her bottom, and the swish of her ponytail were enough to mesmerize him and, for a while, he was able to forget his wife's death.

Michaela veered left and headed onto a new trail. One he'd never hiked. The dirt path twisted between and around boulders, climbing until they were against the rock surface of the cliff wall. By the time they reached the pinnacle he was out of breath. Jasen bent over, his hands on his legs, inhaling deeply. But the smile of satisfaction on Michaela's lips was worth every labored breath.

He hadn't been to the overlook since Dee died. They'd hiked to the shelter where he'd proposed and she accepted. Hand in hand, they had reached the overlook. They hadn't come this far up the trail. He glanced over the expanse, wowed by the height.

"Beautiful, isn't it?" Michaela asked. The wind blew strands of her hair. Her green eyes entranced by the panoramic scenery, she scanned the riverscape and the trees, then lifted her eyes to the sky. Her brow bunched.

"Yes, you are."

Michaela faced him, reaching for his hand. The soft touch had his heart hammering. His body intrinsically reacted to her.

"Thanks," she said. They walked the cliff edge trail. She stopped to pick up a beer can and candy wrapper. "Not the best hiking fare."

"No. But good date fare."

"You'd bring beer and candy up here on a date?" she asked.

"This is a great place to watch the sun set." He glanced over the edge toward the descending sun.

She gasped. "That would be awesome, but we'd have to walk back in the dark."

*We.* He couldn't help the smile frozen on his face.

"The pine trees smell great," she said.

Tall pines edged one side of the trail, like the nightmare. His heartbeat pounded in his ears.

"Jasen?" Michaela called. Even though she skimmed the back of his hand with her thumb, he half expected her to emerge from the tree line, struggling to reach him. Sweat peppered his forehead. He hesitated, and Michaela jerked to a stop.

"What is it?" she asked.

Air clogged in his throat. His gaze darted around, searching for Dee's ghost. Jasen couldn't verbalize the terror or the debilitating guilt. He stumbled forward and leaned against a large stone. It was a mistake. The drop off loomed precariously close. Air became nonexistent.

"Oh no," Michaela uttered.

Jasen jerked his gaze from her upturned face toward the sky. Clouds hurried over the trees as if they fled from something. Thunder rumbled. He closed his eyes and rubbed his face.

"We've got to get out of here," he groaned. The only thing was... his legs, hell, maybe his heart refused to work.

Michaela's concern morphed into determination. She paced for a moment then, with her hands on her hips, she stepped to the edge of the chasm. He opened his mouth, but it was hard to talk around his heart lodged in his throat.

Jasen didn't know what to make of the devilish glint in her eyes. He swallowed. She shucked off her backpack and dropped it next to the boulder. "Close your eyes and relax, Jasen."

He snorted. Michaela gave him the stink eye before she leaned to tie her shoe. He rolled his tight shoulders then stretched out his arms with palms on the cool rough stone as if he held it in place. A hoarse laugh rumbled out of his throat, and he tipped his head back.

He felt a tug on his shorts waistband, and suddenly they were around his ankles. He whipped his head down, his chin against his chest. The damp wind whirled over his exposure.

Michaela kneeled at his feet, her head bowed as if she worshiped his shoes.

"Michaela?"

She turned to the side, a small smile on her lips. "It's time for therapy." Her husky tone made him twitch.

"Oh?" Jasen asked, still unable to move.

"One rule. You must keep your eyes on the view."

"But—" he started.

"I'm not working on your butt today. That's another therapy session." She gazed up, rising to her knees.

Suddenly, he was encased in her warm, wet mouth. Breathless for another reason, he curled his fingers and gasped. Her tongue worked his length. He did as she had asked and studied the landscape. "Take down your hair," he rasped.

She pulled out the band holding her ponytail. Jasen thrust his fingers into her luxurious waves, holding her head. He moved with her, and she hummed against him. His blood raced. "Oh God, I'm close."

Heavy drops of rain fell, but he didn't slow. Lightning flashed, followed by thunder. Jasen glanced down into Michaela's hooded emerald eyes and found his sweet release. Therapy had worked.

# CHAPTER 21

## *Michaela*

MICHAELA STOOD, WIPING HER KNEES, and streaking her palms with mud. She picked up the backpack, shifting awkwardly.

Jasen pulled up his basketball shorts and adjusted his manhood. Even with his fear, she'd been able to satisfy him. It thrilled her, remembering the way he'd moved with her and plunged his long fingers into her hair. He had moaned her name. The sound had warmed her, making her feel beautiful and desired. Something she hadn't felt in a long time.

"Let's go," Jasen said, taking her hand. "We need to get to the shelter." The wind had picked up, and the rain turned the path to mud. The trail would be treacherous near the edge. The trees bowed, and leaf debris showered on them.

Exposed on a high point, they were targets for lightning. This wasn't exactly how she planned the day to go. In fact, she had no intention of de-pantsing her boss, but she'd needed to get Jasen to concentrate on anything else.

"This is one hell of a storm," he said.

"I'm sorry," Michaela hollered over the wind. "The Weather Channel said less than a thirty percent chance. I wouldn't have come to the cliff if I..."

"So the therapy wasn't premeditative?" Jasen asked, holding her as she stepped down a stone stair.

"No, it just kind of came to me," she smiled up at him then wiped the rain from her eyes.

"You mean, came in you," Jasen teased.

"That's another session," she replied, passing him when he stumbled.

Jasen held her hand but stopped. He stared at her with a stunned expression. He was right.

She was a contrary person, always spouting how she didn't want a relationship with a boss but kept flirting and teasing with him. Oh my God, she'd just sucked him off out in the open. Anyone on the path could have seen them.

Michaela rubbed her head. "I need therapy."

"That can be arranged," he said with a wry grin and began walking again.

The light had waned by the time they spotted the shelter. It had a roof and one full wall with a stone fireplace grill. The shelter held six picnic tables. In good weather Dry Run creek was visible from the far corner. The rainy night had created an opaque curtain, but the churning water reminded her it was there.

Several people waited at the shelter. The older couple they had seen before cuddled at the back table. A young man and his father talked with their heads over a device, trying to get a signal. The rest were joggers or hikers caught in the deluge.

Michaela shook off her arms and stomped the mud off her feet. She plopped her backpack on the nearest tabletop and rolled her shoulders. Soaked through to the skin, she shivered.

The wind wailed, and she hugged herself. She couldn't risk returning along the river trail, even if Jasen wouldn't object. The sound of the angry river magnified the danger. She had never heard the river from the shelter. Grateful the building had been constructed halfway up the cliff side, Michaela didn't fear the floodwaters.

She faced Jasen, and he frowned. He'd taken off his shirt and squeezed the excess water out. She wanted to run her fingers over his damp chest, but he thrust the shirt at her.

Jasen put his arm around her in a loose embrace. His breath warmed her ear. "Put it on," he insisted.

She slipped it over her head even though it clung to her skin. "Why?" she asked.

They sat on a tabletop, their feet on the bench. Jasen pulled her close, sharing body heat. "You're wearing a wet white shirt."

Michaela nuzzled his neck. "Thanks for looking out for me." She could keep warm if her body was in a constant state of need.

The low rumble of his laugh vibrated. "I don't want to share."

Lightning flashed and thunder rolled. The father played country music on his phone, but the downpour drumming on the roof drowned the words.

"Should we eat?" she asked, rubbing her stomach.

"What I'm hungry for, I can't get here," Jasen mumbled.

"We aren't going to make it to the Weiner Wagon tonight." Michaela laughed. "You weren't talking about food were you?"

"No."

She searched in her bag, then handed him a sandwich. Turkey, cheddar, and mayo on wheat. They shared a water bottle.

As the storm raged and night settled, little hope remained that the group would escape the shelter before sunrise. Michaela sat with her head on Jasen's shoulder. She whispered, "Do you know any of these people?"

"The father and son look familiar. People come from all over to hike the park." He shrugged. "Why?"

"I just worry that they saw…"

"Your therapy session?" Jasen chuckled, and the couple glanced over at them.

Michaela's face grew hot. And she playfully hit his shoulder.

"I doubt it," he rubbed his chin. "But I didn't see anyone looking up at us." Suddenly he grew pensive.

"What is it?" Her heart sank.

Jasen turned his head away, staring into the dark. His voice barely a whisper, he said, "Dee haunts my dreams. I know I wasn't responsible for her death, but I dream about being there. Not reaching her in time. Unable to move because I freeze."

He faced Michaela again, his eyes haunted. "Ever since the rumors of a lady haunting the canyon started, my dreams have turned to nightmares. It's like she doesn't want me to be happy. Especially with you."

"With me?" Michaela gasped.

"You've been in my dreams. You try to rescue me." Jasen glanced down at their threaded fingers.

"Jasen," she whispered. "What do I rescue you from?"

He squeezed his eyes shut. "Her ghost. I know it seems silly, but she's always trying to pull me off the cliff or into the water."

"How do I rescue you?"

"You don't. She gets me first." Jasen shook his head. "It's like she doesn't want us to get together."

"Do you want us together?" she asked, staring at their hands. It was his subconscious mind keeping them apart—not his dead wife. Her heart raced. Did she want to know the answer?

She swallowed, his lack of response solidifying the heaviness in her heart.

Jasen rubbed the back of his head. "I don't know." He sighed again. "That's not true. I feel a connection with you and want to explore it, but I know you want to wait until this temporary contract is finished. That's less than four months. I can wait. The night the contract expires I'm going to take you out."

Michaela sucked in a deep breath and nodded. He canted his head and leaned close, touching her face with a gentle caress. A shiver ran down her spine. Could she trust him with her heart? She leaned into his warmth, happy and content, eventually falling asleep in his arms.

# CHAPTER 22

## *Jasen*

AFTER THEIR OVERNIGHT AT THE shelter, Jasen didn't see Michaela until Monday morning. She'd answered his texts but not his phone call. He'd dropped the bomb of dating after she'd dropped his pants. Had he moved too soon? Did she only want a physical relationship?

The computer screen had been open for half an hour, but he couldn't concentrate on the email he was penning. He saved the draft and closed the screen. Rubbing his eyes, he leaned back.

"Long night?" Jacklyn asked from the doorway.

"Yeah, I didn't get much sleep." He yawned, which he hastily covered.

"Do you know what's wrong with Michaela?" Hands on her hips, Jacklyn's gaze narrowed on him, eying him suspiciously.

Jasen popped out of his seat. "What's wrong with her?"

A lopsided grin formed, and she shrugged. Jasen hurried to Michaela's office. She held her head in her hands as she leaned over the desk.

"Rough night?" he asked, startling her.

Wide red-rimmed eyes took him in. She blinked and glanced back at the computer. "It's Darren."

At that, Jasen entered her office and closed the door. He took the empty seat across from her and waited.

She folded her arms over her chest and huffed. "He's taken the job in Nockerville. He wants to share ideas with me and work together to build up the two towns."

Jasen nodded, not knowing if she liked the idea or not. Was she frazzled or excited? "When does he want to meet you?"

She grimaced as if she tasted something bad. "Soon." She shook her head.

"Michaela," Jasen said as a warning. "How soon?"

"Tomorrow."

"Christ." Jasen stood and started pacing her small office. Her eyes trailed him as he moved. He stopped and faced her. She'd gone pale. "There's more?"

With a small nod, she said, "There's a fundraising ball, and you and the mayor of Nockerville are doing something together."

Jasen sat down in the chair. "I've forgotten about that. It's not until the end of the year. Between Christmas and New Year's. It's a charity event and black tie. There will be a formal dinner and dancing. And folks will have the opportunity to bid on silent auctions throughout the room."

Jasen rubbed his chin. "Darren is going?"

"He wants me to be his date." She gulped, looking as if the thought horrified her.

Jasen stood again with his hands on his hips. "You don't have to go. It's not mandatory for your position. I'd ask you, but I know you don't want to date your boss."

She glanced away.

Thoughts of her in the green elvish gown made him warm. "Would you wear a push-up bra?"

Michaela whipped her head around, gaping. Heat washed over him. He was an ass. Then her lips slowly quirked into a smirk. "Maybe. Depends on the dress." She shrugged then continued, "I might not need a bra." She flashed a teasing smile, but it dropped off when her phone rang.

Jasen leaned over the table and noticed a picture of bare chested Darren flashing on the screen. "Want me...?"

"Sure."

"Hello?" Jasen said.

"Hello, is Michaela there?"

"Whom may I say is calling?"

"Her husband." Darren said in a clipped voice.

Jasen chuckled. "I didn't know she'd gotten remarried. I'll have to congratulate her," he drawled. "Would you like to leave a message?"

"Sure. Please tell her that Darren called and that I love and miss her. Got that?"

"Yes, sir. I'll be sure to tell her. You have yourself a nice day." Jasen ended the call and handed her the phone. "What a jerk," he mumbled.

Michaela had quieted and seemed a shell of herself.

"What are you worried about?" Jasen asked softly.

Her eyes shifted and locked on his gaze. "I'm afraid."

"Why? He can't bother you."

"I'm afraid of me, not Darren." Michaela swallowed and her lip quivered.

"He's charming, and I can tell he's scheming to get me."

"Get you how?"

"To get me to sleep with him."

The simplicity of the statement and her honesty floored him. Jasen inspected her. Red eyes with bags, wrinkled clothes, disheveled hair and minimal makeup, Michaela hadn't slept well either. "Don't worry."

She chuckled. "You don't know him. If he wants something, he gets it. He'll work and work until it's his." She hugged herself again.

"He's done this to you before," Jasen growled. His eyes narrowed.

Jasen pushed the chair backward and rounded the desk. He pulled her into his arms. She gasped when he tipped her chin and claimed her lips. She fisted his shirt and tugged him closer, opening for him. He delved in. The moment stretched, their breathing ragged and hearts racing until someone cleared their throat. She buried her face against his neck and breathed deeply. He swiveled his head, spotting B.J.

"Can I join this party?" B.J. asked, laughing as he disappeared from view.

Jasen kissed her forehead then broke the embrace. "I better see what that rogue wants."

Michaela's cheeks had blossomed pink and she nodded, returning to her desk chair. "He probably has a book for you. Another office romance novel." Jasen was glad her eyes sparkled with mischief.

B.J. stared at an oil painting with his hands behind his back when Jasen approached. "This is a pretty good likeness," he said. When he turned he wore a large smile. "Congratulations on your girlfriend."

"She's not my—"

"Whatever, Romeo. Tell that to her tonsils." B.J. laughed, and they walked to Jasen's office.

Jasen felt heat creep to his face. "What's happening?"

B.J.'s smile faded. "This." He placed a small article he'd cut out of the Fortuna Forum.

"Lady Ghost Thought to be Dee DeLay by Nellie Neus" Jasen read with a frown. The panic that ought to have accompanied the article did not manifest. Instead, he read the four paragraphs, reaching the end. "Ridiculous."

"That's it?" B.J. asked through narrowed eyes.

"Do you think I should call Nellie or let it go?" Jasen asked, glancing up at his friend.

"Oh hell," B.J. said, feeling backward for the guest chair and lowering himself onto it. "Are you feeling okay?"

Now Jasen began to worry, tilting his head he scanned B.J. "What's going on?"

"Nothing." B.J. appeared shocked. "Absolutely nothing." He scrubbed his hand down his face then smiled. A bright-watted smile. "It's Michaela.

She's fixed you."

Jasen frowned and leaned back. Then he relaxed, realizing he wasn't riding waves of guilt. A smile broke through. "I guess therapy worked," he mumbled.

"You've had therapy?" B.J. asked.

Jasen waved his hand as his cheeks warmed.

"Oh, hm." B.J. started to laugh in earnest. "So how are you two? Is she still upset about nosy Nellie?"

"It's her ex-husband. She thinks he is interested in her as a challenge."

B.J.'s brow furrowed. "How can she be a challenge if she's already been married to him? I don't get it."

Jasen kept his hands in his lap, fumbling with a pen. "She's frightened he'll try to seduce her. Apparently, he's charming."

"So charming, he'll charm her pants off?" B.J. chuckled again. "If I were so lucky."

"I think she's afraid she'll give in."

B.J. pointed at Jasen. "No, that's what you fear. You are terrified she'll fall back in love with that slime-ball and leave town. Give her some credit, Jasen. She's a smart lady, and she's been played by that cad before. She'll be wary of him this time around."

"It's the fundraising ball. He's invited Michaela to the dance. But I told her she isn't required to attend. She shouldn't feel obligated."

"Wait. Did you ask her to go?" B.J. asked.

"No, she doesn't want to go out with me yet."

"Yet?"

Jasen smiled and leaned back in the chair. "I'm taking her out on the final night of her contract."

"What are you going to do?"

"I have no idea. Any suggestions?" Jasen asked.

"A movie and dinner?"

Jasen shook his head. "No. I want it to me more than that."

"What about the theater? The Upstage Center Theater always has some show or another."

"Thanks, B.J., that will work. I'll order the tickets today." With a nod, he pulled up the website for the very last night of her contract. It was a Friday. He remembered the date because it fell on his wedding anniversary.

"Oh no. It's sold out," Jasen said, closing his laptop. He combed his face.

"Well shit. Sorry, bro," B.J. said, rubbing his chin. He glanced toward the ceiling then back at Jasen. "Sorry to bring this up now, but Larry's roof is leaking."

Jasen blinked and leaned against the back of his chair. "Larry who?"

"Larry from Larry's Erection Company, next door to Longfellow's." B.J.

folded his hands on his lap.

"Ah. So it's the same building, right?" Jasen stood and stretched.

"Yes."

"So have it fixed," Jasen said, drumming his fingers on the desktop.

B.J. raised his hand. "This isn't the first time we've had issues—"

"Aren't you Longfellow's property manager? And manager of my other properties? Whether it's a patch or the whole roof needs replaced—just fix it. I trust you." Jasen returned to his seat. "You know the drill: send me the bill once the job's done."

"Yes, sir!" B.J. saluted as he left the office.

A sudden ache formed at the back of Jasen's head. Maybe he needed more therapy.

# CHAPTER 23

## *Michaela*

THE SPONTANEOUS LUNCH DATE AT the Pink Taco had Michaela nervously glancing around. She sipped her tea and waited for her guest.

Across the restaurant, Nellie dipped chips into salsa, keeping Michaela in her sights.

B.J. Johnson swaggered through the entry. Michaela studied him. Dark hair, eyes, and lashes, broad shoulders, and tapered waist. Of course, she'd seen his bare chest. Sculptured as if he had nothing to do but crunches. His full lips tweaked up into a smirk as he caught her staring.

Her neutral expression was practiced, but the color creeping to her face she could only imagine. Hot all over, she gulped her iced tea. B.J. slid in the booth across from her.

"Thanks for meeting me" she said softly then cleared her throat.

"A smart man does not ignore the summons of a pretty lady." His toothy grin made her heart race.

A server took their order and set a fresh basket of chips on the table. Michaela leaned forward conspiring. "Is Nellie still over there? " she asked.

"Yes, ma'am." B.J. winked at Nellie and growled through a fake smile. "I really hate that bitch."

Michaela's brows rose, and she reached across, patting his hand. "I'm guessing there's a story. And I'd love to hear it sometime, but I'm on my lunch."

B.J. tilted his head and a genuine smile appeared. "What can I do for you?"

"This fundraiser, do you know about it?"

"Yeah, it's a big shindig. All the suits come out of the woodwork to donate. It's nice that they give, don't get me wrong, but they'd rather throw money than get their hands dirty and work. If you know what I mean."

"I've read the website and know it's formal, but what else can you tell me?" Michaela pulled her sweet tea close and sipped.

"There are auctions. The ticket money goes to a charity, but the auctions sometimes go to multiple charities. It depends who's on the committee." He tapped his chin. "Last year it was a Veteran affairs foundation. All the money raised went there. They collected clothes and canned goods upon entry."

"This year it's going to help foster kids. I've met one of the social workers in Fortuna, Morgan Topp. She's told me good things about the charity. I like knowing the funds are actually going to help the kids."

B.J. nodded. "I like Morgan. She's a kind soul."

The server delivered their meal, and they began to eat. B.J. cut his steak burrito. As Michaela put a bite of chimichanga in her mouth, the bell above the door chimed and Nellie called out loudly, "Jasen, over here." Nellie waved a slender hand. He scanned the restaurant seeing Michaela and B.J.

Michaela started coughing and grabbed her drink.

"You okay?" B.J. asked, his brow furrowed. He nodded at Jasen.

"I didn't tell him I'd planned to meet you," she said, staring at her plate.

"Why should you? Besides, did he tell you he was meeting Nellie?" B.J. asked, tilting his head in Nellie's direction.

Michaela met B.J.'s gaze. "No, he did not."

"See. It's all good."

Michaela toyed with the napkin on her lap. "I have something to ask you, B.J."

"Shoot."

"Would you like to go to the fundraiser with me?"

His jaw had dropped open, but he snapped it shut, glancing over at Jasen. Then slowly, a smile formed until he practically glowed. "Why certainly, I'd love to." B.J. leaned back. "Are you going to wear your green dress?" He chuckled when she gasped.

"I guess I could. Should I wear the pointy ears too?" Michaela giggled.

"Why not?" B.J. pushed his plate forward and plucked another chip from the basket. "Don't look now, but I think Jasen is jealous."

Michaela tilted her head slightly, trying to see Jasen.

"I told you not to look." B.J. sighed when Michaela pursed her lips. "Jasen looks as if he swallowed a lemon. No, maybe his appendix is going to bust."

Michaela covered her mouth to hide a giggle. "I hope it doesn't. I'd have to pick up his work. Actually, Jacklyn would do most of it."

"So what's this really about? Why me? Why not Jasen? You two have chemistry."

Michaela sighed and glanced over at the mayor, who drummed his fingers on the table. Nellie leaned close and, for the first time Michaela noticed, Nellie wore a low-cut blouse that exposed mega cleavage. B.J. was right, Jasen appeared in pain. The fake smile appeared more of a grimace and wasn't the usual one he used when talking city business.

"I have a rule not to date coworkers or my boss, so I will not be going out with Jasen." Michaela waved an arm. "At last company I worked for I fell in love with and married my boss. However, he was married to the company. I was the mistress. I don't want a repeat."

"Jasen's not the same man." B.J. crossed his arms.

She shifted food around on her plate. "I know. And I'm sorry if you took my invitation the wrong way. I know Jasen considers you his friend, so I was hoping you'd help me."

B.J. leaned forward, intent on her words. "Thank you."

Michaela nodded. "My ex-husband has accepted a job in Nockerville, and he has asked me to go to the ball. There's no way in hell I'd go with him. And believe me, he's trying to charm his way back into my life."

"Does he miss you or your talent? You must have been an asset in the company." B.J. rubbed his chin. "So you want to snub your ex and let him know what he's missing."

"That sounds good." Michaela nodded, a smirk forming.

"And I suppose you'd like to tease Jasen. Show him what he could have if he plays his cards right." Again B.J. rubbed his chin. "We can do this."

Michaela grinned, feeling giddy. She clasped her hands and forced them still. "Thank you for understanding. You're a good friend."

B.J.'s cheeks turned pink as he gazed at his plate. "Thanks. Let's pray I don't forget I'm acting." He met her gaze with a wolfish grin that stole her breath.

Michaela fingered her glass. Daren might have serious competition. Good grief! Half the women in the Pink Taco swooned when B.J. ran his fingers through his thick hair. The other half watched mesmerized.

B.J. took the bill even though Michaela had invited him. "You're making Nellie's day," B.J. said, tipping his head in the smiley reporter's direction.

On the sidewalk, Michaela hugged B.J. before heading toward the courthouse. She'd caught one glance at Jasen's scowl before she walked out of his line of sight.

# CHAPTER 24

## *Michaela*

"GO AHEAD," MICHAELA SAID, SHOOING Kim away.

Kim shifted, cocking her hip. "I'm not going to leave you here alone." She glanced at Glen with his friends at the trailhead.

"We've spent all day together. Jasen should be here any second, and I'm sure you want to snuggle with Glen," Michaela said, wiggling her brows. When Kim opened her mouth to protest again, Michaela continued, "Besides, neither of us have been here before and we don't know the way. You go ahead with Glen. I already told Jasen I'd be waiting in the shallows." She pointed to a sign, next to a small brown building.

"I don't want to leave you, but I don't want to abandon Glen either. Fine," Kim said, throwing her hands in the air. She shined a flirty smile toward Glen. "Just hurry."

Killing time, Michaela read the park sign that explained the hot spring. Jasen had agreed to meet them there, but he had been waylaid at the office. Michaela cradled her towel as she studied the area where families waded. Laying her towel on a rock, she stepped into the tepid water.

Twilight clung to the sky as the families started to leave. A truckload of young men arrived, what her father would call rednecks. She sunk deeper as one guy approached her. "Hey there, darlin', wanna get wild?"

"Schleimscheisser," Michaela mumbled, pretending to be a German tourist.

"Come on, baby," he grinned, scooting closer. "Let me show you a good time."

"Mein boyfreund coming," she said, trying to mimic Darren's grandfather's accent.

"Let's go where it's hot and I'll show you my wiener schnitzel," the doofus said, earning laughter from his buddies.

Surprised he guessed the correct language, Michaela replied, "Nein. Du bist Bauchnabelfussel."

"I don't know what yer sayin', but yer awfully pretty." He had moved close enough that she could smell alcohol on his breath.

A car door slammed, and Michaela turned toward the parking lot. Jasen's profile against the twilight made her heart sing. She exited the water, wrapped the towel around her, and then raised her hand in greeting.

"Du kommst spät mein Dampfnudel," she growled, then continued speaking German, hoping he'd catch the hint. "Wir sprechen auf Deutsch! Ja? Eins, zwei, drei, vier, fünf, sechs, sieben, acht, neun, zehn. Oktober. Volkswagen. Scheisse. Strudel."

"Gesundheit? Danke?" Jasen said, shrugging.

"Ach, zee? Mein boyfreund." Michaela said, pointing. She giggled and wrapped her arms around him. "I'm so glad you're here. That guy was getting a little too chummy," she whispered.

The cretin returned to his friends. Jasen led her upstream along the path.

"I don't know what I would have done if you'd been any later," Michaela said.

"I've got good timing, huh?" Jasen grinned.

She playfully swatted him. "You're late. I wouldn't have had to deal with that Dummkopf if you would have been on time."

"What all did you say in German?" Jasen asked.

"I counted and some other stuff," she said, watching his backside. No shoes, no shirt, just pastel striped swim trunks. She longed to touch the smooth skin of his back.

"Whoa. It's steep here," he said, stopping. She bumped into him, her face brushing his back. She clutched his waist to steady herself and caught a hint of his cologne.

"Where are the others?" Michaela heard Kim's peal of laughter but couldn't see the group yet.

"They're in the crazy hot zone. We can try to work our way up, if you'd like."

"Let's see. Hot tub temp should be fine for me."

She followed Jasen down the rocky bank and into water until they were waist deep. "Oh God, this is awesome."

Jasen held her hand and kept moving upstream. The running water fluctuated temperatures, cool, warm, hot, and cold. The further upstream Jasen tugged her, the warmer the brook. He found a good place to sit on a submerged rock within earshot of the others.

Darkness fell like a blanket and Michaela leaned back against a smooth rock, stretching her legs. A soft sigh escaped. "I can get used to this." She wiggled her toes. "My new shoes have been killing me. I'll have to come here every day until they're broken in."

Jasen moved before her and lifted her leg. He started to rub the ball of her foot. "You're hired," she purred. Something light floated between their bodies, and Michaela snatched it out of the water, lifting it. Her eyes widened as she gazed at Jasen.

"Is that—" he asked.

"Yes, it is." Michaela giggled and wadded the fabric into a ball. "Somebody is getting frisky."

"Yeah, that can happen here sometimes. Especially, in the dark." His voice had gone low, sending shivers to Michaela's core. Thank God for the cover of darkness.

"Hey, Kim," Michaela called.

"Yeah, Mick, where are you?"

"I'm getting a foot massage. You?"

Kim laughed. "I'm getting something else massaged."

Michaela chuckled and shook her head. "I found *my* bikini floating downstream."

Kim squeaked what sounded like a cuss word. "Keep it for me. We'll get it when we leave."

"*Your* bikini?" Jasen asked, moving to her calf.

"Kim didn't bring a suit this trip, and she likes the strings."

"I think Glen likes pulling the strings," Jasen said, moving to her thigh. When he reached her pinnacle, his movement brushed against her sweet spot. Suddenly overheated, she sat upright, her shoulders out of the water.

Jasen switched to her other foot. But a few moments later he was at her apex again. Jasen traced the edge of her bikini bottom and she gasped. Kim's laughter grew louder, stymieing the temptation to let Michaela's bottoms float away. Jasen sat next to her and pulled her onto his lap.

Michaela lay her head against his shoulder and sighed. With one hand playing with the hair on his chest, she was totally flirting with her boss. Not even flirting, but cuddling. That was worse, wasn't it?

Glen popped above water near them, startling Michaela. "Hiya Mick, where's the bikini?"

"You should be more careful with other people's property," Michaela scolded, dangling the bikini top.

Glen's lopsided grin flashed.

"For Christ's sake, Mick. Let me have my top," Kim groused.

Jasen's fingers edged Michaela's suit along her leg again and Michaela gasped, wanting Kim and Glen to evaporate.

"Here." Michaela handed Kim the suit. Glen helped to tie it as Kim faced away from them. She lifted her hair.

Jasen's fingers worked around the edge of her inner right leg. It tickled, and Michaela squirmed.

"How long are you in town?" Jasen asked Kim.

Properly attired, Kim faced them again. "Just for a long weekend. I'm touring the firehouse with the contractor and getting estimates for remodeling."

"The dude who owns the building wouldn't sell," Glen said, splashing Jasen.

"But at least he let us lease it for a year." Kim waved her wet hand, flinging water into Michaela's eye.

"Rezoning was easy enough," Michaela said, rubbing her eye.

"Yes, lucky us," Kim giggled. "It's a good thing the mayor has the hots for my BFF."

"It won't be forever if I murder you, bestie," Michaela mumbled.

"We're going to go. Do you need a lift or do you have a ride?" Kim asked, her voice fading.

"I've got her. Don't worry." Jasen waved with his free hand.

"Enjoy your time with mayor Hottie McHot," Kim shouted then giggled.

Michaela buried her face against Jasen. "I'm going to kill her. Slowly and painfully."

Jasen laughed. "How about we move the town hall books to the coffee shop once it opens?"

Michaela pushed backward and glanced into his sparkling eyes. "That sounds awesome."

Michaela pulled to a stop at the edge of the parking lot. Only Jasen's car remained. "I can't believe Kim left and took my stuff."

"It's okay."

"It's not my clothes, Jasen. Kim has my keys to the house and car. And my cell phone. I don't remember her number to call her, and she'll probably go to Glen's and I don't know where he lives." The breeze, a damp towel, and dropping temperatures had Michaela hugging herself. She crossed her arms and frowned.

Jasen unlocked and opened the door for her. He tugged her wet towel off her and handed over his dry towel then started the car to warm it. Once she'd finished with his towel, he gave her his T-shirt.

"You're welcome to stay with me, or I can get you a room at the bed-and-breakfast. I'm sure Ben and Kelly would be happy to let you stay."

Her brow creased with worry, Michaela shook her head. "I don't think I should. They're remodeling. If you wouldn't mind, I think it would be best if I stay with you."

He nodded, shifting the car into gear. The heater blasted warm air on Michaela's bare toes, and she relaxed. "This is the second time I ended up wet and wearing your shirt."

"We're starting a new tradition." Jasen chuckled, pulling into a cul-de-sac. He pulled into the driveway of a brown contemporary wood-sided house then eased into the garage.

Jasen flipped the light switch before they stepped into a small family room. A tan leather sofa and recliner along with cluttered coffee and end tables filled the room. The family room opened to a large kitchen with cherry cabinets, black granite countertops, and sleek stainless steel appliances. Jasen turned on the lights as they walked through a cozy great room.

"Oh, I love the fireplace." Michaela stopped to admire the stone wall with the rough-hewn beam. "Do you use it much?"

"Not really." Jasen rubbed his chin. "Actually, I don't know the last time I used it."

"I guess winters don't get that cold here." She turned away from the eye-catching room element and followed him up the open stairwell.

Jasen gestured to a door. "This room is where Dee kept all of her clothes. I'm sure you'll find something to wear."

Michaela bit her lip but nodded.

Jasen reached into the linen closet and picked a fresh towel for her. "You can use the master bath if you'd like to shower. I'll put your bikini in the dryer while you bathe."

"Okay, thanks." She hugged the fluffy towel to her chest and shadowed him into the master bedroom. The bathroom had dual vanities and an over-sized walk-in shower with glass walls.

Jasen's T-shirt hit her mid-thigh, so she pushed the bottoms down and kicked them. They landed at his feet. Wide-eyed, he watched as she unhooked the top through the fabric. It fell to her waist. She twisted the back to the front and unhooked it.

Having both bikini pieces he had no reason to stay, yet he hesitated, staring at her legs.

Michaela moved toward him and gently nudged him out of the room.

Once he'd left, she opened the bathroom door and peered around. She crept to the stairwell, listening. Jasen shut the refrigerator.

Michaela took a deep breath and crossed the hall to Dee's room. She pushed the stiff door. The room smelled musty. She flicked on the light and gasped, astounded by the level of clothes heaped onto the bed. A fuchsia and orange striped shirt topped the pile. She stepped further inside, noticing a thick layer of grime on the dresser and cobwebs draping the corners and curtains. She pivoted, causing dust to take flight and leaving footprints where she'd walked. Coughing, she lifted the shirt over her nose and backed out of the room.

After the shower, Michaela rooted around in Jasen's dresser until she found a gray Hammered T-shirt and slipped it over her head. A pair of his boxer briefs worked like cycling shorts.

Warm and content, Michaela went in search of her host. She hoped Jasen wouldn't mind she borrowed his clothes, but she couldn't disturb Dee's mausoleum.

# CHAPTER 25

## *Jasen*

JASEN CREPT DOWN THE STAIRS, trying to avoid the steps that creaked. He lifted his feet so the slippers wouldn't scrape. There was no movement from the lumpy blankets on the sofa.

He tiptoed to the kitchen. The scent of coffee hung in the air. The sunlight filtered through the window. On the deck, Michaela sat holding a mug to her lips. She sipped then placed the coffee on the round table. She leaned back in the seat and stretched her legs onto another chair. Like a flower, she lifted her face toward the sun. A serene smile graced her lips. Wisps of her wavy chestnut hair fluttered, catching the sun like fairy dust.

The simplicity of her beauty stunned Jasen. He swallowed and turned away. He needed caffeine and shuffled to the cabinet, picking his favorite mug and coffee pod. Waiting for the machine to brew, he remembered their night.

They had relaxed on the sofa and watched the fire. He'd wanted to create new memories in the house.

Jasen opened the fridge and grabbed the milk. As he doctored his coffee, he smiled. The crackling of the fire and dancing flames were a peaceful backdrop to their conversation. They could have made love. He would have liked to, especially when she came downstairs wearing his clothes. He hadn't understood the depth of their relationship until she reclined on the sofa with a glass of wine and her feet on his lap. She swirled the liquid then sipped.

Jasen had described his dreams, recalling vivid details. He wished they'd fade, but Dee had never really left him. He should be grateful to see her, youthful and showing him attention, but he couldn't shake the malevolence.

With Jasen's head on her lap, Michaela had stroked his head like a mother comforts a child.

Once he wasn't facing her, she spoke of her failed marriage. A wayward tear dropped onto his forehead. Jasen realized Michaela still cared for her ex and he didn't want to lose her. She'd loved Darren. Dedicated herself to him and the business then grown jealous of the company.

Dee had been jealous too, but he hadn't cheated on her. She'd been right about one thing, though; he stayed away on purpose. He'd made excuses to eat with a friend, work later, or hang with the guys at Hammered.

Dee had become demanding. She had to have the best purses and the fanciest shoes. She never accompanied him to any formal dinners. No, she strutted at the mall dressed in over-finery. Her slender form was nice and from a distance her unnatural blond hair was perfect, but it felt like straw. She caked on expensive makeup, even though she was pretty without it.

Jasen shook his head. He slid the glass door open and stepped out into the brisk morning air. The sun felt good, but coolness bit him.

"Good morning," Michaela said, blinking her green eyes like a happy cat.

Jasen sat next to her, cupping his mug in his hands. "Good morning. Did you sleep well?" Because of her allergies, Michaela decided not to sleep in Dee's room.

"I did until you crept through the living room in the middle of the night." Michaela pulled the cup under her nose, inhaling then sipping it.

Jasen scratched his chin. "I didn't get up."

"That's weird. I could have swore... Oh well, I must have been dreaming." She shook her head. "How about you?"

"I slept fairly well; that is, until this morning."

Michaela frowned. "Another nightmare?"

Jasen nodded but kept his gaze on his java. His wife's image from his nightmare still haunted him.

"If I lived here, I would be out on this deck every morning. It's peaceful. I love the burbling brook and the birdsong. And the sun hits it just right." After she placed the mug on the table, she reached over her head and stretched. He was unable to catch a glimpse of her belly, but the coolness affected her breasts, making him long to warm them.

"The house my mom and dad used to have when I was a kid had a huge deck. It didn't have a creek, but I had a swing set. I loved stomping on the deck and pretending that underneath was a cave I could explore." She pulled her knees to her chest and shifted to gaze at him.

"Was it a big house?" he asked.

"Seemed like it to me, but I was little." She shrugged and sighed.

Jasen placed his hand over hers, caressing the back of her hand with his thumb.

"What's happening here?" Michaela asked.

"What do you mean?" He leaned toward her.

"This." She motioned between them.

His heart leaped. His face heated, and an uncontrollable smile appeared. "Our friendship?"

Michaela quirked a brow. "So we're friends with benefits?"

Jasen stuck a finger into the air. "Therapeutic benefits."

She giggled and placed a hand over his and squeezed. "I suppose those are better than other types of benefits."

"Like what?"

"Friends who share peanut butter sandwiches." She shrugged and smiled.

"I am open to other benefits. Like friends who get each other coffee." Jasen raised an empty mug.

She chuckled and swiped his coffee cup. As she refilled the water reservoir, he came up behind her and hugged her. Her curves molded to his body and her warmth excited him. He lifted her hair and kissed her neck. She almost dropped the water.

"Watch it or you'll get baptized." She tilted her head as if listening. "Shh. Did you hear that?"

A faint ringing.

Jasen padded across the kitchen and pulled open the garage door. The ring, louder now, came from his car. He found the phone, along with Michaela's clothes and keys, on the floor behind the passenger seat.

"What the...?" she asked, taking the items he handed her.

"I guess your friend didn't leave you naked and stranded like you thought." Jasen chuckled.

"I guess not. I should have looked in the backseat last night." Michaela set the items on the kitchenette table and checked her phone. "Kim texted wanting to know if I found everything." She laughed and called Kim.

Jasen watched as the pile of clothes shifted and slid to the floor one item at a time. A red bra landed on top. It radiated femininity. He bent to pick it up by the strap. The cups were edged with delicate lace and the print had a tone on tone swirl pattern. Sticking out of her shorts was another piece of red. He scooped up the garment and inspected the fabric. String bikini undies. "These have to be Jessie's handy work," he mumbled to himself.

"Yes, they are," Michaela said, plucking the underwear from his hand.

His face heated. "They're a work of art. Care to model?"

She leaned in and kissed his nose. "Some other time. I need to go meet Kim. Can you take me?"

In a restaurant in Nockerville, Michaela and Kim discussed the details of the upcoming hearing for the coffee shop. Jasen sipped his latte, listening while studying the bookshelf on the wall. There was no way Cam Payne would deny the improvements. The trendy business would give Fortuna residents a chance at variety.

Jasen tuned out the conversation, envisioning Michaela wearing the red bra. Goodness knows after he'd seen her in the bikini he could easily picture the Double D Intimates' bra and panty set.

The bell over the door rang and a man entered. He placed a book on the shelf then chose another. Jasen leaned back and smiled. "So, Glen, what do you like to read?"

"I prefer sci-fi," he said timidly and leaned toward Jasen. "Don't tell Kim. She thinks I like romance."

"You know, there's a bunch of sci-fi romance. Cool aliens, gadgets, and worlds." Jasen beckoned Glen to follow him to the bookshelf. He immediately found an alien slave book and pulled it out, handing it to the other man. Jasen checked the spines, running his finger along them. "Ah!" he pulled out an author he'd read. "Try this one. The author has excellent world building, and she doesn't do cliché things."

Glen flipped the book and scanned the back. Jasen glanced over at the table, discovering both women watching them. He gave a sheepish wave. Lowering his voice, he said, "Watch out or Kim will want you to act things out, if you know what I mean?" Jasen wiggled his brows, and Glen blushed.

"That's what she wants. The women of Fortuna are spoiled. They've been telling her things and filling her head with ideas."

"Are they so bad?" Jasen asked then chuckled at the shocked expression on Glen's face.

With a one-shoulder shrug, Glen grinned. "I guess not."

They rejoined the table, and Kim immediately wanted to see the book. The woman on the cover appeared to be an intergalactic harem undercover cop. It would make for interesting cos-play.

Michaela didn't share Kim's interest in the books. She flipped pages in a magazine. Finding the right decor and equipment for the coffee house seemed a priority. He placed an arm across her back, and she sighed against him. She ate the last bite of her gourmet mac and cheese.

Jasen wiped a tad of cheese from the corner of her mouth and she blushed, glancing away. Kim spied him with a quizzical expression.

Kim tapped the table with a finger. "So Jasen, how long are you going to grow the beard?"

Michaela moved her leg and must have kicked Kim, because Kim jerked back with an "Ow" and rubbed her shin.

"Why?" he asked.

Michaela's hands shot to her face, covering it. She groaned before Kim said a word. Her actions made Kim grin and clap her hands.

"Well, Michaela thinks you're super sexy without the beard." Kim spoke just loud enough for him to hear. "She's not a facial hair girl. It scratches her—Ouch!" Kim jerked back again. "Damn, girl, I was going to say face." She burst out laughing.

Michaela groaned again, her face bright red. Jasen smiled and leaned, whispering in her ear. "Do you think I'm sexy?" Her hands stayed on her face and she groaned a third time.

"I'm going to murder you when you least expect it," she snapped at Kim.

Kim waved her hand. "Whatever. The man needs to know if he's going to compete with Darren or that new hottie. What's his name—oh yeah—B.J. Johnson."

Michaela threw her head back and stared at the ceiling. "I'm going to kill myself," she uttered.

Jasen pasted on his political smile, but his heart turned to lead. "What about B.J.?" he asked, trying to sound as if he really couldn't care less.

Michaela's head snapped forward. "Not another word, Kim, or so help me..." She glared.

Kim threw her hands in the air. "Fine, but you should tell him."

"You just did." Michaela crossed her arms and stared at the table as if she could burn a hole into the top.

Glen gaped as his gaze volleyed from Kim to Michaela then slid to Jasen. He shut his mouth, shrugged one shoulder then continued reading his book.

Michaela sat stiffly, and when Jasen touched her arm, she jumped. She tried to hide her trembling lip, staring at the floor.

# CHAPTER 26

## *Michaela*

IT WOULDN'T BE NICE TO chuck a latte into Kim's sassy face, so instead Michaela balled her fists in her lap and kept her head down. Her gut churned as she clenched her teeth. Kim's divulgence of Michaela's date with B.J. was utterly out of context and uncalled for.

Tears pooled in Michaela's eyes. Jasen touched her arm, more of a concerned graze. The emotional dam sprung a leak. She squeezed her eyes shut, dabbing the tears away with a napkin.

"Michaela," Jasen uttered. "Walk with me." When she hesitated, he added, "Now."

She shoved back from the table and headed for the exit. Jasen followed on her heels then pushed the door open for her. She squinted at the bright light and he took her by the elbow. Jasen led her down the street to Nockerville's square. He halted in front of Barnabas "Buster" Hyman's bronze statue, staring at the plaque.

"I wonder if Fortuna's founder William Stoker and Buster were pals," Jasen mused.

"Jasen," Michaela started in a soft voice.

"Michaela. Don't." He stuck his hands in his front pockets. "You don't need to explain anything. I know Kim was teasing you."

She shook her head and stared down at the pavement. Sucking in her bottom lip, she reached for his hand and threaded her fingers with his.

"I do find you attractive." Michaela met his gaze and tilted her head. "With or without the beard."

Jasen blushed and his gaze shifted to her lips.

"I need to explain about B.J. too. Kim made it sound so bad."

"You mean your date to the fund-raising ball?" Jasen quirked a brow, frowning.

She gasped. "He told you?"

Jasen nodded and turned away from her. She reached for his elbow, stopping him. "Jasen, I chose him for three reasons. The first is that it will dispel any preconceived ideas regarding you and I having a relationship. Little miss nosy newspaper will not get a story from me."

"And the second?" he asked, his forehead crinkled.

"The second is that B.J. can compete with Darren when it comes to ego. They both have swollen heads." Michaela nodded.

"And the third?" Jasen asked.

"You trust B.J."

Jasen appeared neither happy nor upset. He wore a mask.

"You do trust him, right?" Michaela's heart raced.

"Who, Johnson or your ex-husband?"

"I… uh," Michaela swallowed. "B.J. of course. You don't know Darren."

Jasen glanced away and frowned. "I know Darren treated you with less respect than his stupid business. He deserves to be alone with his mistress forever. I can't believe he's making a play for you now. You complained, filed, divorced, and now he wants you back. I don't buy it. He's a jerk."

"You'll find you have a lot in common with B.J. His wife preferred someone else even though B.J. thought she hung the moon. You can commiserate together." Jasen's sad hazel eyes studied her.

"Jasen," Michaela whispered. "I don't like B.J. in that way. He reminds me of Darren." She closed her eyes and rubbed her head. "Part of the reason Darren's ego is uber-inflated is because of his assistant Rodney. I think Rodney Butkus lives up to his name."

When she opened her eyes Jasen wore a crooked smirk.

Michaela couldn't resist him, beard or no. She launched herself into his arms. His lips claimed her with a ferocity that shot straight to her core. Heat exploded within and flames lapped her skin. Their tongues dueled, and she struggled to breathe.

Someone clapped.

Jasen pulled back and touched his forehead to hers, his breathing ragged. "Why do they always clap when we kiss?" Michaela giggled and pressed her face into his chest.

"Oh God," Jasen groaned and released her. He stepped away, red faced, and wearing a sheepish grin.

"What is it?' Michaela whispered. He frowned and she slowly turned.

Nellie stood with a triumphant sneer on her lips and a phone in her hands. "This is fine news. Gotcha." She waved the phone.

"Holy crap," Michaela breathed and stomped off in the opposite direction, leaving a cackling Nellie behind. Jasen remained with his hands on his hips, watching her go.

Michaela had only been to Nockerville a handful of times and didn't know where she was going. She saw Jessie Barnes heading into a fabric shop and followed.

"Hi Michaela," Jessie smiled, but the smile fell off her face when she peered into Michaela's eyes. "What's wrong?"

Tears welled, but she shook her head, smiling. "I feel contrary." A tear escaped.

Jessie turned to the owner. "Margie, put some tea on for us." The woman nodded and disappeared into the back. Jessie took Michaela's hand and led her into the break room. They sat and Margie handed Michaela a cup of tea. "Thanks."

The bell rang and Margie left to help the customer.

"Now out with it," Jessie said. "You can't hold these things inside"

Michaela sighed and glanced up at the ceiling. Resigning to explain, she started, "I just had the best kiss ever."

Jessie smiled with wide eyes. She leaned back. "And...?"

Michaela glanced at her hands. "And Nellie Neus took a picture of Jasen and I."

"Oh no. Not that wench." Jessie blew out a frustrated breath. She shook her head and her auburn hair flared. "We've had trouble with her before. She wrote a horrid piece about Piper and her ex-fiancé. He stalked her in Chicago and followed her to Fortuna."

"I know. What a horrible situation. Piper told me about her experience after Nellie released the article about me. Piper sympathized and helped boost my confidence." Michaela sighed and glanced up. "I shouldn't be kissing my boss."

"I wouldn't be married if my employee wouldn't have kissed me." Jessie laughed at the look on Michaela's face. "My Josiah is quite the kisser too." Jessie spun a tale about carving Josiah's name on a hayloft post.

"What can I do about that picture?" Michaela groaned, rubbing her forehead.

"Write a counter article." Jessie suggested then shrugged. "Are there any special events that haven't been announced?"

"I don't know... we have a release schedule." Michaela scratched her arm. "After what I've said about not wanting to date my boss, I've made a fool of myself."

"Well..." Jessie drawled, "technically, Jasen isn't your boss, is he? It's some council and the taxpayers."

Michaela opened her mouth but snapped it shut. She grinned at Jessie. "Thanks, that makes me feel better."

"Any time." Jessie patted her arm. "So you and Jasen—it's something special, isn't it?"

The smile on Michaela's face hurt her cheeks, but she couldn't wipe it off. "I think so, but my ex-husband is coming to the fund-raising event and he wanted to go with me."

Jessie's brows shot upward. "What are you going to do?"

"I plan to go with B.J. Johnson."

"Why?" Jessie gasped. "What about Jasen?"

"B.J. is Jasen's friend. I thought..." she shrugged. "A diversion. I wanted to mislead Nellie. I was afraid for Jasen's career after what she wrote about me; it would only harm him and his aspirations. B.J. also likes dares."

"Tell me about it." Jessie rolled her eyes. "I can't believe you dared B.J."

"Totally," Michaela giggled then sighed. "I wanted B.J. to piss Darren off and also make Jasen jealous."

"If you don't want to date Jasen, why make him jealous?" Jessie quirked her head to the side.

Michaela bit her lip and shrugged. "I told you I was contrary. I like him, but he's hung up on his wife. It's hard to compete with the canyon ghost."

"It's tragic." Jessie lowered her voice. "They never found her body. He buried an empty box."

Michaela blinked and gasped. "No wonder she haunts him."

"I lost over half my herd in that gully-washer. The ranch is still building up the herd." Jessie shook her head. "If I hadn't had Josiah helping me, I would have given up." She sighed, her lips forming a thin line. "I'm sure you don't have to go to the dance with B.J. now."

"It will still throw Darren off his game."

"Not if Nellie sends him the picture," Jessie said.

Michaela's phone vibrated. She glanced at it and groaned, "Oh, crapplesauce."

"What's the matter?" Jessie asked. "Did she post the picture on social media?"

"No. Worse." Michaela shook her head. "Jasen's in-laws need something."

# CHAPTER 27

## *Michaela*

MICHAELA TRIED TO KEEP HER nose from crinkling as she stepped over the threshold into the mobile home. The bouquet was greasy spoon meets abandoned bar. Legit velvet paintings hung on yellowed nicotine-stained walls. The sofa was more duct tape than fabric.

"Hello again, little lady," Jerry hollered.

"Who's there?" Sally called from the other room. A chair scraped against the floor as Sally jumped to her feet, a cigarette hanging from her lips.

"It's Jasen and his girlfriend." Jerry smiled a gap-toothed grin.

"Oh, it's her again," Sally huffed, returning to her seat.

Michaela and Jasen exchanged a look. She squared her shoulders and touched Jerry's arm. "Thank you for having us."

Jerry blushed and nodded. "Come on in. It ain't much, but it's home."

"That's all that matters," Michaela said.

"What's the problem with the water heater?" Jasen asked.

"Straight to business," Jerry said, shaking his head. "Follow me. The water is cold. It's been cold since yesterday, and Sally don't like to take a cold shower." He beckoned Jasen to follow and led him down a dark hallway.

Michaela stood awkwardly in the middle of the living room, tracing the pattern on the olive green carpet with her gaze. It could use a vacuum or a burning.

The chair scooted again as Sally rose. Michaela slowly joined her in the kitchen area. The older woman waddled to the refrigerator and pulled open the door. "I s'pect you want fed."

"No ma'am," Michaela said, scanning the counter top. Dusty ceramic pig canisters stared up at the cobwebs.

Sally straightened. "Oh ho. Ma'am. Ain't you fancy?"

Michaela glanced at her hands. "I'm sorry for how I behaved toward you on my last visit," she said. Glancing at Sally, she found her frowning. "I hope you can forgive me."

Michaela bit her lip. Sally's tone more than her words had brought out Michaela's protective nature.

"I'm also sorry about Dee." Michaela hadn't experienced the loss of someone close except her mother.

Sally's eyes narrowed briefly before she turned to the counter and opened a whiskey bottle. She poured the clear liquid into a Solo cup. "Thank you."

"I've seen her picture on Jasen's desk. She was very beautiful. She must have your genes."

Sally blushed under her rouge. She twittered and returned to her chair at the small laminated table. "She won pageants, you know?"

"Actually, I didn't know." Michaela took a seat in a wobbly chair across from Sally. "Did she start when she was young?"

Sally smiled, flashing more teeth than her husband had. "She was just a baby when she got her first ribbon." She stood and walked to a shadow box. "This here's the first. We got fifty dollars. That's when we knew our Dee was meant to make money."

Sally hobbled to the coffee table and picked up a pile of albums. She dropped the pile on the kitchen table, swirling the cigarette ashes. She pulled her chair close to Michaela and opened the top album. "Here she is on the day we had her."

Michaela stared at the round-faced infant. "She was a cute baby. Such chubby cheeks."

Sally laughed, her eyes crinkling. "I thought so too, but don't let Dee hear you say that. She wants to believe she is forever thin."

Michaela blinked, wanting to correct Sally's tense, but she turned the page and started on a new anecdote. When they reached the end of the high school book Michaela had a smile pasted on her face that rivaled Jasen's politician smile. It was clear Dee's beauty was the family's ticket to a better life. And she had landed the good-looking mayor of Fortuna.

"Once she was married, we didn't see her as much, but Jasen brought her to us on the weekends," Sally said.

"That was nice of him," Michaela said.

Jasen and Jerry entered the living space, dirt smudged and hair askew. They washed at the sink.

"Did you get it fixed?" Sally asked, lighting another cigarette.

"We need to get a new pan," Jerry said.

"There's perfectly good pans in the cupboard." Sally pointed to a cabinet.

Jasen smirked and met Michaela's eyes.

Jerry dried his hands on his white tank top. He guffawed. "No. It's a big metal pan."

"You can use the old cheesecake tin I saved."

Jerry put his hands on his hips. "Come and look at it then you can see if you have a pan the right size." He winked at Michaela.

"Oh, all right." She hoisted her girth to standing and followed her husband.

Jasen rubbed a spot on his shirt. "It's filthy back there."

Michaela giggled. "Just like the rest of the place." She walked near him and studied the photos on the fridge. Several pictures of Dee, with her faux blond, overly tanned body, wearing a cheesy grin, hung by insurance and realtor's magnets.

"I take it you and Sally are getting along," Jasen said, tucking his shirt into his khakis.

"Yes. I haven't said much. She's gone on and on about her daughter's fabulous pageant career." Michaela stopped herself from saying more. Jasen's wife was dead.

Michaela zoned in on a picture. At a beach wearing a familiar fuchsia and orange halter top, Dee's head was thrown back, laughing. A magazine on a towel, caught Michaela's attention, and she peeled the photo off the sticky fridge. "Huh?"

"Jasen, can we go to the hardware store and get a pan?" Jerry asked. He lowered his voice but everyone could still hear, "Sally doesn't want to chance a cold shower."

"Sure." Jasen turned to Michaela. "Want to ride along? The hardware store Nailed is next to Hammered."

"No, Michaela can stay with me and I'll show her some pageant videos." Sally rubbed her hands like a mad scientist.

Michaela swallowed and glanced helplessly at Jasen. Her tongue stuck to the roof of her mouth. She would rather have dinner with her disappearing mother and the home-wrecker who stole her than sit through the torture of beauty-queen-hell.

Jasen scratched the back of his head as Jerry buttoned a plaid flannel shirt over his stained undershirt.

"We'll be back," Jerry said with a wave. The aluminum screen door screeched shut.

The sound of a VCR machine slurping a VHS tape in split the silence. Sally dropped to the sofa and patted the cushion next to her. "Just you wait until you see how pretty Dee is. She has the walk down pat."

The grainy fragmented footage reminded Michaela of a scene from *The Ring* movie, except these creepy kids wore makeup. The five-year-olds looked like twenty-two-year-olds.

Dee strutted across the stage in various dresses, recited poems, and sang. The singing wasn't horrid, but she wouldn't make it onto *American Idol*.

After forty-five minutes, Michaela mentally cursed Jasen. Where was that man? She begged a bathroom break, and Sally paused the recording. How long could she remain locked in the bathroom before being considered rude?

When Michaela appeared next to the sofa, she found Sally mesmerized by the beautiful paused face of her daughter. "I think you need a refill," Michaela said, pointing to the empty cup.

Sally blinked and nodded. She edged to the end of the sofa.

"Let me get it for you," Michaela offered.

"Thank you," Sally said, lifting the cup.

Michaela entered the kitchen and set the cup on the counter. Pouring the whiskey, she spied an envelope with more beach pictures sticking out of it.

She returned to Sally's side and handed her the whiskey. "Do you mind if I try some?" Michaela asked. "I've never had that brand."

"Heavens. Never?" Sally's gaze skittered around as if deciding she could spare a few drops of the good stuff.

"I just want a taste," Michaela said. "Please."

"You can taste it," Sally nodded. "The red cups are on the microwave."

Michaela grinned and picked up her purse. As a guise, she put on lip balm then picked up her phone. She took a cup but hastily glanced through the photos spreading them over the counter. Using her phone, she clicked photos of the pictures.

Guilt bubbled up. Michaela stalked a dead girl, but something gnawed at her. She couldn't figure the mystery out now but she wanted to when she had time.

Twisting the cap of the bottle, she brought it to her nose and grimaced. It smelled like rubbing alcohol. She poured a little and took a sip. She swallowed and coughed.

Sally guffawed from the sofa. "It'll put hair on your chest."

"Yes." Michaela's throat burned and she cleared it. "I'm sure it's an acquired taste." She shuffled the pictures, keeping one out while tucking the others back into the envelope. Her eyes narrowed on the time-stamp in the corner.

On reflex, she grabbed the photo and placed it in her hand under her phone. She stowed the items in her purse then returned to her seat.

"Well?" Sally said, raising her thick painted brows.

"I'll save it for you." Michaela stuck out her tongue. "Yuck."

Sally laughed again and hit play. Dee sashayed across the screen once more, making Michaela wish she had downed the whole bottle.

# CHAPTER 28

## *Jasen*

JASEN PULLED HIS COLLAR UP then stuffed his hands into his pockets. The bitter evening wind chilled him.

Across the park, Michaela flitted around, smiling and making sure the vendors had everything they needed. She passed out programs and pointed toward the public bathrooms.

The temperature hovered in the upper 40s. Kids wore layers as they climbed on the new playground equipment. Parents huddled in groups as they watched the children.

Jasen glanced at his watch, only minutes until the concert started. With a church choir preforming holiday classics, carriage rides around the square, and food trucks with hot beverages and yuletide treats, the atmosphere felt Christmassy.

Jasen smiled. It had been years since the holidays felt welcoming. Jasen had dreaded the holiday season thanks to Dee's overspending. He started depositing money in a secret account so he could make the mortgage payments. They'd fight and she'd cry.

"Don't I deserve nice things—a good life?" Dee would whine. "I shop the clearance rack," she'd argue.

When Dee died, Jasen had expected to return or donate bags of new clothes but there was nothing but used items. The items, like his money, had vanished into some mysterious financial black hole.

When the choir started, Michaela paused to listen. She had a red nose, and her breath came in smoky puffs, her lips parted in a smile as she stared at the group of singers. Her eyes slid shut and she swayed with the music. Jasen watched, transfixed. The stage lighting cast an ethereal glow over her face. A stark contrast to the banshee-like ghost of his wife.

Jasen sighed and leaned against the metal lamp pole. The melodic sounds of the voices lifted and swirled, reminding him of a simpler time.

"Damn, you've got it bad," B.J. said from beside him. His dark hair was windblown, and Jasen envied the look. With his hands in the pockets of his leather jacket, B.J. looked warm, especially with the crimson scarf around his neck.

"Shut up," Jasen said, turning from the lamppost. "Here. Take it to her, please."

B.J. bobbed his head and grabbed the red envelope. He moseyed toward Michaela, stopping to have words with Desire Hardmann. B.J. started away from the old woman, but she swatted his rear. Jasen chuckled, and B.J. shook his head, not even turning around.

When B.J. reached Michaela, she did a double take then rewarded him with a beguiling smile. He leaned and whispered in her ear un-sanctimoniously, pointing the envelope in Jasen's direction. She laughed, glancing down to take it. She placed a kiss on B.J.'s cheek. Jasen balled his hands.

B.J. walked back toward Jasen wearing a sly grin.

Jasen's gaze swung back to Michaela as she opened the card. She gasped, reading the front, then covered her mouth as she laughed. She glanced around then found him leaning against the lamppost. The chill of the metal bit his arm. Jasen held her gaze as she dipped her head slightly. He couldn't tell if she blushed, but he imagined her rouge-tinged cheeks.

B.J. arrived at his side once more. "Man, I can't believe she likes you."

Jasen couldn't stop smiling. "What did she say?"

B.J. chuckled. "She gave me a kiss to pass on but forget that."

"You disappoint."

"Whatever."

"Anything else?" Jasen broke eye contact with Michaela and glanced at his friend.

"I handed her your card and she said 'thank you'." B.J. huffed, "What are we, ten and passing notes in class?"

Jasen laughed and clapped his friend on the back. "Ten-year-olds can't buy their buddies a beer. What do you say?"

"All right, I'm in." B.J. rubbed his face but smiled.

"You're easy."

"Please pass it on to all the ladies," B.J. laughed.

They walked the block to Hammered and he and B.J. stood at the long, carved wood bar. The owner Holden Dix paused to discuss the unusual weather.

"It's going to snow. My knee is aching," Holden said.

Jasen glanced at B.J., who wore a placating smile. He didn't buy it either.

# CHAPTER 29

## *Michaela*

WHEN MICHAELA OPENED THE DOOR, B.J. stood in a tux. Long curling lashes framed dark sultry eyes. His strong square jaw had a spattering of hair and he was right to leave it. She sucked in a breath and nearly coughed because of his overpowering cologne.

B.J. stepped into the living room and whistled, inspecting her long gown. "I love the dress, especially the back. So, no bra?" His fingers skimmed her backbone, giving her the chills.

The backless Champagne halter-styled dress had intricate beading with delicate lace around the neckline. Jessie Barnes had made her something special, so Michaela would have support. She smiled and picked up her clutch and wrap. "A gentleman doesn't ask such questions."

"Who said I was a gentleman?" B.J. chuckled and offered his elbow.

"You look like a spy," she giggled.

"Johnson, B.J. Johnson," he said, leading her to the car.

She squirmed as B.J. drove. She'd chosen to wear four-inch heels. Her feet would ache tomorrow, but she'd be the same height as Darren.

Entering the grand building, she glanced up at the ornate coffered ceiling. Couples lingered in the outer room perusing the items up for auction. She and B.J. inspected the baskets. The first auction was for a membership for the Nockerville country club, Twin Hills. Another was for a spa treatment. Most were local goods or services. B.J. bid on a cleaning service. The company he worked for had provided a framed aerial photo of the Dry Run creek canyon.

"Michaela." Darren's voice floated over the noise.

Michaela gripped B.J.'s arm, and he covered her fingers with a supportive hand. "Here we go," she uttered, and B.J.'s face morphed into a formidable scowl. She sucked in a deep breath and turned to face her ex. "Darren."

Darren placed a kiss on her cheek. He scanned her from head to toe. An easy lopsided grin twisted his lips. "God, you look hot."

"Thank you." She inspected him. As always, he looked as if he modeled expensive clothing. "Nice bow tie. Purple, huh?"

"It's the color of royalty." Darren waved his hand and bowed.

B.J. snorted and smirked. Darren cleared his throat. She leaned closer to B.J. "Oh, Darren, this is B.J. Johnson, B.J., this is Darren Arschfick."

The men gripped hands. Each wore a dominant smile and squeezed. Michaela glanced away rolling her eyes.

A blond woman in a long royal blue dress threw back her head, braying like a donkey. Familiarity nagged Michaela. She'd heard the laugh before. Yet the woman's face, high tight cheek bones, cerulean blue eyes, and stenciled brows, weren't familiar.

Michaela left B.J. and Darren talking over property values and circumvented the woman who spoke with a group of gentlemen. Michaela studied an auction box within earshot.

The woman in blue guffawed regally. "So do you know what I did? When he unwrapped the bandage, I pretended I couldn't see." She tossed her hair as she laughed and placed a dainty hand on the man on her right's arm. The men laughed politely.

Michaela continued to examine the box and its contents, pretending to read about the donor.

"What did the doctor do?" one man asked.

"He called for the nurse. And said to get a syringe. He wanted to give me a shot. Like that would give someone their sight."

Michaela chuckled: the doctor had seen through her prank and the blond didn't understand.

"I let the poor man in on the joke then and gave him a big kiss." The woman winked at the men.

Something one of them said made her toss her long locks again and Michaela snapped her head. "Oh my God," Michaela uttered. After watching hours of pageant videos, she recognized Dee's laugh.

The woman wiped a tear of mirth from her eye then sobered, glancing over to the entry. She paled, but recovered by excusing herself.

Michaela shifted to see what had frightened the woman. Jasen had entered the building and talked with B.J. by the door. "Son of a bitch," Michaela uttered.

"Tsk," Nellie Neus chided. "What a mouth."

Michaela spun and blinked. "I... uh. Maybe you can help me." She tilted her head and inspected the reporter. Nellie's jaw dropped. Michaela stepped forward and touched her arm.

"You're going to think I'm crazy." Michaela leaned close, making sure she had Nellie's full attention. "How well did you know the mayor's wife?"

"Dee? I didn't, really. I just knew her reputation." Nellie tilted her head. "What's going on?"

The woman in blue reappeared in another group of men. She vied for their attention while scanning the room on high alert.

Michaela took Nellie's arm and shifted so the woman in blue was behind her and Nellie could see over her shoulder. "See that lady in the royal blue gown?"

Nellie nodded. Her eyes narrowed as she scanned the woman. "What about her?"

"She was regaling the men with an anecdote about a prank she pulled on her plastic surgeon, but didn't realize the guy was on to her. She's not too bright."

"And...?" Nellie drawled.

"And her laugh. Does it sound familiar to you?" Michaela hoped that the odd sounding laugh was distinct enough to ring her recollection.

As if on cue, the woman tossed her head, cackling at something a young man had said. Nellie once again narrowed her eyes and hummed. "It sounds familiar." Nellie tapped her chin with a finger, her gaze sliding to Michaela. "How do you know Dee's laugh?"

"I've been to meet her parents." Michaela shifted her eyes and scanned the room. "Something didn't sit right about the parents. They talk as if she's still living, and I saw this." She opened her clutch and pulled out a small photo.

Nellie glanced at it. "It's a picture of Dee. So?"

"Look at the date."

Nellie snatched the photo with a grimace then scanned it. She pulled it close. "It's Dee and a bunch of people at the beach. She's smiling and drinking beer."

"The year is wrong. This was taken after she 'died'."

Nellie gasped and stared at the date again, calculating. "But a camera can easily have the wrong time stamp. Her parents are buffoons."

Michaela giggled and put her hands together in front of her. "Her parents are clueless about technology, and I believe they'd muddle the camera date, but this isn't the sort of party they'd attend."

"No, too sophisticated. They don't bother to leave their trailer unless it's bingo or the fish fry." Nellie studied the people in the photo. "None of these people are Fortuna. At least, locals nowadays. I'm sorry, I can't use this as solid evidence." Nellie handed the photo back.

"I know the date is right." Michaela took the photo but pointed to a magazine sitting on a towel, a small obscure item. "See that magazine? It's from the July issue." Using her phone to find a website, Michaela handed over the photo and her phone so Nellie could compare them.

"Holy moly." Nellie's eyes narrowed on the woman in blue. "I can't believe it. You're on to something. You've got a good nose for clues."

Michaela stifled a giggle and accepted the compliment with a nod.

"Where d'you get the incriminating photo?" Nellie asked.

"From Mr. and Mrs. Mander's. They had more. I only snatched the one, but took photos of the others with my phone."

Nellie crinkled her nose. "Can you send them to me?"

"Uh, sure."

Nellie nodded then glanced around the room. "I'm going to go snoop."

"I'll keep my eyes and ears open too."

With a quick grin, Nellie disappeared into the sea of people.

Michaela turned her attention to a table of hors d'oeuvres; she needed something sweet and a drink to wash it down. She plucked a strawberry from the plate. And when she bit the delectable berry, she sighed, closing her eyes. The taste of summer at Christmas. When she opened her eyes, Jasen stood before her with a strange, suspicious look.

"Michaela," he greeted.

Her stomach churned, his relatively cool welcome chilled her. "Mayor DeLay."

His gaze traveled down her body then back up again. The room's temperature rose and she swallowed. "That's a beautiful dress."

"Thank you." Michaela scanned his tailored black suit. His hazel eyes remained guarded.

"Something wrong?" she asked.

"Nothing tomorrow won't cure." He muttered something else and regrouped his smile as a Nockerville council member shook his hand. When the councilman left, Jasen seemed to wilt. "It's like running for office all over again. I've got to keep face."

"I liked your card. Are we still on?" she asked, giving him a peripheral glance.

A sheepish grin on his red face, Jasen answered, "Oh, hell yes."

She giggled, but jumped when B.J. touched her arm.

"I've got something for you." He handed her a glass of blush wine.

She took the glass and a large gulp. "Bless you. This is just what the doctor ordered." She took another long sip and smiled. She'd probably need a lot more alcohol to get through the night.

The mayor of Nockerville whisked Jasen away, leaving her with B.J.

"I saw you were having a grand conversation with my ex," Michaela said.

"Yeah, he knows his stuff." B.J. took a drink of wine. "You were talking with our favorite reporter."

Michaela snorted and rolled her eyes. "You might favor her," she teased, "but she's not my friend. We might have some common ground. I was trying to even things up a bit."

"Is your common ground Jasen?" B.J. quirked a brow.

Michaela nudged him with her elbow, her cheeks warm from the topic and the alcohol. "Maybe."

"So Darren…" B.J. started, "wanted to know if I would give you up to dance with him at some point."

"You mean we actually have to dance?" she grimaced. Her toes already ached. The shiny parquet floor clacked with all the dress shoes and high heel shoes.

B.J. led her to a table and they sat to eat while she kicked off her heels. She waved at Jessie and Josiah Barnes.

B.J. introduced several people as they filtered by. Names swam in Michaela's mind. She nodded and shook hands, hearing stories about how B.J. was their romance novel pimp.

After a second glass of wine, B.J. said, "I read about happily ever after all the time. I'm not sure when it'll happen to me, though."

Michaela reached over and placed a hand on his. "Don't worry. Your time is coming." She tilted her head. "I have a suggestion for you. Tone down the cologne. It's potent."

B.J. nodded. "It's European."

Michaela glanced at her watch, counting the minutes until she could meet up with Jasen. Her heart sped up at the thought of their clandestine rendezvous.

Darren appeared table side. "Care to dance with me?" he asked.

Michaela frowned and nudged B.J. "Is he talking to you or me?"

B.J. laughed, and Darren's brows dipped slightly. "Please?"

Michaela sighed and slipped on her shoes. Darren led her to the dance floor. "You look beautiful tonight. I wish you would have agreed to be my date, but I understand why you chose a local." He rambled on about the pros and cons of local dates, reminding her of a nervous kid.

She scanned the other couples as they swooshed past. She had to admit Darren was a marvelous dancer. "We should have done more dancing," Michaela let the sentiment slip out.

"If you would have—"

"Don't even," Michaela uttered. "You will not lie to me."

His face turned red, and Darren scowled. Then he shook it off and smiled again. "I wish I would have listened to you more."

Okay. That lament had her biting her lip. Was it a manipulation or a true regret? It didn't matter. "Just pay attention to the next one."

"I want you back," he said, twirling her out.

Michaela swallowed, scanning the crowd for B.J. Where was her damn date when she needed him? She circled back into Darren's embrace. He leaned to kiss her. She pushed back on his chest just as B.J. arrived, tapping on his shoulder.

"God bless you," she said as she slipped into B.J.'s arms. The man could dance better than Darren. She glanced over to see her ex swinging the woman in blue around the dance floor.

Jasen passed, leading Desire in his arms. The old woman winked at Michaela and slapped Jasen's rear. He pretended not to notice.

"I think I need another drink," Michaela said.

B.J. chuckled and led her off the dance floor. "Ms. Hardmann does that to all the guys."

"Sexual harassment."

"What are you going to do, throw her in jail? She's a hundred and twenty." He laughed and handed her another glass of wine.

"I suppose not, but if it was a guy he'd get slapped," Michaela said.

"That's true. Ms. Hardmann is harmless unless you're a man's ass." B.J. laughed, but the laugh choked in his throat when Nellie came sashaying up to them.

"Mind if I steal your date?" she asked, raking B.J. with her gaze. He shifted his feet.

"He's all yours, Nellie. I need a break, anyway. Please wear him out for me." She laughed as B.J. glared when Nellie jerked him onto the dance floor. Michaela checked the time and scanned the room.

Michaela met Jasen at the far side of the Christmas tree like he'd asked. "Go down to the end of the room with the auctions then turn right at the hallway. The third door is where we'll meet. There's a small recess you can stand in so you're not seen," Jasen said as he admired the decorated tree.

Michaela nodded and returned to the crowded room. Checking the item she'd bid on, she found she'd been outbid. She bid again then moved down the line. At the end, she turned down the hallway like he'd instructed. When she reached the third door about halfway down the corridor, she stepped out of sight into the door recess. She tried the handle, but it was locked. She heard footsteps and backed against the door.

Jasen stepped in front of her and she sighed. "Took you long enough," she whispered.

He said nothing but stepped forward and pulled her into his arms. He buried his nose in her up-do and sighed against her. "I've been wanting to do that all night." Warm hands caressed her back, and he pressed her backward toward the door. She tipped her head up and claimed his lips. Jasen moaned as she opened her mouth for him. He swept in, exploring.

Slow steps started down the hall, and they broke apart. He fumbled in his pocket for something, pulling out a key. The door pushed in and they retreated. He quietly closed and locked the door. The handle jiggled.

Michaela held her breath and glanced around. It was a small conference room. She faced the wall of windows. Streetlights illuminated the parking lot and gave the room enough light to see. She put her palms on the cool wood of the long oval table.

What were they doing here? She couldn't refuse him. If Jasen wanted to take her on the table, so help her, she'd let him. She needed to run before it was too late. She sat the clutch down and was about to utter her worries when his hands trailed down her bare back to her zipper. He unzipped the dress as much as it would go. The halter kept it on.

"What are you—?"

"Shh," he whispered. He began kissing her neck, and she tilted her head, granting him access. His hands outlined the edge of the dress back until his fingers slid under the fabric. He massaged her lower back, working his way around the loosened material until he stroked her belly. She sighed against him, enjoying his touch.

He nipped her neck and her body warmed. "Jasen," she purred.

Jasen's hands strayed upward until they cupped her breasts. With a gasp, she arched into his touch. He broke the kiss. "I thought you'd be braless."

"I wish I was," she rasped.

# CHAPTER 30

## *Jasen*

FOOTSTEPS RETURNED AND A SOFT knock sounded. Jasen zipped Michaela's dress and kissed her neck. As he approached the door, Michaela followed wide-eyed, her hand on her throat.

"Michaela?" her ex-husband's muffled voice called.

She dropped her hand and kicked off her shoes. Swinging the door open, Michaela stood with one hand on her hip. "What do you want now?"

Darren's eyes narrowed when he saw Jasen. "Him again." Darren snorted and strutted into the room. "I wanted to talk to you about us." He faced Jasen, "Do you mind giving us a minute?"

Michaela sighed and pinched the bridge of her nose.

"You're not doing yourself any favors," Jasen said to Darren, earning a superior sneer. Jasen moved toward the door, his feet lead. He paused before Michaela, tracing her collarbone. "I'll be right outside the door."

Michaela flicked a small smile and nodded. She strolled back into the center of the room and pulled out a chair. She sat and offered her ex another.

Jasen stood in the dimly lit hallway, gazing down the tunnel toward the throng of bidders. The charities would be cashing in. He glanced at his watch. He had to help Mayor Baals announce the winners. Good thing Darren had interrupted them.

Out of the ex's line of sight, Jasen stood where Michaela could see him and leaned against the wall with his arms crossed.

"Out with it, Darren," she sighed.

"I remember you enjoy conference rooms. Care to… for old times' sake?" Darren's buttery voice asked.

"No. And conference tables make a piss-poor bed. You should have come home," she stood and raised her finger to poke him. "You should have taken me out to dinner. Away from the damn office and the security cameras. It wasn't personal, but rushed. Maybe it had been fun and daring, in the beginning, but after a year of marriage, if I wanted my husband to touch me I had to parade myself before him naked at work. Do you see how that's wrong?" Her hands rested on her hips.

"It was hot sex. You know how to turn me on."

"But I was never enough. You didn't love me," Michaela said in a sorrowful voice that twisted Jasen's heart. She covered her face with her hands. Michaela's shoulders shook. *That bastard made her cry.*

Jasen pushed off the wall going to her, but stopped short, remaining in the hall. Darren had embraced her. At least Darren wasn't a complete ass. He held Michaela as she wept. Michaela laid her head on his shoulder. Her hand snaked up his back and rested there.

Heaviness settled in his gut, but Jasen couldn't lose what he never had. He sighed, staring at his shoes. He jammed his hands into his pockets, about to leave, when he glanced at Michaela.

She blinked frightened green eyes, holding his gaze. Inhaling, Jasen wrapped on the door jamb. "Knock-knock," he said. "I need to lock up the conference room then find Mayor Baals."

Michaela pushed away from Darren and glided to Jasen's side. "Sorry to hold you up. The winners will be announced soon."

"My apologies. We got caught up in the moment," Darren said, offering his hand to Jasen.

Michaela's eye roll brought a smile to Jasen's lips. He locked the door and followed the others to the auction room. Volunteers gathered items, taking them through the room to the stage area. The attendees milled around, waiting.

Mayor Krystal Baals stepped onto the platform and tapped the mic. "Are we on? Good. Ladies and gentlemen, thank you for making this benefit a success. We will begin announcing the winners soon, but first I would like to take a moment to thank our sponsors and volunteers."

The crowd clapped, and Krystal glanced around before continuing. "I would like to thank the Nocker family for providing the space for the event and for donating multiple items, including a family membership to Twin Hills country club."

Jasen edged to the platform's side where the mayor saw him. She motioned for him to join her. "This is the honorable Jasen DeLay, mayor of Fortuna. Many of the residents of Fortuna are in attendance and have donated items for bidding. I'd like to thank the volunteers from the Rotary and Optimist clubs. We couldn't do it without you! Refer to the backside of the auction list for the complete list of donors, sponsors, and volunteers."

"Good evening," Jasen said stepping up to the mic. "I love reading, so this charity is near and dear to my heart. Illiteracy is a tragic thing." He quoted the region statistics provided and then listed how the charity would combat illiteracy. "Once again, thank you for coming out tonight. Y'all look fabulous."

Jasen moved to the side as Krystal took the mic. "On to the auctions!" A volunteer carried a basket wrapped in cellophane onto the stage. She grinned, glancing over the ballroom.

"Six books in the *Looking Good* series by Paige Turner. They are signed by the author." Krystal smiled, reading the description. "The basket was donated by the Fortuna Dare Society."

Jasen's face heated as he glanced at B.J., who smirked.

"The winner is Liam Nocker. Congratulations." Krystal continued, announcing several more winners.

"We're going to break for a half an hour. Please place your final bids on any remaining items. We have several packages of new books signed by the authors; I saw a spa treatment and massage package too."

Frustrated by his honor bound duties, Jasen shifted waiting for the night to end. B.J. had brought Michaela, but Jasen planned to take her home. He longed to touch her smooth stomach again. He wondered how he'd keep his hands to himself on the return to Fortuna.

Jasen parked in Michaela's driveway and opened the door for her. "I can't wait to get these shoes off." Yawning, she fumbled for the key and pushed the door open. She kicked her heels into the corner.

Jasen took her into his arms and buried his nose in her hair. He unfastened the clip, letting her length free. "I love your hair. It smells better than the house."

She leaned against him and giggled. "I'm so incredibly tired." She yawned again.

"Want to watch a movie?" he shrugged.

"Either that or get naked, huh?" she arched her eyebrows.

"Are you channeling Kim?" he asked, laughing.

"Ms. Hardmann." Michaela giggled and turned in his arms. "Unzip me."

Jasen swallowed and did as she asked. She lifted her hair to the side, "Now the fasteners." He unhooked the small clasps at the neck and the dress fell to the floor, pooling at her feet. Michaela stepped out of it and glanced over her shoulder.

Michaela wore a champagne-colored thong matching her dress. He traced the soft lacy edge, her back bare except for one low strap and a strap around her neck. Jasen froze, mesmerized by the sway of her hips. She crooked her finger, beckoning him to follow. He cleared his throat and, turning, he locked the door and clicked off the living room light.

"You better have fewer clothes on when you arrive in my room," she called from down the hallway.

Jasen kicked off his shoes and hung his jacket on a doorknob, his tie on another. In the bedroom, she'd turned down the queen bed.

Jasen started to unbutton his dress shirt. "Stop," she said from the bathroom doorway.

Jasen admired the youthful curve of her breasts and deep plunge of the bra. He longed to run his tongue over the cleft of her breasts.

"Allow me," she grinned. Every place her fingers grazed his skin it burned, sparking desire. He kept watch on her eyes as she focused on each button then the part of his flesh she'd uncovered. He shrugged out of the shirt. Her sultry eyes made him want to pick her up and toss her on the bed.

She tugged on his belt, and his pants fell to the floor. His erection strained his boxer briefs. Her fingers traced the band at his waist, her greedy gaze scanning his package.

"Wait," Jasen said.

She paused glancing at him, her emerald eyes sparkling with want. "Yes, sir?" She inclined her head to the side like a curious puppy.

"Are you sure?" he asked. "Do you want this? Us? Me?" He bit his lip. Michaela cupped his face. He pressed into her warm hand, closing his eyes. "I had to be sure. I don't want to hurt you."

"Jasen," she whispered as her other hand cradled his manhood.

He gasped, snapping his eyes open. Her warmth cocooning him jumpstarted his heart.

"I want to figure your bra out," he said.

Michaela thrust her chest out. His fingertips traced the beaded scalloped edge of the deep plunge where the cups met. The bottom of the cups crisscrossed and circled her sides, meeting in the rear then roping around her stomach.

"It's a low back bra. The things we girls do to look beautiful," Michaela said, a wicked smile forming.

Jasen's fingers lingered on her face. "You don't need the bra to be beautiful."

"Is that so?" She covered his hand.

"I'm about ninety-nine point nine nine percent sure, but just to make it one hundred percent, let's remove the bra."

"I'm one hundred percent sure you're just as sexy without boxers." Quick as a snake bite, she pushed his boxers off. Michaela smiled at him before glancing down. Her chest heaved in a silent gasp.

"Michaela," Jasen whispered, straining not to throw her on the bed and ravage her. "The bra."

She grinned and slowly spun, her hand grazing his erection. Jasen hissed. Staring at her back, he touched her round cheeks, appreciating the Double D Intimate's custom design. He traced the lines of the thong.

Michaela pointed to the low strap. "You can unhook it." Jasen found the latch. The intricate design hid the clever clasp. He slid the metal hook out.

She lifted her hair. Jasen unclasped the bra and it fell forward onto the bed. He stepped closer and encircled her waist. He kissed her neck. She moaned, pressing her backside into his erection.

Jasen spun her around, pressing his chest against her soft breasts. Their kiss started sweet, but when she opened for him, he couldn't get enough. He pushed the edge of her thong until it fell to her feet. He lifted her and she hooked her legs behind him. Jasen was on fire, but before he could embed himself in her, he wanted to preform therapy. His challenge, as any man, especially a Fortuna man, was to pleasure his partner. Jasen lowered her to the bed, keeping their kiss hot.

Michaela's hair splayed around her head like a flame, and her hooded eyes dared him not to stop. He worked his way nipping and kissing down her chest. His finger found her core, warm, wet, and welcoming. God, he almost came undone.

"Jasen, please," she begged in rapid, short pants.

"I'm hungry," he grinned. Jasen glanced at her pleasure zone, his blood burning in his veins. He licked her seam, making her squirm. He dove between her legs, his administrations making her mewl.

"Jasen." She threw her head back." I'm close." He smiled then worked faster, sucking, licking, and nipping.

"Jasen," she moaned, thrusting her fingers into his hair and holding him there. A moment later, she hit the pinnacle.

Michaela relaxed her hands and closed her eyes, gulping air. A final flick of his tongue, and she squeaked. He laid beside her and stroked her arm as her breathing slowed. Michaela rolled toward him and touched his face.

"Did you like part one of your therapy?" Jasen asked.

Her brow rose. "Therapy? I thought I was being reconditioned."

Jasen laughed and reached for her, holding her against his chest in a tender embrace. She captured his length and he flinched.

"Part one. If that was part one, what's part two?' she asked, exploring his manhood.

He hissed. "That's part three."

"What's—"

"It starts with this," he leaned forward and kissed her, a chaste kiss, then kissed her nose. "Open your mouth."

She complied. He traced her bottom lip with his tongue then sucked it in. He shifted her onto her back, proceeding to ravage her mouth. His erection pressed her hip, and a leg rested between hers. His hand continued to caress her arm up and down until he plunged his fingers into her hair. He loved her silky waves.

He abandoned her hair, working his way down toward her apex. She inhaled sharply. Without breaking their kiss, she fell apart at his hand and once more became a rag-doll.

Michaela pushed him onto his back and started nibbling and sucking his chest and neck, her one leg between his, grazing him like he'd done to her. He groaned, a feral needy sound. A sound foreign to his ears.

His blood boiled, and he needed to unite with Michaela. He tried to sit up, but she held him.

"I need to go get my wallet," he murmured.

She pecked his lips before smiling sweetly. "Check the nightstand drawer."

Jasen rolled over and tugged it open. Inside was a brand new box of condoms. He retrieved a package. "Part three."

Michaela opened her arms to him, and he obliged. "I can kiss you all night."

"Not a problem," he replied. He lined up, making eye contact before easing in. She gasped, clasping him with her body. He moaned at her warmth. She embraced him and pulled him closer. They fit together. "Part three."

"This time you'll join me, right?" he asked. He started to move in her, and she moaned.

"Oh, hell yeah."

Michaela touched his face, and he dipped to kiss her again. He picked up the pace and her hips met his. She moaned and tightened around him as another orgasm hit, causing him to explode. Winded, and thoroughly spent, he rolled off her and went to throw the condom away.

She followed him into the bathroom. "Will you stay the night?"

"Do you want me to?" he asked as she hugged him.

"Yes," she said, glancing at his reflection in the mirror. Her cheeks flushed.

"What the lady wants, the lady gets," Jasen said. He held her as she drifted to sleep, her lily scented hair spread over his pillow and her soft body spooning his. He sighed and wished the morning would never come.

# CHAPTER 31

## *Michaela*

MICHAELA OPENED HER OFFICE DOOR a crack and peeped out. Jacklyn tapped at her keyboard then paused, glancing around. Michaela ducked out of sight.

She'd let her relationship with Jasen go too far. Especially if his wife was still living. Michaela scanned her watch and sighed. Squaring her shoulders, she shifted her purse then pulled the door open.

Jacklyn glanced up and smiled. "Early lunch?"

Michaela nodded. "I've got a meeting. It was the only time we could agree on. Might as well eat." With a shrug, she hurried toward the exit.

"Michaela," Jasen called.

She reached the front door but stopped, her hand on the handle. She'd have to face Jasen sometime, but she needed to get her emotions in check. Each time she gazed at him, her body ignited with desire. The timbre of his voice—the longing in it—sent her pulse racing. Willing her feet to ignore her heart, she squeezed her eyes shut, refusing to turn toward him.

"We need to talk," he said, his voice closer.

"Not now. Sorry. I've got a meeting." She pushed the door, escaping into the bright Texas day.

Michaela strode down the sidewalk. She shouldn't have made love to Jasen until she knew if his wife was alive. Thinking of laying skin to skin next to his long body drove her blood to boil. A breeze caressed her face, cooling the heat.

Across the street, Nellie Neus entered Hammered. Michaela plodded toward the restaurant with a melancholy heart. Her stomach twisted as she sat in the same booth with the nosy news reporter.

"Hey girl," Nellie grinned.

"Hey, Nellie." Michaela surveyed the restaurant, not seeing any of Jasen's book club or council members.

Sharon Dix waddled to the table with glasses of water and menus. "The Fortuna fish is the special today," she said, pointing to the paper clipped to the menu. "It comes with two sides but the lunch portion has one side." She took their orders and left.

Nellie started, "So I've done some digging and—Jackpot!"

Michaela couldn't help but smile at Nellie's enthusiasm. "What is it?"

Nellie's smile widened.

"Oh, come on. Don't make me read it in tomorrow's Forum." Michaela rolled her eyes.

"Maybe I will," Nellie laughed.

"No, you're going to spill it. You can't wait to tell someone."

"I know." Nellie leaned over the table and lowered her voice. "I searched the public records for Dee Mander and her parents. Nothing unusual about her parents, but Dee—that's another story."

Michaela blinked and held her breath.

"She's been married twice before Jasen. No kids."

Michaela exhaled. "That's no big deal. I'm divorced."

Nellie stuck a finger into the air. "I never said she got divorced."

Michaela slapped her palms on the table. "What?"

Nellie leaned back against the hunter green booth and crossed her arms. "That's right. There's no record of her divorce."

"Holy cow." Michaela rubbed her forehead. Rational though stalled.

"Dee is a fraud. Jasen was never married," Nellie said with a smug expression.

Michaela hadn't committed adultery. Her heart raced as a wave of elation rolled over her. She sipped her sweet tea.

"Can you go back to the Manders' pit and get more evidence?" Nellie asked. "They don't like me. They call me a snoop."

"Well, it's true."

Nellie giggled. "You're right. I've put a call into her first and second husbands. I'll keep searching the records."

"Maybe try her married names with her middle name too," Michaela suggested.

"Great idea. You'd make an excellent reporter." Nellie winked.

"I don't know about that," Michaela said, heat radiating from her cheeks.

"So can you go to the Manders' dump?"

"I'll try. Jasen will have to take me," she said hesitantly. "I don't think I can take watching another pageant video." Michaela covered her face and shivered.

A newspaper slapped the table, making the women jump. "What's this bullshit?" B.J. Johnson pointed to the headline on the front page.

"It's all in there." Nellie narrowed her eyes. "I can't help it if you can't read."

B.J. scowled and sat next to Michaela. "Why don't you explain it to me."

Michaela fingered the paper, turning it so she could read it. "Canyon Ghost Strikes Again."

"Another sighting," Nellie said.

"They saw her?" B.J. asked.

"No. They heard her."

"Was she asking Jasen for money so she can buy shoes?" B.J. asked.

"Shh," Michaela said, reading the article. She flipped to another section and finished. "Wow. Just like the kids at Halloween. This has happened to at least ten other people?"

"Yes. It's been reported that many times to the police. They searched for an injured person but thought it might be a prank. The ghostly voice is haunting the same area of the trail along the creek."

"During the day?" Michaela asked.

"Mostly."

"The article said they heard howls," Michaela said, staring at Nellie. "What did it sound like?"

Nellie glanced around then moaned, low and long.

B.J. shifted on the booth. "Are you sure it wasn't a couple making love?"

Nellie's mouth flopped open, and her cheeks flamed crimson. Michaela nudged B.J. "Seriously?"

"Well, hell, this is Fortuna. Somebody could be acting out a book scene. It wouldn't be the first time." B.J. crossed his arms.

"That's true, but everyone that I've interviewed imitated the sound the exact same way," Nellie said, her eyes bright.

"Exactly? That's odd," Michaela said.

"Hmm. That can't be a coincidence," B.J. said.

Michaela and Nellie glanced at each other and smirked. "I'll check the police reports again and look for a pattern in the day and times," Nellie said.

"Let's suppose Dee is alive. Why would she do this?" Michaela asked, tapping her chin.

Nellie shrugged. "To keep the ruse that she's dead?"

"Wait. You two think Dee is alive?" B.J. shook his head. "Don't say anything to Jasen unless you have proof. I mean proof as in the archangel Gabriel hands you a sealed envelope from the Big Cheese himself. Got it?" He looked each woman in the eye before changing the subject. "Michaela, are you still afraid of magicians?"

"Oh my God," Michaela groaned. "I am not afraid of magicians!"

B.J. raised his hands in surrender. "I didn't write it." His gaze slid to

Nellie.

"Listen, my mom left me and my dad for a guy who could pull a rabbit out of his hat, so I don't like them. Okay?" Michaela's throat tightened.

"Gotcha," B.J. said. "Sorry to upset you." He scowled at Nellie again.

"Yeah, I'm sorry too. Darren spun it that way," Nellie said with a pout.

"Hearsay is inadmissible in court. Get your facts straight if you want to be a great reporter and not just propagate sensationalism," B.J. said.

"Don't you have to go hash out plot points and character traits with your book club buddies?" Nellie said, matching B.J.'s scowl.

B.J. rolled his eyes then waved as Jasen entered the restaurant. His brows shot up, recognizing Nellie. "Ladies," B.J. said rising. "Enjoy your day." He sauntered over to Jasen at the bookshelf.

"I appreciate the apology," Michaela said with a nod. She studied Jasen's hindquarters, remembering the contour of his body.

"You're welcome." Nellie glanced at the men as B.J. pointed to the book in Jasen's hand.

"You know," Michaela said with a wry grin, "the Forum should have a weekly book review. It should be submitted by random men or, I suppose, it could be a regular column."

"Wow, what a great idea." Nellie's eyes lit up. "You really are good at your job."

"Gee thanks," Michaela said, glancing down at her food. "I love Fortuna. I want to make it the best it can be."

"Yes, I know that now."

Michaela shot a glance at Jasen before looking at Nellie. "I have an idea for the town, but it needs to get approved by the council. Maybe you can help?"

"How?" Nellie tilted her head, making her blond curls bob.

"If the public wants it, then they'll have to approve it." Michaela watched as Jasen and B.J. sat at the bar and ordered.

"Ah." Nellie's hawk-like expression zeroed in on Michaela's face. "Pray tell, how can I help you?"

"I'd like to bring in romance authors for a book signing event."

"That's some golden hearsay," Nellie said with a smirk.

"Can you sensationalize the book event propaganda?"

"I can propagate the hell out of it." They clinked their plastic glasses and giggled.

# CHAPTER 32

## *Michaela*

MICHAELA CALLED AND MESSAGED SEVERAL regional authors, wanting to find out availability and interest. Optimistic about the council meeting's outcome, she first had to speak to the city manager.

Jasen peeked his head in her office as she retrieved papers from the printer. She stapled the packet then glanced up. "Bad time?" he asked, stepping into the room.

"I have an appointment with Cam." Michaela stood, glancing into his penetrating hazel eyes. "He wanted to hear about the idea."

"Our idea?" Jasen smirked.

She hesitated, quelling the desire to throw herself into his arms. She nodded but smiled. While snuggling, they had joked about the Fortuna men and which character Jasen could dress up as and act out. Their conversation had taken several twists until it settled on the romance conference.

Rom-con ideas swirled around in Michaela's head like ingredients in a stew. It would turn out awesome, but it needed a chance to simmer. There wasn't much time. Michaela glanced at her watch. "I need to go. Especially if this is going to become a reality."

"You can do it," Jasen said, moving to the side so she could pass.

"Thanks." She paused next to him. "I'll let you know how it goes."

He touched her elbow before she could move away. "Dinner tonight?"

Michaela's heart rate quickened. Dinner would turn into more. *Breathe.*

"I can't—" she stammered. "I have plans." She pulled her arm away and entered the hall. Jasen didn't follow her, and Michaela slowed until she stopped. With another glance at her watch, she huffed then spun on her heels. Peering into her office, she found him staring into the distance with a frown, his shoulders drooped and his hands stuffed into his pockets.

"Jasen?" she whispered.

He glanced up.

"I just need time." Michaela couldn't voice her emotions because they clogged her throat. "Just give me some time."

Jasen nodded but gave her a lopsided smile that threatened to make her insides melt.

The engraved brass sign claimed the desk belonged to Cam Payne. Hunched, he read the proposal, his bald spot tipping toward Michaela.

"You are thorough," Cam said over his reading glasses. "This doesn't leave you much time to get this big of a shindig together."

"I know but, as you can see, there are several interested authors and vendors already," Michaela said. "It's a matter of getting approval, the permits, and the tents."

"My brother-in-law runs a party supply store in Bald Knob. I bet we can get the tents there, and if not he'll be willing to help us find another vendor." Cam straightened, rubbing his chin. "I want you to find out exact costs on the rentals. Also talk to the police and see about closing the roads and parking. I'm sure the crowd will cause a headache."

"I'm on it." Michaela jotted Cam's list on her notepad. Her stomach rumbled. But excitement, not anxiety, made it churn. The small window of time gave her a challenge, and the rom-con event was a challenge worth winning. She rushed out of the meeting, returning to her office. Closing the door, she took a deep breath. In the solitude of the cramped space, she focused. Grabbing a dry erase marker, she transferred the list of qualifiers to the whiteboard.

She stood back, thinking of the time-line. First things first. She pushed a contact on her phone. "Hello, Ben. Who do I speak to regarding an event that may disrupt traffic through the town?" Michaela smiled. Fate had placed her at the officer's bed-and-breakfast.

"That's not me, but I know who you need to talk to. Wait just a sec," Ben said, putting her on hold. "Okay. I'll transfer you now."

"Thanks, Ben. Have a great day."

"You too." The line began ringing, and a feminine voice greeted Michaela.

Working out the details appeared simple, though the event thus far was hypothetical.

Onto the next item on her list. Michaela rubbed her hands together and spun around in her chair.

Avoiding Jasen had been hard, especially after she'd texted him regarding the meeting, but Michaela had made it through the day. She hurried home for a quick meal and to change into running clothes. When she reached Stanton Cove Park, she studied the information board with the map. According to Nellie's research, the hikers all heard the ghost in the same section of the park.

Michaela started her run, knowing she probably wouldn't be lucky enough to hear the ghost. She was too late in the day, but curiosity had her moving toward the haunted location.

She'd sent her father and Nellie a text before leaving the parking lot. Nellie replied fifteen minutes later with a thumbs-up emoji.

The flat gravel trail following the Dry Run creek forked. Michaela took the left spur. The path narrowed and steepened, winding through tall trees as it neared the base of the cliff. In the cliff's shadow, she paused for a water break. Her phone rang, piercing the evening air and echoing off the rock surface.

"Hello, Dad," she answered.

"Hey baby-doll, what's this about a ghost?" Tim asked.

"People have heard haunting moans, and rumor has it that it's the spirit of Jasen's wife." Michaela took a deep breath.

"I've seen an article about the specter of Stanton Cove Park. Do you think it's real?" he asked.

"The ghost? No. But multiple people have reported hearing the wailing. Everyone imitates the same sound. They aren't coordinated sightings, and according to Nellie, the hikers aren't ones to report phony phenomenon to the police."

"Interesting."

"Yeah, it is. That's why I'm here."

"Why did you text me about it?" Her father's voice turned softer with a touch of concern.

"I just wanted someone to know where I was going," she admitted.

"What about Jasen? Did you two have a falling out?"

"No, Dad. It's complicated," she said with a sigh.

Her father chuckled. "Love usually is."

*Love?* Michaela pinched the bridge of her nose.

"When I met your—"

"Shh—" Michaela turned around listening. The wind carried a low moan. "Holy hauntings, Dad, I hear it. I need to go."

"Don't hang up. Just go and I'll stay with you."

"Thanks, Dad." Michaela turned on the video hoping, to capture the sound then continued forward. She ventured off the main path onto a narrow dirt trail. It rounded a boulder, and the sound stopped. She froze, straining her ears. Minutes later the groan started again, and Michaela once more followed the noise. She quickened her pace but watched her steps as the sun waned.

The moan abruptly stopped and Michaela held her breath, listening. Eerie silence. After a moment, she bent over, holding her knees and sharply inhaled.

"Mick? Are you okay?" her father asked.

Michaela glanced at the phone, realizing she'd recorded the ghost. She giggled. "I'm fine." She waited a few more minutes before prancing toward her car.

# CHAPTER 33

## *Jasen*

JASEN GLANCED AT THE CLOCK again. He had over an hour before the town hall meeting. Announced New Year's Day, he'd been getting calls and emails of support. He sighed and rubbed his eyes before refocusing on the screen of his computer.

"Knock, knock," Nellie said from the door. She kept a hand on her chartreuse shoulder bag.

"Good evening," Jasen said, hoping he kept the irritation out of his voice. He stood. "What can I do for you, Nellie?"

"Well..." Nellie glanced down the hallway before stepping into his office.

Jasen motioned to the chairs across from his desk. As she sat, she smoothed her short yellow skirt. She frowned and stared at her hands. This wasn't the plucky Nellie who usually bounced into any situation with confidence.

"It's a touchy subject." Chin up, Nellie met his eyes. "I need you to keep an open mind."

Jasen leaned back, nodding.

"It has to do with Dee Mander."

Jasen's jaw dropped open. He recovered and clamped his teeth together.

"As you know, there have been several people who've encountered something unusual in Stanton Cove Park."

"Yes," Jasen grunted.

"I've been researching the phenomenon. That includes Dee, since—" Nellie waved her hand. "Most think it's her ghost."

"I don't—"

"Please, Jasen. Hear me out." She blinked puppy-dog eyes.

He sighed and crossed his arms.

"I'll get right to it, then. Did you know she had been married?" Nellie asked.

"To me."

"No, before you."

Jasen shook his head. "I was her first." He leaned in, wondering where Nellie planned to take him on her fanciful trip.

"According to my research, she'd been married at least twice and engaged one other time before you came along." Nellie plunged her hand into the large satchel and pulled out a folder. "She married her high school sweetheart. Captain of the Nockerville football team, Mike Hunt." Nellie pushed the folder toward him.

Jasen flipped it open and found photocopied newspaper articles with Dee and Mike's engagement and wedding announcements. He rubbed his chin. Dee had lied to him about being married. But Mike could have been a jerk.

"Okay. She was married before. So what?"

"Turn the marriage announcement over." Nellie chewed her lip and tugged on the hem of her floral-patterned shirt.

He flipped the paper, and Dee's smiling face mocked him with two different men. Another wedding announcement dated after Mike. The engagement dated after the second marriage.

*What the hell.* Did he know his wife at all? Still, she was dead. What did it matter?

"Forgive me, Jasen," Nellie said, placing her phone on the desk and pushing the screen to speaker. It rang.

"Hello," a deep masculine voice answered.

"Hiya, Mike, it's Nellie."

"Oh yeah. Did you find Dee yet?" Mike asked.

"Not yet. I'm with Jasen, another of her husbands," Nellie said, glancing at Jasen.

"I'm her husband. No one else. She's mine," Mike snarled.

"Why did you two split then?" Jasen couldn't help asking.

"I don't know," Mike said, his voice soft. "I thought we were happy. She up and disappeared. Then Nellie calls and tells me Dee married someone else. That's not possible."

"People remarry all the time," Jasen said incredulously, leaning over the phone.

"Not without divorcing first," Mike harrumphed.

"What? You never divorced her?" Jasen said, flabbergasted. He stood wiping his damp palms on his khakis.

"No. Why would I divorce Dee?" Mike asked.

"But it's been years," Nellie said.

"I don't care how long it's been, I love her. I want her to come home," Mike said with longing.

Mike's words echoed in Jasen's mind. A wave of sadness filled him as he slumped into his chair. "I have some bad news for you."

"Oh no," Mike groaned.

"Dee was killed in a flash flood." Jasen swallowed a bitter taste.

"That's not what Nellie says," Mike said.

Jasen's gaze snapped to Nellie's red face. "What does Nellie say?"

"Dee is alive," Mike replied.

Jasen rubbed his face. Not another theory.

"Listen, Jasen, they didn't find a body or any of her personal stuff besides her car and the items from her gym bag that she kept in the car. None of her IDs or credit cards were found. Also look at this—" Nellie said, placing a photograph of Dee on the desk. "That magazine in the picture is from this year. How is that possible?"

"That has to be wrong," he said, examining the photo. He could see the title but not a month.

Nellie slapped the magazine on the table. "Here it is."

Jasen couldn't make sense of it. "No," he mumbled.

"There's more," Nellie said. She stood, placing more paperwork on his desk.

His vision swam, and he found it hard to breathe. Jasen closed his eyes trying to calm his racing heart.

Nellie rattled on, but Jasen tried to tune her out. He glanced at the clock, wishing the hands moved faster. He let her explain and he'd nod, but it was hogwash. Something to write in the Forum to boost sales, he'd wager.

Jasen gazed over the heads of the Fortuna residents toward the back wall where Michaela shook hands with a man. Jasen recognized the man as familiar but couldn't place him.

Cam nudged his arm. "The people have rallied on this one."

"Yes, it appears we may have a riot if things don't go their way," Jasen said, glancing at his book club men in the front row. B.J. scowled with his arms crossed. Parker and Forrest had their heads together.

"At this rate, the hall will fill before the meeting starts," Sandy Beach said, moving around the table on the raised platform. She took a seat next to Bunny Hopkins, who waved at her husband and daughters in the audience.

Desire walked through the entrance, leading the posse of first pew ladies.

Notorious do-gooders, the group of widows and spinsters volunteered everywhere. Jasen and his book club guys theorized the women got involved to learn all the juicy town gossip.

Milo and Artis greeted townsfolk like celebrities. Kim and Glen smiled and waved to Michaela. Kim's T-shirt was smeared with paint from the firehouse remodel.

Brad slipped a book to Ophelia. She inspected the cover and beamed.

Walter Mellan stalked up the aisle toward the group, only stopping to shake hands with Collin Copper, the chief of police. Once on the platform, Walter approached Cam and Jasen. "I had to park three blocks away. What's going on? Why this meeting?" he grumbled.

"It's the article the Forum published yesterday," Jasen said.

"Yes. Fortuna having a romance author convention would get most of the locals out of their homes," Cam agreed.

Walter nodded and rubbed his chin. "But it isn't fact—yet." He smirked and glanced at the others seated at the table facing the audience.

"I want to know who the informant is," Cam said, scanning the room.

"I have an idea," Jasen said, finding Michaela speaking with Nellie. Michaela met his eyes then her gaze darted back to the reporter. Nellie pushed something into Michaela's hands; it was small and blue.

He fingered the small baggie in his pocket. It held a fortune cookie that Michaela had given him when they entered the room. All she had said was, "Read it later." Curiosity would suck the life from him minute by minute.

"Oh?" Cam's brows rose as he stared expectantly.

"It was me," Jacklyn said. Cam, Walter, and Jasen pivoted to stare at her. Jacklyn put her hands on her hips.

"That nosy newspaper reporter called to speak with you, Jasen, but you were in a meeting. She started asking me questions. Then I thought *why not?* I was vague, mind you. Well, I don't know the details. I'd only heard bits of things here and there. I suppose Nellie embellished enough to get the community excited." She shrugged and turned around before the men reacted.

"I didn't see that coming," Cam said with a dry laugh.

Jasen nodded.

The community filled the chairs until the overflow lined the perimeter. At seven, Cam approached the mic and the murmurs faded.

"Welcome to the council meeting. Thank you for joining us tonight. What a turnout! We have business to conduct first, then we will open the floor to your questions and concerns." Cam returned to his seat.

Between the treasurer's report, minutes approval, and various updates, Jasen's thoughts wandered. As he watched Fortuna's citizens he noticed bouncing knees, people inspecting the ceiling or their phones, and a few wiggling side to side. They were antsy like him. Before the council voted on the event, they would hear from Michaela and open the floor to the concerned citizens.

Jasen shifted, and the cookie broke. He pulled the bag out and saw a slip of yellow paper with the crumbs.

"Now, as to the event mentioned in yesterday's newspaper," Sandy said, catching the room's attention. "We welcome your thoughts and concerns."

B.J. Johnson jumped to his feet. "Ma'am," he greeted, "when is it?"

Jasen chuckled. "You don't beat around the bush."

"He could around my bush," Desire Hardmann yelled.

B.J.'s mouth flopped open, and he turned scarlet as the room burst out laughing. He lowered himself to the chair and crossed his arms again.

Michaela stood at the podium and waited until the room quieted. She inhaled, glancing around, but avoided Desire's row. "If approved, the author's event will be held on Valentine's weekend."

The crowd broke out in conversation. Michaela glanced over at Jasen with a smirk. His insides heated. He shifted but returned a grin.

She listed proposed plans, including food vendors, fundraising, and the main draw: romance authors. "You've asked me several times this evening if local author Paige Turner will come. I say we ask him." Her gaze narrowed in on a short man who rose. Recognition dawned on Jasen. "Ladies and gentlemen, this is Paul Ennis. He writes under the pseudonym Paige Turner. Paul, are you available?"

"Thank you, Ms. Arschfick. I have some good news. I am available that weekend."

The room burst into applause with whistles and whoops of excitement.

Michaela motioned for Paul to join her. As the room once more gained composure, Paul adjusted the mic.

"That's not the only good news. I am a member of Writers of Romance. I've spoken with my local branch of WOR, and many members are available that weekend. They've given their information to Ms. Arschfick. There is a variety of subgenres in our group including high and urban fantasy, MC, western, historical, paranormal, and contemporary."

The crowd broke out in cheers, whistles, and clapping. The deafening noise covered the crinkling of the cookie bag as Jasen opened it and retrieved the paper.

Paul continued, "I'm working with the talented Jessie Barnes of Double D Intimates again. If you'll remember, she created a gown that matched a cover. She'll be working hard on a new item for another cover available only at this Fortuna romance author event."

Gasps, joyful shrieks, and murmuring filled the room.

Jasen unfolded the slip of paper. It read: *Tonight you're mine.*

Jasen found it hard to swallow around his heart in his throat. He glanced at the ceiling fans to make sure they'd been switched on.

Michaela thanked Paul and then listed a few other names of romance authors interested in attending the event. Jasen's heart swelled. In her element, Michaela had accomplished much in a short time.

"I have one final question to you," Michaela said to the group. "If the council approves this event, please raise your hand if you would attend."

Every hand shot skyward. "Hell yeah," B.J. whooped, thrusting his fist into the air.

The romance convention was an excellent way to draw the community into the heart of Fortuna. It took an Ohioan to envision and implement the event. With a grin, Jasen shook his head.

# CHAPTER 34

## *Jasen*

FROM THE KITCHEN TO THE living room, around the sofa and coffee table, then back to the kitchen, Jasen paced. He could hear his mother's voice inside his head, "You'll wear a groove into the floor and ruin it."

Michaela puzzled Jasen. Trying to reason out her actions brought a wash of longing and excitement over him.

He sat at the kitchenette, his knee bouncing. He hopped up and opened the fridge. Twisting the cap off a long neck bottle, he slid the patio door and stepped onto the deck. The sounds of the effervescent stream and wind caressing the leaves helped calm his restless spirit. He tipped the amber bottle and cool brew slid down his throat.

Michaela had shined at the council meeting, lighting the townsfolk with hope and excitement. The people seemed to respect her and listened to her plans highlighting the coming event like a sponge soaking in every word. The residents accepted her as if she was one of them.

Even Nellie appeared to like Michaela now. And that was why he worried. While he could appreciate not seeing Nellie as much, the lack of her in his life meant she was probably harassing someone else.

Until Jacklyn had fessed about leaking the event details, Jasen had been certain Michaela had slipped the information to Nellie.

The doorbell sounded. Jasen hurried to the front door and threw it open. Michaela stood holding a small bag. Wearing a sheepish grin, she tossed the bag into the room and launched herself into his arms.

Jasen wrapped his arms around her, relishing her warmth. He closed his eyes, savoring the feel of her.

"Jasen?" Michaela glanced up. She cupped his cheek. The tender touch sent a quiver of desire down his spine.

"I'm happy to see you." Jasen nuzzled her hair, recognizing the familiar scent of lilies.

"I'm happy to see you too, but can we go inside?" she asked, pushing him gently backward until the door could close.

"What do you have in mind?" he asked, waggling his brows.

She fingered the buttons on his polo shirt as her passionate gaze caught his. "I was thinking you could kiss every square inch of my body while I return the favor."

"So—" Jasen's voice cracked, and he cleared his throat. "Okay. If that's what you want. I planned an exciting night of puzzles and reading."

Michaela's eyes widened then narrowed again. Her hand dropped to his zipper and stroked him. "Are you sure?"

He groaned. "No. I like your plan better." Jasen bent, consuming her lips. She opened for him, and he swept in. He pushed her a step toward the stairs then another. Holding her head, he pressed her against the wall.

"A biotch is calling. A biotch is calling," his phone wailed from the kitchen.

They broke apart. Michaela stared blankly.

"It's Sally's ringtone," he said. When it stopped, Jasen lowered his head again.

Michaela giggled until she snorted. "I'm sorry," she said, covering her mouth and nose. "It's so appropriate for your mother-in-law."

"A biotch is calling," the phone alerted again.

Jasen sighed and pushed away from Michaela. "I better answer or the biotch won't stop calling."

Michaela giggled again, following him into the kitchen. "It's okay. We've got all night."

"Hello, Sally. What can I do for you?" Jasen listened as Sally rambled. "You want me to grab some bug killer, right now?" He ran his fingers through his hair, glancing over at Michaela. She nodded and Jasen sighed again. "Fine. We'll be there soon."

The headlights panned the brown sign for Stanton Cove Park, and Michaela shifted in the passenger seat. As Jasen passed the park's entry, Michaela sighed.

"What's wrong?" he asked.

Michaela's gaze slid toward him but stopped at the steering wheel. She leaned forward and swallowed. "Did Nellie talk to you?"

Jasen clenched the wheel then relaxed. He blew a breath out as he turned the car onto a road out of Fortuna. "She did." He hoped his clipped answer would nip the topic short.

"She talked to me too. What did you think of her theory?" Michaela tugged her shoulder belt.

"Which one?" Jasen said, sneaking a glance.

"That Dee is alive," she said softly. Michaela faced the window.

"I don't believe it. Do you?"

Silence eroded Jasen's nerves. "How can you believe her? Especially after what Nellie published about you in the Forum."

Michaela twisted toward him. "Because of the overwhelming evidence. I've seen the photograph. I know the magazine."

Jasen shook his head. "It's weak."

"And she was married twice or three times."

"You were married before too," Jasen frowned.

"Yes I was, but I got a divorce and didn't fake my death."

"I still don't buy it."

Michaela pursed her lips then said, "I slept with you. Can you imagine how I felt when I found out your wife might be living?"

Jasen shook his head, refusing to look at her.

"I committed adultery and felt guilty. Of course, I didn't tell Nellie we'd made love, but when she started researching Dee's lack of divorce records, I can honestly say I was relieved."

"I guess I would be too," Jasen said. "But she's dead. You don't have to worry about her coming back."

"I think she's alive, and I believe her parents know it." Michaela leaned closer and placed her hand on his thigh. "I have an idea. I want to set a trap for Dee to expose herself."

"How?"

"Using the biotch and Jerry to lure Dee out," Michaela said with a wicked smile.

Her twisted lips and the twinkle in her eyes made him pause. "You have a plan."

"Oh yeah," Michaela giggled. "I'll need to stay at your house for the weekend, maybe longer. Are you okay with that?" Her brows rose as she fingered his zipper again.

"Maybe," he said.

"How can I convince you?" she said, breathing on his neck.

"I think I need therapy," he said. She unzipped his pants. "Tonight. Not now."

"That's a shame," she pouted.

"I know, but we're here." Jasen turned onto the street. He adjusted himself then turned off the car. "I can't go in there with a boner." He stared at his tent.

"Just think of Sally naked," Michaela said, jumping out of the car.

"That'll do it," Jasen mumbled and grimaced as he pushed open the door.

Jasen took her hand as they climbed up the rickety porch. "Will you tell me your plan on the way home?"

She smirked. "In detail, and if you approve, I will therapy the hell out of you."

Jasen smiled at the promise. Although he knew it wouldn't be hell, it would be heaven.

# CHAPTER 35

## *Michaela*

MICHAELA STARED INTO THE DARK while Jasen dozed next to her. Her blood raced thinking of his hands and lips loving her. She flipped the quilt down to her waist, wishing the night air to cool her.

Anger, mixed with a smidgen of guilt, gnawed, keeping sleep at bay. She turned away from Jasen and picked up her phone. It was 3:24 AM.

The thankless trip out to Jasen's in-law's trailer park replayed in her mind. Sally Mander was a piece of work, demanding Jasen attend to her and Jerry's every whim. Guilt-ridden, Jasen usually acquiesced.

Over a New Year's luncheon with Kim and Nellie, an ill-conceived plan formed from idle chatter. When the opportunity had come, Michaela had agreed to go, interrupting her and Jasen's love-session for the impromptu insect-spray-shopping spree.

At the Mander's, the oily smell of fried food and cigarette smoke permeated the air. Jasen and Jerry had gone to work spraying the perimeter of the living room. Michaela had watched the men, gleeful Sally had been missing.

All too soon, Sally had stepped from the hall wearing a faded blue housecoat and curlers covered by a purple and olive plaid scarf. Her fuchsia lipstick had rubbed off onto her front tooth. Sally had waddled to the kitchen and poured herself a glass of the cheap liquor. When offered a plastic cup, Michaela vehemently shook her head, earning a guffaw from Sally. Lighting a cigarette, she motioned to the kitchen table, and Michaela had joined her.

"I hate bugs," Sally said, blowing smoke.

The kitchen had crumbs of food everywhere. Bug heaven.

"Especially the kind that bite." Michaela kept her smile hidden.

Jasen and Jerry had continued to the bedrooms.

While Sally recalled—in detail—the bug sightings and Jerry's feeble attempts to exterminate them, Michaela waited for the opportunity to set the trap. It came when Sally mentioned Dee's dislike of spiders.

"Speaking of Dee, did you know Jasen has kept her room exactly the same?" Before Sally started on pageant stories, Michaela had continued, "Nothing has changed. Her clothes are all there. Her makeup and jewelry too. He hasn't been in there since... You know. When he opened the door—Ack! You should have seen the dust swirl." Michaela had shivered.

Kim would have applauded Michaela's acting skills.

"Anyway. There's a small, velvet jewelry box on the dresser. I thought it might be her wedding ring but, of course, she would've been wearing it. Jasen said it was a custom piece he had made for an anniversary gift. He showed it to me. It was exquisite and looked *very* expensive with *loads* of diamonds."

Sally stared at her, enthralled. Mirth percolated under Michaela's poker face.

"It's sad, but I've encouraged him to donate her clothes to a women's center. The jewelry, too."

"Why?" Sally asked, lighting a new cigarette.

"It's not good for his allergies. Once the stuff is donated, then he can clean out the dust. And maybe get on with his life."

Sally had nodded, but she stared off as if she contemplated which numbers she'd pick for the lottery. She'd asked Michaela detailed questions about the location of the box. Michaela had cautioned Sally not to say anything to Jasen as to not upset him.

Michaela flopped onto her back and rubbed dry eyes. She'd tricked Sally, stretching the truth about the jewelry box on the dresser.

Michaela, Nellie, and Kim had theorized mentioning expensive baubles destined to belong to Dee would prompt Sally to call her daughter. Trying to flush Dee out of hiding had been Nellie's idea. Theoretically, if Dee still lived she could have the keys to Jasen's house. Michaela eventually agreed to help because exposing Dee's scam would help Jasen and also protect others from her ploys.

Michaela's jaw ached. She released the corner of the quilt she'd fisted and sat up. On the floor, she picked up the first thing her foot kicked. It was Jasen's T-shirt. She slipped it over her head, then took her phone and used the dim light to pad toward the hall.

Michaela paused at the door, straining her hearing. A creak. She twisted the doorknob and pulled the door open a crack. Another noise came from the end of the hallway. The porch light illuminated the stairwell enough to spot a shadow creeping along the wall.

She should wake Jasen or frighten the intruder by turning on the light, but her heart had turned to ice and her feet refused to move.

A head peered down the hallway, but Michaela remained unnoticed in the dark. She wrinkled her nose at the potent scent of musky perfume. A slender form stepped into view. Something reflected near the carpet, catching Michaela's attention. Leave it to Dee to break in wearing bedazzled high heels. Light, long hair cascaded over her dark clothes. She stalked toward the spare room.

Michaela held her breath. She could spring out, take a picture, and scare the crap out of Dee, exposing her, or she could wait to see if Dee took the bait.

Michaela began recording.

Dee paused outside her room. She twisted the knob then froze when it popped. After a moment, she pushed the door, taking hesitant steps Dee disappeared inside. A dim light illuminated the sliver under the door.

Dee coughed then muttered. Michaela bit her tongue to keep from laughing. The light clicked off. It seemed like forever. Was Dee asthmatic?

The knob rattled as Dee once more handled it. She pulled the door open only enough to escape then closed it again.

It was the moment to act, but Michaela couldn't move. There was more at stake. A plan.

The intruder headed toward the stairwell but gave a fleeting glance down the hallway. Michaela shifted her feet, and the floor squeaked. Dee's brows rose, and she fled down the stairs. The front door latched.

Was Dee gone or waiting to confront Jasen? Michaela tiptoed toward the steps and peered down them. The front door was closed, and everything appeared in its place. Michaela turned around and entered Jasen's bedroom once more. She locked the door and returned to the bed, her heart pounding in her ears.

Michaela laid awake, waiting for Jasen to stir. As the sun crested the eastern horizon, he shifted beside her.

"Good morning," he said sleepily. His erection pressed against her thigh as he nuzzled her neck. He caressed her hip, promising pleasure.

She bit her lip. When she didn't return his affection, he pulled away and inspected her. "What's wrong?"

Michaela sighed. "Dee came last night," she whispered.

Jasen threw the blanket back and sat up. He rubbed his face.

His naked torso seized her attention. The toned muscle moved under his tanned skin as if in a harmonious symphony.

"I can't believe it," Jasen groaned. He studied Michaela, noticing his shirt.

"I wouldn't lie," she said, pushing the covers away and putting her feet on the ground.

"I know." Jasen stood and stretched. "It's just surreal." He slipped on his boxers and sweatpants.

"We will have proof now," Michaela said. "You'll see."

Jasen nodded, staring at the floor. The evidence would expunge his doubt. Michaela pressed her lips together and strode to the door.

"Come on," she said, gesturing for him to follow. He slunk to her side. She twisted the handle but stopped him from entering the hallway. "Look," she said, pointing to the floor.

"What the hell?" Jasen stepped into the narrow space, careful not to step in the white splotches on the floor. "Is this what you needed the baby powder for?"

"Yes." Michaela grinned and stepped over the trail of triangles and dots. "I can't believe she wore heels to break in."

"Dee would've worn heels mountain climbing. I'll have to take your word on the mess," Jasen said, studying the marks on the carpet.

Michaela shook her head. "What's it going to take to convince you, Jasen?" She opened the spare room but didn't step inside. She glanced at the dusty, powdered floor and the mess of steps everywhere.

"Don't worry. I'll clean it." Michaela couldn't help the wide smile that grew. She pointed to the dresser. A dust-free square remained where the box had been. "Holy hoodwinks! She took it."

Michaela punched her fist in the air. "Yes!" She danced into the hall then to his room. She jumped on the bed and kicked her feet in the air.

Jasen watched with a twinkle in his eye and a smirk. He held any questions, but she couldn't start on the explanations until she documented the evidence. She snapped pictures with her phone. Giddiness threatened to erupt as she hopped from room to room.

Jasen followed her downstairs. Michaela turned on the coffeemaker while Jasen retrieved clean cups from the cabinet. "So Nellie gave me a necklace to put in that box I told you about."

"That's what I saw her give you at the meeting," Jasen rubbed his chin.

Michaela glanced up at him. "You were watching me?"

Jasen closed the space between them. His hazel gaze touched her soul, and she found it hard to breathe. He moved a curl off her forehead and tucked it behind her ear. His fingers sliding over her skin gave her goosebumps. "Yes ma'am, I did." He stooped and kissed her forehead.

Forgetting caffeine, she wrapped her arms around his waist and sighed against him.

"What about the necklace?" he asked as he nuzzled her hair.

Michaela sighed again. "I didn't know when I would get over to the Mander's, but the biotch made it easy. I had to bait Sally, hoping she'd contact Dee."

"And the necklace was the bait?"

Michaela pulled away, brewing a mug for him then one for herself. They sat at the kitchenette and sipped coffee. She stared into the dark liquid. "I don't know why we thought of the idea. I guess Nellie has done something similar before."

Jasen crossed his arms and leaned back.

"Do you know those GPS key finders?" Michaela asked. Jasen nodded, and she continued, "Well, at the center of the necklace is one of those locators."

"What?" Jasen frowned. "Don't you need more of those things to triangulate the location?"

"Yes. Nellie and I have one. Kim has one at the coffee shop. Nellie also keeps them in her car and in her office at the Forum." Michaela shrugged. "Dee might toss it if she recognizes the tech."

Michaela scrolled through the pictures on her phone to show Jasen the necklace. She zoomed in on the hot glued mess of rhinestones and gold wire. Nellie's jewelry-making friend had done a decent job. It felt the right weight around the neck, and a few small blue stones, supposed to be laboratory made sapphires, balanced the faux diamonds.

A smile crept to his face. "That's gaudy enough to be her style. Big and flashy, that's Dee."

Michaela studied Jasen's face. He did not deserve the way Dee treated him. She reached her hand across the table and took his. His long fingers curled around hers. His penetrating gaze melted her heart, and Michaela decided Dee would never hurt Jasen again.

# CHAPTER 36

## *Michaela*

MICHAELA PARKED AT THE END of the lot in the last empty spot. She jogged toward the crowd gathering around the Stanton Cove Park sign. Desire Hardmann raised her hand in greeting. The elderly woman wore an eighties-era neon pink jumpsuit and white sneakers.

Kim tapped Michaela's shoulder. With her long black hair in pigtails on the side of her head, T-shirt, and short-shorts, Kim appeared ready to cheer on the Fire Ants. "So Mr. Hottie McHot is in a book club?" she giggled. "Lucky he had a meeting today, or I'd be searching for the ghost without you."

"I'm glad we could tear you away from our hunk of a mayor," Desire said, nudging Michaela. "I don't blame you one bit. If he had any interest in me, I'd keep him in the bedroom until we starved to death. From food, mind you."

Michaela covered her mouth to staunch a giggle. "I have to let him eat to keep his energy up."

A smile broke out on Desire's fuchsia lips. "That's my girl."

Michaela's face flamed hot, and she tried to focus on Ben Moore, who had jumped onto a boulder. He spoke into a megaphone, "Thank you for joining us on this crisp morning. Please keep warm." In a squad coat, wool hat, and gloves, Ben appeared ready to face the frozen tundra.

Michaela smiled. The temperature was warm compared to Ohio. She'd brought a lightweight jacket in case her bare arms got the chills in the cliff's shadow.

"We will search the park in groups. Do not go on your own. Group leaders will contact me if they hear or see anything." Ben continued on, but

Michaela glanced around spotting Nellie and B.J. near his truck.

Nellie poked B.J. in his chest as her mouth moved nonstop. Stoic, B.J. crossed his arms, wearing a patronizing smirk. Nellie threw her arms up and spun. B.J. stepped toward her, but she twirled again only to bounce off his chest and fall onto her rear. She blinked up at him. He helped Nellie to her feet then attempted to dust off her bottom. She smacked B.J.'s hand away and started yelling again.

"Feel the sexual tension between those two," Kim said, giggling. Michaela heard the squawking but couldn't make out the words.

"Hey, you two. B.J. Nellie," Ben said through the loudspeaker, "Cut it out. We can't hear ourselves think."

Nellie and B.J. stared, owl-eyed. Nellie placed her hands on her hips, her face bright red. Wearing a sheepish grin, B.J. crossed his arms again.

"Okay, crew," Ben said, catching the group's attention once more. "Ms. Hardmann has offered a box of donuts to the group who finds the ghost."

Michaela listened to Ben but watched as Nellie shoved an envelope toward B.J. then hurried away before he could give it back. He shook his head and walked toward his truck.

Nellie caught up to Michaela, rubbing her hands. "What have I missed?"

Michaela glanced at Kim. "Everything."

Nellie laughed and raised her hand. "Ben, what do you expect we'll find?"

Ben pursed his lips before replying, "We won't know until we look."

"Dead bodies?" Nellie asked, tilting her head. The crowd murmured.

"Most likely not," Ben said, rubbing his forehead.

"But possible?" she pressed.

"Anything is possible, but it's not probable." Ben pointed to a man in the front. "Do you have a list of the leaders?"

"Thank you, Officer Moore," Nellie mumbled as she grinned and texted something on her phone.

"You don't want to find a body, do you?" Kim asked.

Nellie snapped a few pictures of the crowd. She grimaced. "Ew. No way. That would be totally gross." She shifted, facing Kim and Michaela. "Maybe. Yes, it would be gross but make a great story."

Michaela shook her head.

"Speaking of stories," Nellie said, linking her elbow with Michaela's. "Tell us about last night's visitor."

Kim gasped and leaned in. "What the hell? Dee came and you didn't call your best friend?"

"It was three in the morning," Michaela said, rolling her eyes.

"Okay. Thanks for not calling your best friend," Kim said.

Michaela yawned, and the group filtered closer to the volunteers who'd set up the search.

Ben glanced at a clipboard then at the three women. "Nellie, you can join the group over there with Walter. Mic—"

"No. I'm staying with Michaela and her friend, Kim." Nellie cocked her head and glared, daring Ben to argue.

Ben swung his gaze to Michaela. "I think she wants to needle me until I spill the list of authors coming to the Fortuna author event," Michaela said.

Nellie's head snapped around, making her blond curls bounce. "Wait, there are more?"

Michaela winked at Ben before turning away and heading toward the trail where Kim waited. Nellie scurried after her.

Michaela led Nellie, Kim, and three other Fortuna residents to the fork in the trail where she first heard the ghost. "I have a video of my search," she said. "You have to listen close, because I'm running through brush and over gravel."

"Can you play it?" asked a teen named Gabe Barnes.

"I'd like to hear it too," Gabe's sister Tori said. The young lady was nearly as tall as her brother.

Michaela adjusted the volume on her phone and played the video. Toward the end the moan became clearer. "This narrow trail is the one I followed," Michaela said, pointing.

The group leader, the teens' father Bridger, stepped toward the passage. "Let's go," he said, motioning the group to follow.

The kids followed their father single file. Nellie clicked pictures of the family disappearing from view.

"We better follow," Kim said. "I want those donuts."

Michaela giggled. "Why don't we trap the ghost?"

Nellie jerked her head up with an evil sneer. "Why don't we."

"I'll tell you why," Kim started. "How many acres is this park?"

"A bazillion and two," Nellie said, rubbing her arm where a stick scratched her.

"Right. I don't think you'd find enough baby powder to sprinkle on the ground," Kim said. "By the way, brilliant idea, Mick."

"How did you talk Jasen into it? He was adamant Dee was dead," Nellie said.

"The Manders," Michaela said, laughing. "If I had to go back there, he had to listen to our scheme. Luckily, he gave me the benefit of the doubt. But thanks to your diligent research, Nellie, I think he was softened up."

"I'm glad it helped," Nellie said.

"I can't believe he married her," Kim said. "The family is money-grubbing scam artists."

Kim had verbalized Michaela's thought. She sighed.

"Dee is blond, pretty, and has big boobs; that's what attracts men," Nellie said.

"I'm screwed," Kim said, holding strands of her raven black hair.

"I don't think Jasen is that shallow, but I didn't know him back then," Michaela said.

"You're right, Michaela. Jasen isn't shallow, but I'm guessing Dee can play the heart strings like Brad Paisley can play guitar," Nellie said.

Bridger stopped and raised his hand. The group gathered behind him. "Did you hear that?"

The teens tilted their heads, listening. Nellie tapped her phone and raised it, posed to capture anything.

"Oh," a voice moaned.

"Son of a gun," Bridger said.

"It sounds like people—" Gabe started.

"Yes," Bridger said. He texted the volunteer headquarters with their location.

"It's exactly like Michaela's recording." Nellie pointed out. "Hopefully, there will be other instances of the sound. It repeated quite a few times. Be ready to move when it starts."

"Other groups have heard it too," Bridger said.

"We have to find it first," Kim said. "I want those donuts."

Silence fell. Michaela studied the underbrush, then the trees, trying to recall details of the evening she'd found the ghost.

"Oh."

"This way," Gabe said, taking off between two trees. Tori kept on his heels.

"We are closer," Bridger huffed, sucking a deep breath before texting HQ.

Michaela pushed through the brambles. "Look! There's a path here."

"Good job, Mick," Kim said. "I smell victory."

"I hope there isn't a mattress up here," Michaela uttered to her friends.

"Whoever or whatever it is, I'm ready," Nellie said, raising her phone. "Anything will make a great picture for the Forum."

Once more, "Oh" echoed through the forest. The group hurried down the path past a giant live oak. Gabe stopped and Tori bumped into him. "It's behind us now."

They turned around and hurried back.

"It's got to be here," Kim said. "It sound like the tree is getting it on."

Michaela rounded the trunk with Nellie in her shadow. "What the...?"

"What is that?" Nellie said, taking a photo of a brown box.

"A wire leads up to that branch." Gabe pointed. "There's a speaker up there."

"Okay. This might be it," Bridger said.

"We'll have to wait until it happens again to be one hundred percent sure," Michaela said.

Bridger informed the others then stood back, studying the mechanism. "Something else is up there. Gabe do you think you can climb up to the branch?"

Gabe took a running jump and grabbed the limb. Hooking his leg around, he hoisted himself on top. He rubbed his hands, removing debris. "Wow."

"Here, take a picture with my phone," Nellie said, tossing her cell at Gabe.

He snapped a few pictures then dropped it back to Nellie. Kim and Michaela leaned close as Nellie examined the photos. She zoomed in.

"Is that a solar panel?" Michaela asked, scrunching her eyes to get a better look.

"That's what it looks like," Nellie said.

"Check this out," Tori said, on her knees next to the box. "There's a message."

"We should have known," Bridger said, kneeling next to his daughter.

Nellie clicked another picture then started recording. "We are out in the middle of Stanton Cove Park searching for the canyon ghost, who is reportedly the ghost of Fortuna's own mayor Jasen DeLay's deceased wife. I'm with residents of Fortuna." Nellie focused briefly on each of the group, introducing them. "Michaela experienced this strange noise before while jogging. We followed the path she took on that fateful evening and have encountered the same moaning. Just now, we have found a message and what we hope is the source of all the hubbub."

Nellie aimed her phone toward the branch. "Up there, what you see is a speaker with a solar panel. A wire leads along the branch..." Gabe waved as she panned over him, "down the live oak's trunk to this small brown box. It's metal, like a toolbox. There's a message from an old Fortuna friend I think you should see."

Nellie stepped closer and lined up the messy letters.

"OH." The sound radiated above them.

Nellie whirled. Aiming the phone at the branch, she walked under it to the other side.

Michaela glanced at Kim, who held her hands over her mouth. Once the recording ended, Nellie pointed to the box. "Can you read it for us, Michaela?"

"I'll try," she giggled. Michaela kneeled and leaned over the box. She glanced up at Nellie, who gave her a thumbs up. She inhaled and released it. "Dear Fortuna, No ghost-tess, just the prankster with the mostess. I hope you've enjoyed what you've found. My favorite bedroom (porno) sound." She glanced up at the group and joined them in laughter.

"Now that's a story," Kim said, helping Michaela to her feet. "Donuts for the win! I see why you like this town, Mick," she giggled then nudged her.

"I'm glad you're here with me," Michaela hugged her friend. "That's one mystery solved. Now we have to expose Dee to solve the other."

# CHAPTER 37

## *Jasen*

JASEN WALKED INTO THE A Hole in One donut shop, lifting a hand in greeting to the men of his book club. After ordering, he took his large coffee and a box of donut holes to share to the table. He slid into the hard, bright-orange booth next to Parker.

"How's it going?" Canon asked through a mouthful of food.

"Good," Jasen said with a smirk.

"Oh, ho!" B.J. leaned across the table pointing. "You're happy, and it's not because of romance books."

Jasen's face heated, and he popped a donut hole into his mouth, not answering.

"Not romance books," Brad said, "just romance."

"He's getting some nooky," Forrest laughed.

"Don't let them bother you," Parker said, slapping Jasen on the back. "They're jealous."

Brad coughed then smoothed his mustache. He placed a book on the table. "So, sci-fi books are interesting."

"Smooth switch," Canon said, offering Brad his knuckles. Nodding, Brad fist bumped him.

"Actually, I enjoyed the world building," B.J. said.

"Did Lisa enjoy the scenes?" Forrest asked Parker.

"Did Ivy?" Parker shot back.

Forrest morphed to a shade of crimson, and the men laughed.

"With all the weird alien probing, I'm okay moving on to something new." Jasen took a sip of his hot drink.

"Have you completed your dare?" B.J. asked Jasen.

"Have you?" Jasen threw back. B.J. scowled and crossed his arms.

"How about something with magic," Brad suggested, putting a few more books on the table.

"That's cool with me," Jasen said.

"Wanting to use your magic wand?" Canon asked Jasen, wiggling his brows.

"How would you know it's magic?" B.J. teased Canon. The young firefighter turned as red as Fortuna engine number forty-three.

"Duh," Forrest said, rolling his eyes. "All ding-dongs are magical."

"Ding-dongs?" B.J. laughed, and Canon snickered.

"Ding-dongs, wieners, schlongs, wankers—whatever. They're all magic," Forrest said, searching the donut hole box. He grinned, finding a chocolate ball of sugary goodness.

"I like this conversation," Desire said, pausing beside the table and rubbing her hands together. Jasen pushed the box toward her and she peered inside. "Forrest is right. Do you know how a one-eyed wonder worm and a genie lamp are the same?" She glanced at the book club men, winking at Brad.

Parker nudged Jasen and whispered, "I don't think I want to know."

Canon's brows knit together. "No. How?"

"You rub them a few times and something will shoot out." Desire threw her head back, cackling like a witch.

Brad covered his face and groaned. Canon nodded and laughed. B.J. met Jasen's eyes and shook his head.

Desire moved on and left the book club to pick the new subgenre. Jasen grabbed the book closest to him and flipped it. The blurb sounded interesting. He'd seen the author's name somewhere recently.

"Oh my gosh," Jasen said, nearly tipping his cup when he jumped up. "This author will be at the author event."

"How do you know?" Forrest asked.

Jasen sighed and handed the book to Parker. "Don't you ever check the Fortuna website or any of the other social media?"

"But the committee just approved the event," Canon said.

"The event has its own page with the author list and volunteer opportunities. Our book club should volunteer," Parker suggested.

B.J. handed his phone to Forrest. "Look here. See the list of authors?"

Forrest scrolled, his eyes widening as he read name after name. "Whoa. That's a crazy long list. Does Michaela have enough help?"

"No. She's appealing to Nockerville civic and church groups," Jasen said, rubbing his chin.

"She's the bomb," Parker said. "I can't believe Michaela was able to make it happen in such a short time."

"You've got a good one," Brad said, meeting Jasen's eyes.

Warmth filled Jasen's chest, and he smiled. Now if he could only convince Michaela she was his.

Parker pointed to Brad's phone. "Here's something we can help with, what do you think?"

Forrest took it and pulled the screen to his face, then burst out laughing. B.J. glanced closer. "You've got to be kidding me. This can't be on the list for volunteering."

B.J. passed the phone to Canon. "No freaking way." He handed Brad the phone then shrugged. "Let's face it—I bet most men in this town have wings."

Parker nodded.

"Well, I've got to head out. It's time to work on my honey-do-list," Forrest said as he scooted to the end of the booth.

"Yeah, me too." Parker stood and they exited together.

"Now it's just us single guys," Canon said, staring out the window with a frown.

B.J. fished in his pocket and pulled out an envelope. "Here," he said, handing it to Jasen.

Jasen opened it. He found two slips of paper and read the small print. "What the—?" He glanced up at his friend, who grinned and shrugged.

"I have connections." B.J.'s face reddened.

"Thank you," Jasen uttered.

B.J. tapped the tickets, knocking on the table. "This is your in for the dare."

Canon smirked. "You had a cowboy. What else, Jasen?"

The temperature of the room rose, and Jasen stared into his cup.

B.J. nudged Canon. "He had a fantasy in a theater."

"Wow." Canon glanced at the tickets. "An illusionist. That's cool. Definitely fantasy, since they morph reality. You just have to wear chaps."

"I'm sure Michaela will appreciate the leather," B.J. said, laughing at Jasen's glare.

Jasen glanced at the date. He and Michaela had already set the day aside for a date to celebrate her time as Fortuna's municipal liaison coming to an end. But was an illusionist too close to a magician? He'd never make her relive her past.

One by one the others left, leaving Jasen to his spiraling thoughts.

# CHAPTER 38

## *Jasen*

JASEN WALKED TO MICHAELA'S DOOR and knocked. He tapped his foot on the concrete step. The light flicked off inside. Michaela opened the door and jumped into his arms.

"I've missed you," she said.

He chuckled as he buried his nose into her lily scented waves. "You only saw me a few hours ago."

"Not soon enough," she murmured against him.

"Come on," he said, leading her to the car. "We are going to the theater."

"Oh? I thought tonight's performance was sold out?" she asked.

"It pays to be mayor. I have connections," Jasen said, turning over the engine.

"Yeah, B.J. told me about it." She snickered at his mock-affronted gasp.

"Did he tell you about the show?" Jasen worried she wouldn't be interested, given her history.

"No. He didn't want to ruin the surprise, and I didn't look it up either." She relaxed back into the seat. Her black dress molded to her body in all the right places.

As they pulled into the restaurant parking lot, he said, "The main act features a contortionist group of acrobats."

"That sounds great," she said.

He held the restaurant door open, and Michaela slipped through. The hostess led them to a table and a server with a black tie took their drink order.

Over the menu, Jasen said, "It's the opening act you might not want to see. If that's the case, we can skip it totally or arrive fashionably late."

"Now I'm curious. What's the act?" she said, studying him.

"It's an illusionist." Jasen held his breath.

"As long as he's not the jerk who stole my mom, we're good," she said.

Jasen exhaled and smiled. "He's not. I looked him up online. He's young and uses all kinds of effects. The clips of his shows are awesome."

"How young?" Michaela asked with raised brows.

"Younger than us."

"Really? Good." She relaxed, closing her menu. "So what's with the cowboy hat?"

After they ordered, he took her hand. "I have a confession to make."

Her thumb swirled a pattern on the back of his hand. The sensation sent shivers up his arm. Her gaze steadied on his eyes. Jasen sighed and continued. "Before you moved here, the book club guys and I went camping. B.J. dared—"

"Oh boy," Michaela smirked, leaning closer. "This is gonna be good."

Jasen rubbed his chin. "He dared us to act out a character, setting, and trope with a date. It posed a problem with the four of us who weren't in a relationship. But then—"

"I came along," Michaela giggled. She tucked a wave behind her ear. "And the cowboy hat is part of the dare?"

"Cowboy is my character. I don't usually wear hats," he said.

"And the rest of the dare...?"

"A fantasy in the theater," Jasen shrugged. "The book club guys want proof I'm actually following through with it."

"Is that why you wanted to see the illusionist?" she frowned.

Jasen's gut ached as if she'd punched him. "No, of course not. He just happened to be the entertainer at the theater tonight. I don't care a rat's ass about the dare. If you don't want to go, we won't go."

"Okay." Michaela glanced at the tablecloth. After a moment, her head shifted, sending her waves cascading over her shoulder. "What happens if you don't follow through with the dare?"

Jasen's mouth fell open. The book club had never specified the consequences for ditching a dare. "I don't know."

Michaela's phone vibrated, and she glanced at a text. "I'm sorry I need to answer this." While she texted, Jasen pulled out his phone and sent Michaela's question to the Fortuna Dare Society's group chat. Suddenly, the chat blew up as the men responded. He gasped as he read their ideas.

"What's wrong?" Michaela asked, her brow knit with concern.

"It's the book club. They're telling me what will happen if I don't complete the dare." Jasen passed her the phone so she could read the responses.

Michaela covered her mouth, but it didn't stop the giggles. "B.J. says if you don't complete it you'll be a lonely, old geezer. Canon wants you to take Desire on a date as punishment." Michaela slapped the table top, jostling the candle and earning stares from the other patrons. "Parker's idea is priceless."

"No, Michaela. I will not run through Stanton Cove Park naked," Jasen said, shaking his head and crossing his arms.

"That's a shame. Parker wants competition." Michaela giggled. handing him the phone.

As Jasen read the new messages, his face heated. He groaned and turned off his phone, then stuffed it into his back pocket.

Jasen held Michaela's elbow as they entered the plush carpeted theater lobby. Several gold frames advertised upcoming events. Jasen retrieved their tickets from his breast coat pocket and handed them to the usher.

Michaela smiled until she glanced over Jasen's shoulder to a poster. "The Great Farquhar? You've got to be kidding me," she mumbled. She glanced at her watch then uttered, "I've got time."

Michaela burst through into the auditorium and stormed down the aisle.

"Miss," the usher called. Michaela didn't slow.

Jasen grabbed the ticket stubs from his hand. "Sorry," he said, hurrying after her. He nodded to a frowning couple as he rushed passed. Michaela had made it to the stage and climbed side steps. She caught his eye and disappeared behind the curtain. He hopped up the stairs and followed her.

She'd paused backstage and stared up into the darkness where people worked.

"What are you doing?" Jasen asked.

Michaela shook her head, her waves flying. "Just be with me. There's something I need to do." Her large, green eyes implored him.

Jasen took her hand. "I'm with you. Let's go."

A faint smile fluttered over her lips, and she squeezed his hand. She continued down the dark hall toward the fitting rooms. Stage crew darted about, passing them without a word.

She pulled him to a stop in front of a door with the name Farquhar on it. She inhaled deeply then raised a fist and knocked. A green-eyed young man opened the door. "Can I help you?" he asked.

"I need to speak to *the Great Farquhar*," her tone dripped sarcasm.

"That's me," he said, scanning Michaela from head to toe. He crossed his arms and leaned against the door frame.

"Right. And I'm a virgin," Michaela said as she shoved passed him into the room.

"Listen lady, I've got a show to do in a few minutes, and you're messing with my vibe," Farquhar shadowed Michaela to his dressing table.

Jasen stepped into the small brightly lit room.

Michaela spun. "You listen. I'm looking for the old bastard Thorston Farquhar who stole my mom away from me." Chest heaving, she stood with her hands on her hips. Jasen wanted to take her into his arms and hold her.

Mouth flopped open, the young man stepped closer. "No way."

Tears filled her eyes. "Where is he?"

Farquhar glanced at Jasen then took another step closer to Michaela. "You're looking for my dad. Look there." He pointed to a photo on his dressing mirror.

Michaela turned and studied the picture. A tall skinny man with a magician's top hat grinned next to a buxom woman in a sequined bodysuit. "That's my mother," she gasped.

"That's my mom too," Farquhar said, glancing over her shoulder at the old photo. He frowned. "My dad died two years ago."

Michaela fingered her mother's smiling face. "And Mom?"

"I don't know. She left me and Dad when I was five," he said. "It was just Dad and I until…"

"Michaela, you and your brother had similar childhoods," Jasen said in a soft voice.

"My," she swallowed, "brother?" Michaela stared at their reflection in the mirror. He had the same color wavy hair and same shape and color eyes. Even the bow shape of his mouth mirrored hers.

Farquhar's lips lifted in a shy smile. "You're Michaela. My father told me you were out there, but I never thought I'd meet you, sis."

Michaela faced him. She touched his face, and a tear escaped. He opened his arms, and she stepped in. They embraced, and Michaela began to weep.

Jasen waited near the room's entrance as the siblings talked, forgetting the show.

A tap sounded at the door, and a tech stuck his head in. "Fifteen minutes Mr. Farquhar."

"Gotcha. Thanks." He waved the man off.

"I guess we need to leave." Michaela held her hands.

"Not before introducing me to… my brother-in-law?" Farquhar offered his hand.

Michaela grinned but turned red. "This is Jasen. He's the mayor of Fortuna. Jasen, can you believe I have a brother?"

"Nice to meet you Jasen. I'm Thor."

Jasen took Thor's hand and shook. "Pleased to meet you. I'll give you a few minutes. Michaela, I'll wait for you in the hall." He nodded, leaving the room. Jasen heard Michaela say, "We don't have much time before the show, but I need your help."

# CHAPTER 39

## *Michaela*

MICHAELA'S MIND REELED. SHE LOWERED Herself into Thor's chair as he glanced at the mirror and smoothed his hair. When she'd stormed backstage, her hatred fueled her, but now her heart had shifted to... love? She had a little brother. Her cheeks hurt with the large smile.

"I'm sorry about Mom," Michaela said, knowing exactly what Thor had experienced.

"You can't help our mother being a bitch," Thor said, taking her hands in his.

"I don't know what's wrong with her," Michaela said, her eyes filling again.

"She's a gold digger/the-grass-is-greener-on-the-other-side-of-the-fence kind of person." He let go and opened the drawer, searching for something. "If she wouldn't have left, I wouldn't have been as close to my father."

Michaela nodded. "Same."

Thor glanced at her. "Is your dad still living?"

She nodded again. "He's a long-distance trucker, but he'd love to meet you."

Thor smiled wistfully. "I'd like that."

Michaela's phone chirped. She glanced at the screen and jumped up, heart racing. "Oh, my gosh."

"Is everything okay?" Thor asked.

She blinked. "I need your help."

A knock sounded, and the door opened. "Mr. Farquhar time to move. You're on in five," a young guy with a headset said. Jasen waited outside the room, and Michaela met his gaze.

169

"Walk with me," Thor said as he made his way toward the stage. "What's going on?"

Michaela explained her relationship with Jasen, and the problems with Nellie and Dee. She expressed her happiness over their date and the goofiness of the dare.

Jasen followed them and the tech to the side stage and waited patiently while she hastily spoke with her brother.

"You love him, don't you?" Thor tilted his head toward Jasen.

"Yes, I do." Michaela glanced at Jasen and heated. "And I don't want him hurt by a gold digger like our mom."

"I understand."

As the tech fit Thor with an earpiece and mic, Michaela checked her phone again. Nellie had messaged her details. It seemed everything was aligning. She sighed and approached Jasen. When he opened his arms, she fell against him. Encircled by his strength and protection, she snuggled into his warmth. He kissed her forehead, and tingles shot down her spine.

Stagehands moved around them, fluttering the light-absorbing black curtains. Reluctant to surrender his embrace, she said, "Thor asked me to watch from backstage, but I didn't want to leave you. Let's grab our seats before he starts." She waved at Thor.

"Break a leg," Jasen said with a salute.

"Thanks, brother," Thor said with a wink. "See you shortly."

Fingers laced, Michaela and Jasen exited the stage area and made their way toward the lobby. "Thanks for coming with me," Michaela smiled. "What a ride."

"Are you okay?" he asked.

Michaela rubbed the place over her heart. "I think so. It's surreal. I can't believe I have a brother."

"Better find your seats," an older gentleman said, holding open the door to the theater.

"Let's go." Jasen offered his arm.

Michaela took it. The auditorium had filled, and a dull murmur of happy voices permeated the room. They advanced toward the front. Jasen stopped and let her in. Seated in the second row, she had a perfect view of center stage.

The lights dimmed and music played. Someone tapped Jasen on the shoulder. B.J. Johnson leaned between Jasen and Michaela. "Fancy meeting you here. I'd be much obliged if you could take that ten gallon tank off your head, so I can see." B.J. said, laughing at Jasen's shocked expression.

"Shh B.J.," Brad Davidson said, nudging him.

"Crap," Jasen mumbled. He sat his hat on his lap.

"Did you know he'd be here?" Michaela asked, leaning toward Jasen.

"No. The whole book club is in the row behind us," Jasen whispered.

"Making sure you follow through with your dare," Michaela giggled.

"I guess."

Michaela twisted and peeked behind Jasen. A young man grinned and nodded, elbowing a red-headed man with a beard. He smiled and finger waved. She giggled again.

"Ladies and gentlemen, welcome the world renowned illusionist the Great Farquhar." Cheers rose as the lights swirled around the room. On a giant screen, galaxies and stars flashed, then the solar system, zooming in on earth. The lights focused on a point in the middle of the stage. Smoke erupted from a small explosion. When the smoke cleared, Thor stood, arms raised, wearing a smirk.

Michaela's heart filled with pride as she watched Thor perform feat after feat. Disappearances or reappearing items wowed her. It had been decades since she'd seen a performance, and his skill amazed her.

A half hour into his show, Thor swept his arms wide. "For my next performance, I need a volunteer from the audience." He closed his eyes and rubbed his temples.

Michaela shifted forward and glanced toward the left aisle, where Nellie sat notepad poised next to a man who held a large black camera. Nellie caught her attention and nodded with an evil grin.

"My assistant is blonde. She's beautiful. She's elevated and—" Thor pulled a ticket out of thin air. "She's sitting in box B, seat three."

A spotlight shot to the box and a woman gasped. Dee stood, her hands covering her mouth. A gaudy bauble hung around her neck. An usher escorted her out of the box. A moment later she was led onto the stage. Her four-inch heels clicked on the wood.

Jasen gasped. "That's the necklace you showed me."

"Holy hell," B.J. uttered.

"Isn't that Jasen's wife?" the young man asked.

"It can't be," Brad said.

Michaela took Jasen's hand. He glanced at her with a pale face.

"So gorgeous, what's your name?" Thor asked.

Dee threw her head back, tossing her hair, and laughed that unforgettable donkey bray. "Mandy," she said, taking his offered hand.

"Son of a bitch," Jasen hissed. "Mandy is Dee's middle name."

B.J. leaned between them again. "You want me to go get her?"

Jasen opened his mouth, but Michaela interjected, "Just wait." She pointed down the row toward Nellie.

"This ought to be good," B.J. mused, sitting back.

"Have you heard about the laws of attraction?" Thor asked Dee. Her doe-in-the-headlights expression spoke volumes, but she nodded anyway. "For those who don't know, basically you focus on something... think about it, and it will come back to you."

He dramatically waved his hand to the right. "If you want to spread peace and goodwill to men, you think good thoughts and focus on bringing peace. Eventually your thoughts will become true." Displayed on the large screen behind him was a peace symbol formed from daisies. "Or if you're into fast cars and you desire a Ferrari F12 Berlinetta, you can use the power of your mind to visualize it into existence." A red sports car zoomed across the screen.

"So, my beauty, what are we going to think into reality?" Thor continued. "Could you end up on the cover of a romance novel? Will it be love?" A heart flashed shades red, to pink, then back to red.

Nellie clapped, and soon others, including Michaela cheered. She motioned to B.J., and he whistled.

Canon cupped his hands around his mouth and yelled, "Yeehaw love!"

"Very well," Thor said. Music rose and the lights flashed. A close up of Dee and Thor appeared on the screen. She placed a hand over her heart.

"Love it is," Thor stalked back and forth on the stage. "Think of your first crush. Let's be more specific. Close your eyes."

Dee closed her eyes, her face flushed and smiling, and she shifted. Thor moved her so she faced away from the crowd.

"Think about your high school love. The teen who took your breath away. Think about his name. Visualize his hair, his eyes, and his smile."

Thor held up a pair of headphones. "Mandy, I want you to wear these headphones. They'll help to concentrate by reducing noise but you'll be able to hear my voice." He slipped headphones over her ears.

Thor rubbed his temples again. "Row M seat fourteen."

A gentleman stood. An assistant walked him down to the stage.

"Nod if you can hear me, Mandy," Thor said. The camera angle changed, focusing on her face. She stood still. Thor repeated, "Nod if you can hear me, Mandy."

She nodded.

"Forget your first love. Envision your first exciting adult relationship. The sound of his voice. His body. Can you remember?"

"Oh yeah," she smiled.

"Very good." Thor turned toward the audience again. "Mandy, can you hear me?"

She stood still.

"Awesome," Thor trilled. "Row H seat three." Again a man was led toward the stage. He stood next to the first man. Both wore khaki pants and white dress shirts.

"Now, Mandy, think of the man who likes to follow rules. Envision his work, his home. Got it?"

Dee grinned and again nodded, her long hair swishing.

"Row B seat eleven," Thor called.

Jasen swallowed and turned toward Michaela. "I can't do this," he murmured.

B.J. clamped a hand on Jasen's shoulder. "Face that bitch," B.J. said quietly but firmly. Jasen stood and inched his way to the end of the row. Thor instructed Dee to recall others in her past, then called them to the stage including her date.

"That's one of the Nocker twins," B.J. said in Michaela's ear. He recorded the act with his phone. "Their family founded Nockerville and they are loaded."

Thor visited the first man. He had his ID ready. Thor held up the ID. Then handed it to the next man. "What does this say?"

"Michael Hunt," the row H man said.

"Mandy, who was your first love? What was his name?" Thor asked.

"Mike Hunt."

The audience clapped.

Thor took the second man's ID and passed it to Jasen.

"What does it read?"

"Barry Maple," Jasen said, frowning. He returned the license to its owner.

"Mandy, who was your first adult love?"

"Barry Maple," she replied.

Thor passed Jasen's license to the man on his left. "Jasen DeLay," he read.

"And Mandy, which man followed the rules," Thor asked.

"Jasen," Dee said.

"Did Nellie give you tickets?" Michaela whispered to B.J.

"The Forum bought a block of tickets. I asked her for some after she gave me Jasen's. The book club wanted to support Jasen on the dare. Of course, I'm glad I'm witnessing the take down of that fraudulent hussy." B.J. sneered. "How did you get Dee here?"

"Nellie found out where she was shacking up. She dropped the tickets in the mail with a note that Dee had won box seats to opening night," Michaela said. She bit her lip, hoping they'd done the right thing. Exposing the truth might hurt several people. Jasen included.

Thor continued until all the men had been named correctly. The audience murmured in awe, unaware of Nellie's meddling.

Thor removed the headphones. "Now, Mandy, are you ready to see what your thoughts have produced?" He dramatically waved his arms.

"Yes," she breathed.

The lights dimmed and the stars swirled on the screen then Dee's face appeared. "Mandy, open your eyes."

Thor turned her around and she faced her past. She gasped then screeched. Thor took her elbow, helping her remain standing. The men varied in appearance from calm to angry. Barry fumed, but the Nocker twin smiled as if he enjoyed being the final choice.

Jasen started to move toward stage left but the stagehand motioned for him to return. He stuffed his hands in his pockets and returned to Barry's side.

Thor took Dee's hand and led her to the front. He raised their hands and the audience clapped and hooted. They bowed. As far as the crowd knew the men on stage only had the names of Mandy's past loves, they were unaware that the participants were victims.

"He's going to kill you," B.J. said.

"Think so?" Michaela glanced at him. "I'll tell him it was your idea."

B.J. scowled and leaned away from her.

The camera man took pictures from the center aisle, and Nellie grinned as she continued to scribble notes.

"Thank you, ladies and gentlemen, you've been a wonderful audience. Give it up for our volunteers." Thor swiped his arm toward the men.

The volume of the theater increased as the house lights rose. B.J. got to his feet and whistled again. The others in the book club made noise as well. Michaela sunk into the velvety red cushioned seat. Her stomach churned. The relief she sought hadn't come.

She glanced at the stage. Jasen had pasted on his political smile and shook hands with the other men. After a moment, he turned his hazel gaze to her. Michaela desired to take him into her arms and never let him go.

# CHAPTER 40

## *Jasen*

JASEN UNCLENCHED HIS JAW, RESPONDING to Barry, Dee's second husband. "Today would have been our anniversary," he said.

"That sucks. Only seven months after she left me," Barry huffed, his forehead forming a V. "Boy, she works fast."

"There wasn't time for her to get a divorce," Jasen mused, glancing toward Michaela in the audience. She chewed on her bottom lip. He offered her a smile, hoping it appeared friendly.

The spotlights shined on the stage, heating Jasen. He rubbed his chin, wanting to disappear into the shadows.

"She's married to me," Mike said, puffing out his chest.

"You can have her," another man said. "She used me to get a nose job then took off with the surgeon." He crossed his arms.

Thor's assistant spoke animatedly, and he nodded. "All right, folks. We need to leave the stage so the next act can begin." He pointed toward stage left. "Miss Mandy there's a Texas Ranger who wants to ask you a few questions. Gentlemen, you are welcome to make a statement as well."

Dee stuck her nose in the air and poked Thor in the chest. "You are a horrible magic person. I can't believe I thought about letting you have this." She planted her hands on her chest then abruptly turned. Batting her lashes, she stomped toward the officer waiting in the shadows. Mike followed, trying to take her hand. Dee jerked away from his touch.

Jasen and the group of men accompanied an officer to a stuffy room. Each man gave a brief statement and contact information. Jasen folded his arms and leaned against the wall, closing his eyes. They had all been duped, but Jasen had been the only victim in Fortuna.

Whether by choice or accident, Dee had not overlapped areas where she fished until the charity ball.

Jasen rubbed his chest. He knew Dee had been guilty of greediness, but he hadn't suspected the scam. She hadn't desired a honeymoon cruise, but demanded it. Her spending on name brand clothes and fancy accessories regardless of how long he'd have to work to pay off the bills. The arguments when he'd set an allowance. All red flares. He shook his head. The flood must have been a lucky fluke for her. "How could someone who says they love you not care if you think they are dead? I grieved for her. And her parents let me believe it."

Jasen balled his fists. The Manders must have known Dee lived, and yet they had continued demanding Jasen take care of them. The subterfuge and betrayal hurt.

"That sucks," Barry replied. "I found a note saying she'd left me for another guy. At first, it upset me. I wondered what was wrong with me. But then I got pissed. Finally, I got over it and moved on. Now I have a wonderful woman who loves me and doesn't want me to springboard her to the next guy. I'm lucky."

Jasen nodded. Michaela's face flashed in his mind, and the ache lifted. Overcome with the desire to find Michaela, he placed his palms on the table. "Are we almost done here?"

Jasen shuffled down the hallway toward the lobby. He pushed open the door. The book club guys waited with Michaela, except Canon who posed with Thor in front of his life-sized poster.

Michaela spotted him first and stepped toward him but hesitated. Jasen moved, and suddenly he was burying his nose in her lily-scented waves. He hugged her against him, breathing deeply. She rubbed his back.

"Geez, Jasen. You're going to break her," B.J. muttered.

"Back off, B.J.," Michaela growled.

B.J. put his hands up in surrender and backed away.

Jasen began to chuckle. Michaela his protector. He nuzzled her neck, and she giggled, "It tickles."

Jasen pulled back to gaze into her deep green eyes. "You're awesome," he said.

Her eyes narrowed. "You deserve the best, that's all." She shrugged.

Jasen cupped her face. "I've got her."

Tears filled her eyes. "You're not mad at me?"

"Hell no," Jasen said. "You liberated me."

He dipped to kiss her. She opened for him with a moan. He plunged his hand into her silky hair. Everything fell away, and Michaela's passion threatened to consume him. He couldn't get enough. His heart raced, and her touch thrilled him.

"Get a room," Parker groused.

"Jealous?" Forrest asked.

"They don't have to get a room," B.J. said.

"You're a perv," Canon said with a laugh.

"Gross. That's my sister," Thor groaned.

Jasen broke the kiss. They touched foreheads, grinning.

"Uh oh," B.J. mumbled. "Here comes trouble."

Nellie sashayed toward the group with a triumphant smile. Michaela stiffened in Jasen's arms. He frowned and released Michaela.

"Thank you, Nellie, for exposing Dee as a fraud," Jasen said, taking her hand. "I'm free."

"You're welcome," Nellie said, blushing. "I couldn't have done it without Michaela's help."

"Michaela," Jasen said, facing her.

"Yes," Michaela said, then bit her lip.

"I love you." Jasen took both her hands and squeezed.

Her eyes sparkled with tears. "I love you too, Jasen."

"I consider this dare fulfilled," Brad said, walking away from them. Parker and Forrest trailed behind him.

"Wait up." Nellie scurried after the men. "What dare?"

"Oh, shit. Not a word," B.J. said, pointing at Canon.

"Hey, Nellie, you gotta hear B.J.'s idea," Canon laughed, dodging B.J.'s swing.

"So it's a crappy idea," Nellie said with her hands on her hips.

Forrest walked into Parker, who hissed to a stop, staring at B.J. Even Brad turned to watch the interaction.

"What do you have against happily ever after?" B.J. countered, stepping into her space and glaring at her upturned face. Her cheeks pinked and she tilted her head, making her curls bob.

"Do you feel the sexual tension?" Michaela asked Jasen softly but loud enough for the book club to overhear.

Parker burst out laughing and the others joined in. Red as a Fortuna fire ant, B.J. stepped back with a scowl. Nellie pressed her lips in a line and slanted her head the other way.

"Most definitely," Jasen said. "Prince Charming needs to work on his dare."

Parker doubled over, wiping tears as B.J. sputtered. Jasen didn't wait for him to find his voice and led Michaela to the exit.

"See you tomorrow," Michaela said, waving at Thor.

Once in the car, she laid her head on Jasen's shoulder. A hint of lily filled the air. He sighed and took her hand.

"Are you really okay?" she asked.

He kept quiet until she glanced into his eyes. "Jasen, are you all right?"

Jasen smirked, rubbing his chin. "I think I need therapy."

"That can be arranged," Michaela giggled, fingering his zipper.

# EPILOGUE

## *Michaela*

LISA FORD SCURRIED OVER, GLANCING up from her clipboard long enough to avoid a collision with Michaela and Jessie Barnes. "Paige Turner's assistant is here." Lisa flipped the paper up. "I can't find her table number."

Michaela breathed through her teeth and closed her eyes. Taking a deep breath, she faced Lisa. "Who did you talk to?"

Lisa pointed toward a short, balding man. Michaela shook her head. "That's Paul Ennis. He gets table number four."

Lisa's eyes scrunched as she scoured the page. "Oh." She turned the paper sideways. "P. Ennis! Found it."

"Paul's pseudonym is Paige Turner," Jessie said with a wink.

"Oh." Lisa blinked. "Oooh." She hurried back to Paul with a bright smile. "Right this way, sir. I love your books. Especially the one with the interior decorator—"

Paul and Lisa appeared to be engaging in a pleasant conversation, but Michaela didn't have time to stop to listen. She arched her back and shifted into the shade of the information tent.

"Drink this," Jasen said, pushing a water bottle into her hand.

"Thanks." She sipped, enjoying the cool liquid as it slid down her throat.

"I gotta run." Jasen kissed her nose.

"Shouldn't you be donning your wings?" Michaela asked, quirking her lips.

Jasen laughed. "Yeah, you wish."

Michaela suddenly felt hot all over. She took another drink as Jasen stepped closer. Heat radiated off his lean body. He tipped her chin. His

179

hazel gaze sparkled with teasing.

"Later," he said, brushing his lips against hers. She watched him walk toward the large concession tent, his jeans clinging to his firm rear.

"Earth to Mick," Kim said, waving a hand in front of her face. Jessie giggled and continued setting up a display.

"Sorry, Kim." Michaela finished the water and glanced down at the iPad.

Kim flicked her hair and pouted her lips. "I know I can't compete with Mr. Hottie McHot, but I'd like to think you'd spare me a minute."

Michaela grinned, studying her friend. Tall and graceful, stylish to a fault, Kim appeared to have stepped out of a 1940s movie. She pushed up the oversized shades.

"Shoot," Michaela said.

Kim tipped her glasses, her mischievous dark eyes sparkling. "I'm not that upset," she giggled. "I just wanted to let you know we are all set at the check-in table."

"That's great." Michaela set the tablet down and hugged her friend. "I'm so glad you came to Texas too. I love having you in my life."

"Oh, don't get mushy on me. I don't want to mess up my mascara." Kim sniffed. "I'm glad I came too. What would you do without me? Don't answer that. I know you have Mr. McHotpants."

Michaela rolled her eyes. "His name is Jasen."

Kim waved her arm. "Pfft. I know." She took Michaela's hand. "I can't wait to watch the show. This town is fabulous!"

"Thanks for your help," Michaela glanced at her watch. "I better go. I have so much to do before I meet Dad."

"Okay, I can take a hint." Kim winked. "When you're hot and need a moment to hide, go try my Bearcat cold brew."

"Bearcat? Are you trying to get Buck to move here?" Michaela giggled.

Rolling her eyes, Kim put her hands on her hips. "No way, you goof. My coffee has cinnamon and cocoa in it. Texans don't seem to like it in chili, so I thought I'd sneak it into the coffee."

"Sounds great," Michaela said. Kim waved as she exited the book event aisle.

"Michaela?" Jessie called, catching her attention. "I just want you to know you're doing a phenomenal job. My grandma would have been tickled pink knowing all these romance authors were descending on Fortuna because of her books."

Tears welled in Michaela's eyes, and she blinked. "Thank you, Jessie. I wish I would have known your grandmother."

"She would have liked you." Jessie spread her arms and twirled. "She would have loved this."

"Jessie," Lisa called, waving her clipboard. "Paul is ready for you to set up your Double D Intimates gowns."

"Great." Jessie hustled toward Lisa.

"Good luck today," Michaela hollered.

Volunteers wore bright blue shirts. They helped authors put the final details on their table displays, arranging swag and stacking books.

When the clock struck the top of the hour, the reader residents of Fortuna flooded the streets. Some dashed to a favorite author's table, others began at the first kiosk, methodically working their way through the vendors. The shops along the square had opened for the festivities.

Michaela fanned herself, observing the throng. The cheerful murmur of the crowd and merry faces of those strolling past made her smile.

"Are you okay?" Tom asked. He wore a blue shirt. Michaela had hired the homeless man to help keep the authors happy. He delivered drinks, snacks, and stayed at their table while they visited the restroom.

"My feet hurt and the event is just starting," she said.

"Sit here," Tom said, leading her to a freshly painted hunter green bench. He returned moments later with a coney from Hamish's Kraut Wagon. "The Michaela coney."

"Thanks," she said, then took a bite. "It's Cincinnati style chili," she hummed in delight.

Tom grimaced as if he stepped in dog poo.

"Have you tried it?" Michaela grinned. She held the coney dog up to her nose. The tantalizing scent of home.

"No way." Tom lowered himself to the bench.

"Do you like mochas or coffee with cinnamon?" Michaela asked. She took a large bite.

"Sure." Tom shrugged.

"So chocolate and cinnamon in coffee are okay but not chili," Michaela said.

"Sounds right."

"Says a man from the state who doesn't like beans in their chili," Michaela said. She took another bite.

"That food truck thing almost got it right," a masculine voice said from behind her.

"Darren," Michaela frowned. "Why are you here?"

He ambled next to the bench. "I've been following Kim on social media. I wanted to support her grand opening."

"You flew from Cincinnati to support Kim's coffee shop?" Michaela glanced at Tom, who shook his head.

Darren sighed, tugging on his shirtsleeve. "I came to see you too. Don't get feisty. I just wanted to see what you've done and how you are doing."

"I'm great," Michaela said with a smile. "I love this community. And I've got a man who loves me like I love him."

Darren nodded, a wistful expression fluttering over his features then disappearing as he plastered on a grin similar to Jasen's political smile. "I'm glad you're happy. I like what you've done to the town. I'll see you around."

Michaela finished her food as Darren disappeared into the crowd. She checked the time again. "Thanks again, Tom. I'll pay you back another time." She rose.

"It's my treat. I appreciate the good word you put in for me with your property developer friend Pete. The job has been a lifesaver. He's a great boss." Tom smiled and gathered her trash.

After hugging Tom, Michaela hastened through the masses, eager to get the refreshing caffeinated drink Kim had mentioned. The bell tinkled when she entered the building. All the tables were filled. Glen and his employees glanced up.

"Hiya, Mick," Glen greeted. "Kim said you'd be in. Give me a sec and I'll get you Kim's mad concoction."

"Don't scare me," Michaela said, inspecting the menu hanging on the reclaimed brick wall.

"You'll love it." Glen disappeared from her view but kept talking. "She said it's sweet like you and cool like her." A moment later, he handed her a cup filled with what looked like a shake. "It's blended cold brew. Kim calls this flavor the Bearcat."

Michaela took a sip and moaned. Hint of mocha and cinnamon blended in the creamy drink. "This is awesome, Glen. Tell Kim I hate it." She laughed and waved, leaving the old firehouse.

Michaela blinked into the sunlight as she stepped across the street to the park's amphitheater.

"You look exhausted, baby doll," Michaela's father said, catching her slumped in the shade of the oak tree. He held hands with a woman named Polly.

"I wanted to enjoy the shade for a moment," Michaela said. Her father clutched a sack from the Gift Spot. "Did you buy a costume?" Michaela closed her eyes. "Never mind. I don't want to know."

Both Polly and her father smiled and blushed. Tim laughed and checked his watch. "It's about time for the big show. Shouldn't you be heading to your seat?"

The music started, and the crowd shifted from the author fair tent, filling the space around the amphitheater. Michaela found her way to her reserved seat and her father followed.

"This is going to be great," Desire Hardmann said, waving a fistful of money. In the third row next to Desire, Jessie covered her face and giggled. Across the aisle, Nellie clutched her phone. She aimed it at Desire, snapping a picture.

The song changed and the city manager, Cam Payne, walked on stage. "Welcome to Fortuna, the most romance readingest town in Texas."

"Yeehaw!" a cowboy yelled from the back.

"Today's show is based on the town's favorite book: *The Visitation*."

The crowd became frenzied, whistling, cheering, clapping, and throwing things in the air. Michaela hadn't read the novel yet, but she decided to buy a copy.

Cam motioned for the audience to settle. He waited until they quieted before continuing. "Volunteering for this afternoon's festivities are the men from the Fortuna Dare Society men's book club and the ranch hands from the Double D and Big Deal Ranches. Without further ado, Fortuna's own visitation."

Base pumped and B.J. Johnson moseyed onto the stage, shirtless but with angel wings.

"Yeah, baby," Desire said, standing up and clapping.

Jessie's brother-in-law Matt followed. Matt, also shirtless, wore jeans, belt but added a black cowboy hat. He hammed it up, swaying to the music.

Like a parody to a Victoria's Secret Fashion Show instead of women in lingerie the shirtless men modeled tight jeans and large feathery wings.

A man stepped onto the stage and the crowd roared.

"What the——?" her father mumbled.

"That's Parker Ford, he's in Jasen's book club and a Fortuna legend. He didn't want feathers. Apparently his wife likes dragon shifters." Michaela covered her mouth to hide a giggle.

Strapped to Parker's shoulders were blue leather wings.

"I think he looks more like a bat," Tim grumbled.

A few other men strutted down the catwalk and back, but Michaela shifted, waiting for Jasen. He wouldn't tell her anything about his costume or the program in general. When she'd handed the project over to B.J. and the Fortuna Dare Society to organize, she thought they would keep her in the loop. However, she'd been too busy to worry much about it until now.

Man after man paraded, but no Jasen. Michaela began to worry. "Where is he?" she uttered. "I better go find him."

"Just wait," her father said, placing a hand on her knee. "The show isn't over yet."

"Ladies and gentlemen, the mayor of Fortuna, Jasen DeLay," Cam announced.

Michaela held her breath. Shirtless like the others but in black dress pants and a black bow tie, Jasen strutted to the end of the catwalk. His tanned chest called to her. She held onto the edge of her seat. He crooked his finger toward her, and she gasped.

"Michaela, please join the mayor on the stage," Cam requested.

Michaela rose, and she glanced at her father. "Go on," Tim said, shooing her toward the front.

Michaela climbed the steps and took Jasen's offered hand. For the first time, Michaela noticed Jasen had a mic and earpiece.

"Good afternoon, Fortuna and guests. Did you enjoy your visitation?" Jasen asked.

The masses cheered. "Encore," Desire yelled.

"I want to introduce you to someone special. This is Michaela Arschfick. She collaborated with the council to implement the changes you've seen in town, from this amphitheater to the repainted park benches. She has worked hard to command an army of volunteers, find and invite authors, and arrange the food, police and a hundred other things I know nothing about. I wanted to recognize Michaela. Thank you for your attention to detail and making Fortuna a better place to live."

B.J. appeared next to her carrying a large bouquet of roses. He handed them to Michaela. Tears filled her eyes as the people cheered a chorus of thank yous. Nellie clicked pictures.

Once the amphitheater had quieted again, Jasen took the bouquet and handed it back to B.J. He then pulled Michaela into his arms.

She sighed against him. Cheek to chest, she relished the warmth of his skin. The steady beat of his heart. He glanced at her with hooded hazel eyes, and her blood ignited. Jasen tipped her chin and brushed his lips against hers.

"I love you," he whispered, but the mic broadcast his declaration to the audience and they *Awwed*.

Michaela giggled, and her face heated. Jasen took her lips once more, plunging his fingers into her hair. She opened for him and his tongue swept in. He moaned.

The crowd clapped, or it could have been her thundering heart or their ragged breathing. Michaela didn't care. She became lost in his kiss.

"Get a room," B.J. muttered.

Without breaking contact with Jasen, Michaela raised her arm and gave B.J. a one-finger salute.

"That's my girl," Desire whooped.

# Love a book?

## Please make sure you leave a review.

## Reviews are virtual hugs for authors

Books by Rochelle Bradley

## THE FORTUNA, TEXAS SERIES
*The Double D Ranch*
*Plumb Twisted*
*More Than a Fantasy*
*Municipal Liaisons*
*Here We Go Again*
*The Playboy's Pretend Fiancée*
*Cole's New Song*

## THE FORTUNA DARE SOCIETY
*Brad*
*Canon*

## LEARNING TO LOVE AGAIN SERIES
*Destionation Escape*
*The 24 Hour Bet*

## THE CARTUBERS MANUAL FOR LOVE SERIES
*Popping the Clutch*

BOOKS by Rochelle Bradley & CJ Warrant
*Pandemonium in Peoria* – Boba Book Babes Mysteries

BOOKS by Rochelle K. Bradley

*Dragonfly Wishes* - Dragons of Ellehcor 1
*Dragunzel* -Dragons of Ellehcor *2*
*Descended* - Secrets of the Fallen *1*
*Charmed by Murphy*

# ABOUT THE AUTHOR

Born and raised in Cincinnati Ohio, Rochelle developed a love of nature and art. She is a Bearcat, a Buckeye, an interior decorator, and fluent in sarcasm. She currently lives in southwest Ohio and shares her home with a black cat, a leash trained orange tabby, and her Prince.

Rochelle co-hosts (with author CJ Warrant) Wednesday Coffee & Books an Instagram Live show where they interview romance authors.

Rochelle is an award winning author including three IHIBRP (Indie Helping Indies Book Review Project) 5-star awards. *Haunted Memories*, a contemporary romance, won a contest from Ellehcor Publishing House. *Against the Laws*, finaled in the Chicago-North's Fire & Ice Contest.

She loves to connect with readers. Scan Rochelle's Linktree (https://linktr.ee/rochellebradley) where you can follow her on TikTok, Facebook, Instagram, and other social media. Visit Rochelle's website to sign up for her newsletter to keep up to date about future novels and book signings: RochelleBradley.com